HEART OF THE MISTS

EVA CHASE

BOUND TO THE FAE

BOOK 9

Heart of the Mists

Book 9 in the Bound to the Fae series

First Digital Edition, 2021

Cover design: Yocla Book Cover Design

Ebook ISBN: 978-1-990338-19-9

Paperback ISBN: 978-1-990338-27-4

Talia

Normally, the carriages Sylas constructs out of juniper wood and magic skim over the ground smoothly even at top speed. I can feel how hastily the one we're riding in now was conjured with every quiver that runs through the frame. There wasn't time for perfection—especially not when every fae capable of conjuring them needed to create not just one but many in that short span.

A force of a few dozen carriages speeds toward the fringelands around us, with more presumably on the way as other packs hear the call for aid. And all of the fae around me have much bigger concerns than how well the vehicles will hold up to the journey. We needed to get going as quickly as possible to face the incoming invasion of Murk.

If everyone hadn't been in such a rush, maybe my

mates would have argued more about my coming along. But when Sylas tried to send me back to our castle, I insisted that I wanted to be a part of this, to see exactly what horrors Orion had brought to the Mists I call home, and he accepted my demand with only a growl of frustration and a nod.

All three of my wolfish Seelie mates are sharing this carriage, along with a retinue of their pack's warriors and the Murk man I claimed as my fifth mate just this morning. Madoc sits next to me near the stern, his hand clasped around mine, his gaze sweeping over the fae around us warily.

Does he anticipate suspicion from the Seelie he's found himself allied with? If so, I haven't seen any yet. The fae of Sylas's pack, and probably many others as well, have already heard how Madoc gave his life to save mine and free me from Orion's final curse—and how the Heart of the Mists brought him back to life after I gave it a stern talking to. When their eyes stray toward us, I see only a kind of startled awe.

My other mates glance back at us regularly, but mostly to check on me, I can tell. August adjusts his weight restlessly on his feet, looking as if he'd have considered carrying me back home right now if his fighting skills weren't so needed at our destination. Mostly, though, they're occupied with making plans for the battle ahead.

"So, that's three domains they struck at once," Whitt is saying, rubbing his jaw. The sly spymaster looks unusually grim.

"And more on the winter side," Sylas says. When he

looks my way this time, it's to include me in the conversation. "Has Corwin reported anything further?"

I've been exchanging occasional thoughts with my Unseelie mate through our soul-twined bond while he races with his flock toward the fringes on the other side of the border. My sense of him right now is hazy because he partly blocked off our connection while he conferred with his coterie. I have a vague sense of worry and anger from him, and an awareness of the larger force of raven shifters who're converging to join him and the other Unseelie arch-lords, but that's all.

I shake my head. "So far, he doesn't know any more than the sentry reported—they attacked the three domains close to the border and the fringes on the winter side."

Astrid frowns. "It must be a massive force for the Murk to have been able to overwhelm that many domains so quickly."

Madoc speaks up from where he's leaned against the side of the carriage. He isn't totally recovered from his death and resurrection yet, but he manages to keep his lightly hoarse voice steady. "Orion always planned on waiting until he could be sure of striking a definitive blow right away. He's been building his army and their arsenal for decades. I'd imagine when he realized that Talia's curse was lifted, he pulled them together in the hopes of moving on the Mists while you were still distracted by her recovery, since he couldn't use her death against you anymore."

A bitter note comes into his tone. There was a time not that long ago when he stood beside the Murk king as one of Orion's knights. He wanted to be over there helping the Murk take the Mists for their own. But we've all realized that not everything we thought about the fae we stood with and the fae we opposed was accurate. And in particular, he's come to terms with the fact that his king is more sadistic than heroic.

"We may not be able to engage with them right away, then," August says to his brothers. "If we go in too outnumbered, we'll only be setting ourselves up for unnecessary casualties. We'll want as large a force as possible assembled before we go up against them."

Sylas nods. "It shouldn't take long to gather warriors from across the realm. Everyone will understand the urgency. And we wouldn't want to rush in immediately anyway. As urgent as the situation is, the Murk have surprised us too many times in the past. We need to take stock and make sure we're tackling them in the most effective way."

Whitt turns to Madoc again. "I don't suppose you have any thoughts on that subject—what tricks your king might have up his sleeve, or what strategies would be most useful for pushing him back?"

Madoc's mouth twists as his gray eyes go distant with thought. "I wasn't around much for the final preparations, so I don't know anything specific about his current plans. But he does like to use his opponents' emotions against them, so if he can find a way to startle or unnerve you, he will. And you shouldn't assume anything you see is real at first glance. I may have been the strongest with illusions among his supporters, but there are plenty others with skills along the same line."

Whitt tips his head in acknowledgment, and Madoc's gaze slides to August. I feel the hesitation in his grip around my hand and squeeze his fingers in case he needs the reassurance. He returns the gesture and clears his throat. "August, could I talk to you about another issue that could become urgent when we confront Orion… and could we discuss it somewhat privately?"

The warrior's brow knits, but he motions the nearby guards toward the front of the carriage and comes closer to perch on the edge of the bench across from us. The sunlight flashes off his auburn hair. With a few quick murmurs, he draws a wall of magic around us that muffles the warble of the breeze and the voices of the other fae in the carriage—as I assume it'll do for ours too.

I look at Madoc, my stomach knotting. "What's wrong?" I have no idea what he'd want to ask August specifically about.

Madoc's mouth stays tensed at its awkward angle. "I haven't had the chance to mention this to you yet. When you were fading—when I was going to offer my blood to cure your curse and August stopped me—I offered him my true name to give him more security that I wouldn't hurt you or anyone else. Well, other than myself." A hint of a wry smile briefly tugs at his lips.

My eyes widen, the understanding of just how big a sacrifice he made washing over me even more powerfully than before. Fae rarely admit their true names to anyone, even their lords or mates, because it essentially gives the other person total power over them. For him to offer it to a man he barely trusted… "You shouldn't have had to do that."

"Well, it is what it is. I didn't think it'd matter, since I didn't expect to be alive to be called by my true name within a few minutes anyway." His gaze travels from me to August. "But here we are."

To his credit, August looks uncomfortable about the whole thing, not the least bit triumphant. "I won't use it again. You don't need to worry that I'd order you around or anything like that."

Madoc lets out a raw chuckle. "Actually, I'm going to ask that you *do* use it again, on a regular basis. You see… Orion knows it too. It's one of his conditions for accepting anyone into his inner circle. He mostly uses it to summon us when he needs us particularly quickly, but obviously he can do more with it if he decides to."

My heart sinks. A memory flickers through my mind of my escape from the Murk colony they call the Refuge, where Orion rules. As Madoc was helping me out into the human world above, he suddenly knew that Orion had realized I'd escaped. He must have gotten that true-name call.

"His power over you wouldn't have ended when your connection to his false Heart was broken?" I ask.

Madoc shakes his head. "Our true names are a part of us, a magic that's tied to our spirits rather than any other source. He hasn't tried to use it yet. He probably assumes I'm dead, whether he can sense that I'm no longer bound to his Heart or because he tried when I was out of commission and got no reaction. But as soon as we confront his army, there'll be an increased chance that he'll either see me or someone else will who'll report it to him."

August's expression has turned even more serious than when he was simply preparing for war. "What do you need me to do?" he asks, simply and steadily.

Madoc blinks at him. Maybe it still surprises him that my other mates are willing to trust *him* now, as if he didn't demonstrate his loyalty in the most undeniable way just this morning.

"Opposing uses of a true name cancel each other out," he says. "You just need to order me not to obey any demands Orion makes of me. But since the effect will fade over time, and we can't be sure when he might attempt to give a command, you'll need to repeat the order regularly. I'd imagine once a day should be enough."

"Of course," August says. "As long as you need me to keep it up." His golden eyes darken. "I hope you don't mind me saying that if I have my way, Orion won't be around to make use of any words at all before many more days have passed."

Madoc's fingers tighten around mine as if he's thinking of all the ways his king tormented me. "I don't mind at all. In fact, I share the sentiment. I only hope that not too many others of my people become collateral damage in this war he's forced on us."

None of us can be sure how the conflict will play out. Madoc is proof that the Murk aren't all malicious villains the way the fae of the seasons have liked to claim. But from the time I spent in the Refuge, I know that a lot of them hate both the Seelie and Unseelie vehemently—and I can't blame them for it, considering the way the other fae have savaged them, even their children.

It was hard enough for Madoc to accept that he might be able to peacefully negotiate some kind of compromise with the fae of the seasons. I don't know how many others we'll be able to persuade to take a more peaceful approach.

But even if those who stand with Madoc now are beyond our reach, there are many other rat shifters who don't agree with Orion or haven't bothered to decide one way or another as they focus on their basic survival. We can at least give them the chance to have the sort of life and home that should have been theirs all along.

"We'll do our best," August says solemnly.

I gently detach my fingers from Madoc's grasp and raise my hands to my ears. "We must be getting close to the fringelands. Why don't you give him the true-name order now? I don't need to hear it." I catch Madoc's gaze. "I realize it's safer for you the fewer people know it."

He gives me a tender smile I've never seen him aim at anyone else, the one that brings a flutter to my chest. I don't think he'd mind me knowing this part of him, but I can tell he appreciates the privacy I'm offering him all the same.

It only takes a moment. I cover my ears and peer over the side of the carriage, August must give his instruction, and then Madoc brushes his knuckles against my arm to tell me it's done. But by then my attention has been captured by the scene up ahead.

Several carriages are soaring toward us from the fringes

across the increasingly rugged terrain. The vehicles themselves don't appear to be in the best of condition, a few of them jerking unsteadily, one trailing sputters of violet smoke.

Sylas and the other arch-lords motion for our brigade to slow. We come to a complete stop when we meet the approaching fleet.

I spot several bodies slumped within the carriages and other fae with blood on their clothes. My throat constricts. I can guess what they're going to say before the woman at the prow of the foremost vehicle speaks.

"We've fled Amberrise. We tried to hold off the Murk that attacked us, but there were too many of them, with vicious powers… We stayed as long as we could, but more than half of my pack has fallen, some never to rise again."

Sylas nods with a look of tense sympathy. "I'm sure you fought honorably and well. I wish we could have reached you sooner to help you before you had to abandon your home." He catches the eyes of Donovan and Celia on their nearby carriages and must get enough of a sense of consensus to ask, "Will you join us now in fighting back with a larger force? We intend to return Amberrise to you as soon as we possibly can."

One of the men behind the lady swipes his hand across his dust-smeared forehead with a weary sag of his shoulders. But the lady raises her chin high. "We'll do what we can. You're almost on their forces. They came after us shortly after we fled—our carriages were faster, but they can't be more than ten minutes distant by now. Do you have healers with you who could see to our injured? My own are exhausted."

The arch-lords motion to a few of the skilled among the gathered packs, who use magic to leap from carriage to carriage until they reach the new arrivals. Sylas keeps August with us, I guess feeling his strength is better preserved for the fight ahead.

The others prepare for battle, most leaving the carriages to get into formation ahead of them. My mates cast a spell around my carriage to shield it from stray attacks before going to join the others, their worried eyes telling me they wish I wasn't here at all.

"They won't even be able to see you," Whitt tells me. "I don't want them targeting you."

I wish there was more I could do right now than sit here watching to see what will happen.

Madoc stays with me, looping his arm around my waist as if bracing himself to haul me away if need be.

"Are you all right?" I ask him quietly. I can't imagine how he feels about facing his people again like this, although I suppose they won't be able to see him right now either. That's probably for the best, since I also can't imagine how they'll react to seeing him on our side.

He exhales roughly. "As all right as I can be. I knew this day was going to come, but I'd have preferred to get more time to brace for it."

"That's why Orion made his move so quickly, isn't it?" I said. "Not because of you, but because all the fae of the seasons have had their mind on other things." Mostly my survival.

"Yes. But that doesn't mean I appreciate his strategy."

A vibration the shield can't deflect passes through the air. I make out a horde of figures in the distance, rushing toward us. All at once, a deluge of shimmering, sizzling bolts of magic rains down on the Seelie army.

Some of the summer fae snap out the words to form shields. Others simply dodge. But as they jerk out of the paths of the blazing spells, several seize up and crumple in on themselves with blood spouting from their limbs or chests.

I shoot forward from my seat, a cry of protest in my throat. Madoc grips my shoulder, but his posture is equally tensed.

"They're mingling illusions," he says, his voice gone ragged. "The spells you can see are nothing, with hidden attacks in between."

He drags in a breath as if to shout a warning, though I'm not sure the army will be able to hear us through the protective magic wrapped around our carriage any more than they can see us. But in the next moment, it becomes clear that the Seelie warriors have figured out the trick for themselves. The arch-lords, August, and Whitt holler instructions to the crowd that others pass on to the farthest reaches.

When the next hail of destructive energy pounds down on them, they all raise their voices in unison to form one huge shield that deflects all of it—the spells both seen and unseen. Seconds later, with another chorus, they hurl magic of their own toward the incoming invaders.

I don't know if it's part of a plan or simply everyone

drawing on their strengths, but a chaos of effects erupts around the advancing army of Murk. Branches and vines burst from the ground to yank some off their feet. Whirlwinds knock others over. Waves of fire roar to the left while a vast torrent of water pummels those on the right.

But the Murk are ready. A few fall, yes, but most of them must snap out defensive spells to block the effects. Then they hurl more magic at our forces. Energy quavers through the air, thick enough to raise the hairs on the backs of my arms.

The fae armies whip their power at each other over and over, neither willing to relent. Cracks start to form in the muddy earth between the lines of soldiers. My heart thumps so hard I'm afraid it's going to leap from my throat.

We're holding them off, but we're not pushing them back—not one inch, from what I've seen. Our people have to be tiring. Are theirs?

I squint, not able to make out much through the clashes of magic and across the distance. The expressions on the faces of the Murk I manage to catch don't look particularly fatigued. But... I don't see the kind of eager furor I can easily imagine lighting up Orion's right now either.

The glimpses I see of narrowed eyes and bared teeth look *desperate*. Determined and fierce, but with an edge of despair. Not because they already doubt their chances, I think, but because they know what their fate will be if they can't pull off this takeover after all.

They all believe their only possible fate is to slaughter the Seelie or be slaughtered in turn.

An uneasy sensation coils around my gut. We have to reach those people somehow, show them there's another path where no blood has to be shed. I know many of them won't listen, but there must be at least a few who will. The more of them we can peel away from Orion's side, the harder it'll be for him to keep up his assault on the Mists.

As I think that, something new is rippling through the Seelie forces. Orders are being called out. The warriors disperse farther along the battle lines. Voices rise again, and a barrier so thick that I can see the glint of it forms along the cracked ground between us and the Murk, thrumming up toward the sky like a thinner version of the border haze.

My Seelie mates come back to the carriage, August's hair damp with sweat, Sylas's dark eye tired while his ghostly one peers into a space none of the rest of us can make out.

"What's happening?" I ask, standing up.

Whitt answers, sinking onto one of the benches with a huff. "We weren't organized enough—we can't take back the domains like this. For now, we're stopping the Murk from getting any farther into the Mists. A significant portion of our warriors will stay here and defend our lands, while the rest of us figure out how the hell we boot the rats off our territory for good."

"Or how to crush all of them where they stand," mutters one of the warriors hopping into the carriage after them, and my men don't even start to argue.

Talia

"We need to act decisively," Laoni insists, her voice echoing off the high ceiling of the border castle's meeting room. "Root them out and exterminate this menace."

Nothing about her comment surprises me, but Madoc tenses where he's sitting next to me at the long table. Most of his recent dealings with the fae of the seasons have been on the Seelie side. He's not as used to the typical Unseelie iciness as I am.

Other than the two of us, it's only arch-lords seated around us. The coterie and cadre members present stand behind their respective lords. But I've earned a place in the discussion by virtue of my experiences with the Murk and my connection to the curse they've inflicted on the Mists, and Madoc... well, Madoc is the closest thing we have to an actual Murk representative, as much as he can speak for his people now that he's cut off from them.

Before either of us has to say anything, Corwin speaks up while sending me a waft of reassurance through our bond. "Simply throwing all our might at them and hoping to smash through their defenses didn't get us very far the first time. I think it's clear that defending the Mists is going to require a more nuanced approach. Decisive, yes, but incisive as well."

The Unseelie faced similar problems to the wolf shifters on their side of the battle. They ended up taking the same tactic of magically walling off the Murk forces and leaving a large contingent of warriors to hold that boundary. But neither summer nor winter knows how long the warriors will be able to withstand the Murk, especially when the Murk may change their own tactics at any moment.

Laoni turns to Corwin with a flash of emotion that looks almost like betrayal in her chilly eyes, as if Corwin owes her any allegiance after the way she's undermined him so often in the past. "I'd expect you to be taking a harder line with the vermin, considering how much they've cost you and your mate."

Her gaze darts to me briefly, and my hand twitches toward my belly automatically. There's no avoiding the punch of grief that hits me at her words. Corwin stiffens in his chair, a similar rush of anguish traveling from him into me, and Sylas's lips draw back in a silent snarl where he's poised at the head of the table.

Because of Orion's curse, I lost what would have been

our first child. It was so early I'd barely had a couple of weeks to start to dream about my future motherhood, but the loss is still a raw wound. My men don't know which of them would have been the father by blood, but they all saw it as their child in spirit. I know they mourn what could have been as deeply as I do.

My teeth set on edge, and my fingers curl toward my palm. I lean forward, catching Laoni's gaze with the movement. "Don't you dare use my pain to advance your agenda. It was my loss more than anyone else's, and *I* don't want to see this war end with an 'extermination.'"

Laoni's expression twitches at the rebuke in my tone. I'm not sure I've ever spoken to her quite so harshly before, but I'm out of patience.

"What would you suggest, then?" Celia asks, looking at both me and Madoc. "With your knowledge of the Murk, how can we hope to win the war and protect the Mists if not by destroying the fae who seek to destroy us?"

The most senior of the Seelie arch-lords isn't any friendlier to the Murk than Laoni is, I know, but at least she's managed to phrase her question politely. And her gaze as it rests on Madoc shows more measured curiosity than anything else, unlike the Unseelie arch-lords who are mostly watching him with eyes narrowed with suspicion.

"Some of them might be won over to our side," I say. "We have to give them the chance to make that decision. As far as they know right now, you'd kill them even if they *weren't* attacking you. To most of them, this war is self-defense for the way you've been slaughtering them whenever you come across them for centuries."

Madoc inclines his head. "What Talia's saying is true. Orion wants blood however he can get it, and I accept that this war won't end until *he's* ended. But many of my people want a real home more than anything else. They want the place in the Mists that's been denied to them for so long, and the ability to live in peace without having to fear wolves or ravens will descend on them at any moment. I think that's a reasonable aspiration."

One of the coterie members makes a faint scoffing sound, but I can't hear it well enough to tell who. I bristle on Madoc's behalf all the same.

"The Murk who've attacked us haven't exactly been in a listening mood," Terisse says, rubbing her mouth. "And it doesn't sound as if they'd be inclined to believe us no matter what we say."

She might have a point there. An idea that occurred to me on the carriage ride as we returned to the Heart bubbles to the surface. "We could go back to the Murk sorceress, Delta—the one who doesn't agree with Orion's rule. The first parlay went badly, but maybe—"

"*Badly?*" Uzziah says with a huff of disbelief. "From what I understand, they attacked the Seelie representatives who went to meet with them."

"Because they believed the Seelie were about to attack them," Madoc puts in. "An impression I can admit I inadvertently added to. I think there's a decent chance she'd listen if you made a solid appeal."

"What, beg this rat queen to come to our aid?" Laoni's nose wrinkles in distaste.

There was a little while when I thought she was

coming around to see my side of things more. But that was only with relations between the Seelie and the Unseelie—and before the man she wouldn't let herself admit she loved fell beneath the Murk's claws. Convincing her to see the rat shifters as worthy of respect is obviously going to be a lot harder.

I turn to Sylas instead. He was the one who led the original parlay anyway. "If we could convince even one colony of the Murk to trust us—and prove ourselves worthy of that trust by making room for them here in the Mists—it would go so far toward showing the Murk there's another way to get what they want. Isn't that worth apologizing for? What does it cost you, really, to be humble, when there were plenty of mistakes made on our side too?"

My mate inhales sharply. "Talia, I understand what you're saying. But we do still have to maintain some air of authority. We don't know this colony of fae at all—even our Murk ally has never dealt with them directly before. We can't leave ourselves vulnerable."

I frown, my heart aching with my frustration that I don't know how to make him see. "Being humble doesn't have to make you vulnerable. Apologizing when you've actually been wrong shouldn't be a weakness. Doesn't it show how confident you are in your authority if you're willing to *admit* where you've misstepped instead of pretending you can never be wrong?"

Sylas pauses, his mismatched gaze searching mine. The scar that marks his face from his forehead to his cheek, bisecting his ghostly eye, was given to him by a Murk woman he underestimated. I can't blame him for hesitating. But now he knows that there's more to the rat shifters than hostility.

"You're right," he says after a moment, to my relief. "For peace in the Mists and for righting past wrongs, I should be willing to take that step—and I am."

"It isn't that simple," Celia points out. "Even if this sorceress agrees to give us a second chance, what land are we going to offer her?"

Donovan shrugged. "There's plenty of unclaimed territory throughout the Mists. I don't think that should be a problem."

"We'll have to be careful about it," Uzziah says. "We wouldn't want them too close to any areas of importance in case she changes her mind about which side she's supporting."

Madoc clears his throat. "It is going to need to be *good* territory. You can't expect any of us to see a peace offering as genuine if you're shunting us off to the fringelands from the start. My people need a chance to reconnect with the Heart of the Mists and enjoy the benefits these realms can offer. It isn't an equal alliance if we're only offered table scraps."

"Of course," Sylas says with a tip of his head. "Since I'll be making the proposal, my cadre and I will look into the possibilities."

"Is that how this works now?" Laoni says. "We're guided by a rat who until recently was working against us? What authority does he have to make these kinds of demands?"

Madoc glowers at her. "I have the authority of having lived among and gotten to know hundreds of my people, including the king you're currently facing off against."

Uzziah's hands fidget on the tabletop before he forces them to still. "We do need to discuss exactly what sort of role the Murk would play here even if some of them can be convinced to back off from their war. We aren't going to raise them up to equal standing with us in an instant, are we? The closest thing they have to an arch-lord is that mad king of theirs."

"Of course we won't rush into handing over power to them," Celia starts.

Corwin breaks in before she can go on. "I think that *is* what we need to be considering already. We have our disputes with the Murk, and they have their own with us. But they are fae, and there's no reason that the Mists shouldn't belong to them just as much as the rest of us if they can coexist with us peacefully. And that includes having control over how their territories are governed."

Laoni's lips curl with increasing disdain. "They haven't yet proven themselves to be more than vermin. They've tied themselves to a twisted copy of our Heart. For all we know, this one sitting at our table is going to go running to his king as soon as he's in a position to earn back his place there." She flings her hand toward Madoc, who goes rigid in his chair.

"Exactly," Uzziah says. "Nothing good can come—"

The frustration that's been building inside me boils over. I push to my feet with a smack of my hands against the table. "Nothing good can come of all this arguing!"

All of the arch-lords fall silent, staring at me. Laoni's mouth presses into a flat line. I focus on her first.

"*You* and the rest of the fae of the seasons haven't proven to the Murk that you're more than bullies and child-murderers yet," I remind her. "We're asking them to make at least as big a leap of faith in us as we are in them. And Madoc gave up his life to save me, so I won't hear any of you questioning whether he deserves to be here. Your own Heart brought him back to life. You couldn't ask for more proof than that."

I sweep my gaze over the rest of the assembled arch-lords. A tremor runs through me, but I hold my posture straight. The words tumble out. "For years, I've been the cure for the curse Orion cast on you. Now I can show you how to finally get a full cure so that you never have to worry about it again. And I say that cure is compassion. Turning on the Murk with nothing but violence and hatred is only going to make them hate *us* more. We *have* to find a way to work with those of them who don't already hate you all so much that they'll never trust you."

"Now look here," Uzziah starts, but I keep going, ignoring him.

"If you're not going to give coexisting a real shot and meet them as equals who have just as much right to the Mists as you do, then I'm not going to stick around here anyway. I'm tired of hearing you all bicker with each other about which fae are more worthy. I'd rather be back in the human world if fae aren't capable of acting better than squabbling kids."

With that, I sink back into my chair. Defiant energy continues to hum through my veins.

I mean it. I'll go back to the human world and stay with my brother if I have to, if having me leave is what it'll take to snap the fae around me out of their old prejudices.

But maybe it won't be necessary for me to go that far. The faces around the table look chagrined.

Corwin speaks up first, with an impression like an embrace through our bond. "I'm sure we can demonstrate to my mate that we're far more reasonable than that."

Donovan looks at Madoc. "Will you be able to appeal to your people? Will they believe that the Heart has accepted you?"

Madoc offers him a crooked smile. "It's already starting to mark me with the true names I've used since it brought me back." He tugs up the sleeve of his shirt to show one of the black tattoo-like marks that's formed on his bicep.

My breath catches, seeing it. It's undeniable proof of the Heart's welcome. A deeper hush falls over the room as the arch-lords take in the sight.

"But I won't be enough on my own," Madoc goes on. "They could see me as a fluke. I'll speak to them and try to convince them to negotiate rather than fight, but we need to be able to show that I'm not the only Murk you've accepted into the Mists. I'll have a much better chance of winning some over if there's already at least one Murk colony settling in."

"Then I'll make my plans to re-establish contact with Delta as quickly as I can," Sylas says. "Our defenses against the current Murk forces appear to be holding well for now, from what I understand?"

Laoni nods and says in a more subdued tone, "We've already set up a rotation of soldiers so that those on the front don't become too exhausted, as well as sending out supplies."

"We're arranging the same for our forces," Celia says. "We've bought ourselves a little time. We do need to see to the refugees from the captured domains—find alternative accommodations for them—now that their most urgent needs have been seen to."

Corwin stands up with an air of authority he's grown over the months since I first met him. "Then I say we pass the rest of the day with Sylas preparing for his overtures and the rest of us taking care of and organizing our people —from our domains and beyond—so that we're ready for whatever else the Murk king might send at us."

To my relief, a murmur of agreement goes around the table, no further arguments raised. I don't for a second believe that I've totally won my own battle, but at least I've gotten a temporary accord.

3

Corwin

The continuing bustle of activity all around me sends an uneasy shiver over my skin. I stop at the edge of the plain where our troops and other Unseelie are gathering into a vast makeshift camp and inhale deeply to settle my nerves.

Next to me, Talia peers out at the vast stretch of icy land that was once vacant and is now dappled with rough buildings of a variety of materials, each cluster marking the specialties of a different flock. "I don't think I've ever seen part of the fae world look this crowded."

I nod. "We like to keep space between our domains so there's less chance of the activities of one flock—or pack, since I suppose the Seelie have a similar policy—conflicting with another's. But a problem on this scale brings us all together."

The fae assembled on the plain just beyond the plateau

around the Heart are only about half of all those who've come to join the fight against the Murk. The other half are stationed along the defensive wall where we're holding the invasion at bay or traveling between there and here. Warriors, healers, and other skilled fae from domains across the winter realm have been gathering here since the call to arms came yesterday.

The energy in the air is fraught with tension. None of us expected to be facing a war like this—ever, and certainly not so suddenly.

Talia sucks in a breath. I can feel her own unsettled emotions through our bond. "You don't need to be here for this," I remind her. "They won't expect my mate to come with me."

She draws up her head with her usual stubbornness. "I'm part of this war. I want to understand what's happening as well as I can and to be there for everyone who needs it. And it seems to help people to see with their own eyes that I'm okay."

Word of her previous illness spread rather quickly through both realms as Orion's curse dug its claws into her. I can say I prefer the sense of tense anticipation that hangs over this haphazard settlement to the hopeless anguish that gripped many of my people when her fate was uncertain.

My soul-twined mate has touched huge numbers of the Unseelie with not just the cure she can offer but her compassion and thoughtfulness as well. Why shouldn't she extend her kindness to our displaced flocks too?

We've set up the rulers and folk of the three flocks

whose homes the Murk overran in hastily constructed dwellings near the base of the plateau, where they're as sheltered as possible from the regular comings and goings of the military camp. Some of their folk are still able to fight, but many are healing from the initial assault. My colleagues and I have attempted to offer them as much tranquillity as we possibly can.

"I don't know either of the lords or the lady of these flocks well," I tell Talia as we weave through the buildings toward that more isolated spot. "For convenience's sake, those on the fringes tend to visit the domains of the Heart less frequently than others do, and I have to admit I may have neglected them some because of the distance. None of them have had any complaints in recent years that required a major intervention. It's mostly been my colleagues on this side of the plateau who oversaw their needs while I focused more on the side of the realm nearer to my flock, but this war involves all of us. I'd like them to know that all of their arch-lords have their interests in mind."

Talia looks down at the basket she's carrying of delicate pastries my human chef and his daughter whipped up. A larger cart of prepared food floats along behind us on a magical current. "I hope they're hungry," she says. "Charles and Beth went all out."

"I'm sure good food will give the flock folk some small comfort." It was the most concrete gift I could offer with the restoration of their homes still so far out of reach.

My gaze catches on Talia's limp, slight at this pace with her foot brace on but noticeable all the same. Part of me longs to snatch the basket out of her hands so she's putting less strain on herself, but I already know what she'd say about that reaction.

It was only yesterday morning that she was wasted away nearly beyond survival. Only the day before that, she lost the child we'd already celebrated with such joy. I know she isn't fragile, but it's difficult to restrain the urge to wrap her up in every protection I can offer.

She must pick up on some of my feelings, because she gives me a soft mental nudge. *Getting out here and being useful makes me feel way better than sitting around in my room would. We will make a life and a family free from Orion's influence, but we all have to do everything we can to work against him first, right?*

I can't argue with her, and the quiver of restrained anguish she doesn't quite manage to suppress brings a jab of guilt into my chest. She's dealing with her own losses and the struggles she's been through the best way she knows how. I wouldn't want to get in the way of that.

The activity around the displaced flocks' settlement is more subdued than in the larger military camp. A few of the flock folk are standing around the edges of their clusters of buildings as sentries. The precaution is hardly needed with so many other fae around, but I can't blame them for keeping it.

The nearest woman's face lights up at the sight of us—more at seeing Talia than me, I observe without resentment. "Arch-lord," she says with a bob of her head. "Lady Talia. It's good of you to check in on us. I'll get my lord."

"Thank you," I say, and she darts off.

Talia watches her go, a bemused expression crossing her face. "She knew who I was. You said that flock hasn't come to the Heart recently."

I smile and ruffle her vivid hair. "I'd imagine word about the woman who's cured so many of us has spread to every domain in the realm. And you're not exactly difficult to pick out of a crowd."

She lets out a little huff of a laugh and walks with me to greet the other sentries, a couple of whom dash off to notify their own lords. As we come to a stop in an open area between the three flocks' houses, several other folk approach to see what's going on and then to exclaim over my mate.

"You're totally well now?" an elderly man asks as she hands him a pastry.

"The curse on me is gone," Talia assures him. "One of the Murk found a way to cure it and risked a lot to accomplish that."

A flicker of apprehension shows in his eyes at the mention of the Murk, but he doesn't say anything against them to her face. "With the help of him and the others of their kind who don't want this war any more than we do, we hope to restore your domain to you soon," I add. "Those who've attacked us will face the full consequences for their crimes."

"May the Heart will it so," the old man says with a dip of his head.

Talia draws her posture a little straighter when a couple who are obviously regal in bearing enter the little clearing. I greet the lord and his mate and offer my condolences for the trauma his people have been through, and he has a few of his flock folk take around their portion of the food I brought. His mate gazes out over the plain beyond us and offers a sad smile. "So many have come to defend the realm. I know it's not only for our sake, but it's uplifting to see all the same."

"We're all doing everything we can to set things right," Talia says, with a tremor of nerves that only I can sense about speaking up unprompted. "Even those of us who can't join the actual fighting."

The lord gives her a little bow. "You've defended us in all sorts of other ways, Lady Talia. We're lucky to have received your blessing."

She smiles back at them, but a twist of regret carries from her into me. She knows her ability to cure the curse isn't a blessing from our Heart but part of Orion's cruel plan.

That doesn't change the fact that you've healed us in every way you can, I say silently. *He had nothing to do with you helping mend relations between summer and winter. And we'd have been much worse off without the cure you could offer, regardless of why you have that power.*

Another of the lords is walking over to us now, with his own mate and a young woman I'm guessing is their daughter from the similarities in their features and coloring. Like her mother, her hair is a deep auburn with strands of maroon and burgundy woven in, her skin pale and her nose pointed like her father's. She looks as though she's barely passed the threshold of adulthood—I have a vague memory of taking a tour around the domains throughout the realm shortly after I took my throne and being introduced to a young adolescent daughter in theirs all those years ago.

The lord exclaims over the food we've brought. "You didn't need to go to the trouble. I can only imagine how hard you're working with this threat encroaching on the Mists."

"It was my chef who went to most of the trouble, and this is the best help he can provide," I say. "You've been through more than anyone should already. Whatever we can do to ease that pain even slightly, I'm happy to offer."

My gaze slides from him to his mate and then their daughter. The daughter meets my eyes with an air of hesitant curiosity—and her posture abruptly stiffens.

I glance around me to ensure nothing startling has happened without my noticing. I can't see what she might have reacted to. But when I return my attention to her, she's still staring, her lips parted. I don't know how to respond.

Talia picks up on my confusion. She steps toward the young woman, holding out a pastry from her basket. "You should try one of these. No one makes them quite like Charles does."

My mate is trying to make an overture of friendliness and set the woman more at ease, but the fae woman's stance only gets more rigid as her gaze flicks between Talia and me. Her parents have noticed now as well. Her mother sets a hand on her shoulder. "Is everything all right, Kara?"

"I—" The young woman blinks hard and focuses on me again. So much emotion whirls in her dark gaze—more than I can make any sense of. She peers at me intently and then says, in a shaky voice, "Can't you feel it?"

I frown. "I'm sorry. I can't say I understand what you're referring to."

"I—you—" She presses her hand to her breastbone, her fingers curling into a fist, and something about that gesture sets off a spark of unsettled recognition in me even though I'm still bewildered.

That spot—right where I felt the bond the moment my gaze caught Talia's that night months ago.

But I'm still not prepared when Kara sucks in a breath and says, "*I* can feel it. You're my soul-twined mate."

"What?" Talia bursts out, her eyes widening. But the icy crash of a realization washes through her at the same time it does me.

We know now that our soul-twined bond was created by Orion. He used his foul magic to create a connection I now cherish regardless of its origins. But by working that magic, he interrupted the natural order of things. Of course I'd have a soul-twined mate among my own people, as any true-blooded Unseelie would.

My bond with Talia drowns out any I might have felt with this woman, though. Nothing stirs in me at all except horror at the situation she's found herself in. I have my mate… and that means she can't have hers.

4

Talia

hen we finally get back to the border castle, Corwin escorts me to my bedroom. "Wait here," he says. "I know you're shaken by this, and we'll talk it through, but I want to speak to Verik to have him see what else might be done to reduce Kara's suffering as much as possible. I'll be back with you in a matter of minutes."

The strain of the situation rings through both his voice and our bond. Our *false* bond that's superseded the one the Heart actually meant for him to have. My own heart lurches all over again at the thought, but I know he means everything he just said. I know he isn't abandoning me, no matter how much the ache inside me is already quavering with the possibility.

I go to the bed and curl up on top of the soft covers. My other mates aren't around, all of them working out the best way to approach Delta—probably deep in conversation in Sylas's study right now. They have no idea how my world was just rocked.

I managed to keep it together in front of the flock leaders and the fae woman who claimed Corwin was supposed to be hers. I suspect we left them with more questions than answers, but there wasn't much Corwin *could* tell them. Through the unsettled haze in my head, I catch snippets of his conversation with Verik, asking him to look into any history of mismatched soul-twined bonds as well as methods for severing a bond that isn't returned.

I already know there isn't any easy way. My Seelie mates spent days searching for a solution when we first found out I was tied to Corwin and turned up nothing that wouldn't put us both through hell. It's so strange to think about that time when I was horrified by the idea of being so closely connected to the Unseelie arch-lord, and now I'm in agony over the possibility of losing our bond.

We worked so hard to find a way to make this relationship work. We've shared so much with each other, come to such a deep understanding. All of that was real, wasn't it, no matter how the bond came into being at the start? All of that should still count.

I'm only vaguely aware of Corwin making his way back to my room. He comes in with a faint click of the door and a rush of fresh concern when he sees my pose on the bed.

I move to push myself upright so I don't make such a pathetic figure, but before I can get very far, he's already there, pulling me into his arms. He even brings out his wings to wrap them around me as if I need the additional embrace.

Maybe I do.

I press my face to his lean chest, breathing in his cool, wintry scent. Tears prick at my eyes. Am I selfish for clinging to this bond so tightly when I have four other men and Kara has no mate at all?

Corwin's arms tighten around me. "No, you're not," he says in answer to the question I didn't voice out loud. "It doesn't matter how our bond was formed. It's *there*, we've been living it, and it's the deepest connection any two people can share. There's a reason it's almost unheard of for soul-twined mates to refuse each other. To be wrenched apart after the bond has already been confirmed and consummated—I only know of it happening through death."

And even that way can prove difficult to deal with, as his mother is clear evidence of.

"It isn't fair to Kara, though, is it?" I say raggedly. "Her whole life as she's been growing up, she's expected to find a soul-twined mate. That's what would have happened if Orion hadn't intervened."

"It can't be the same for her," Corwin says. "It isn't the same loss. She and I *don't* have a connection between our souls—I can't sense her inner state, and she can't sense mine. She just has the impression that she should be able to. She doesn't even know exactly what she's missing."

I'm not sure if that makes the situation better or worse.

Corwin pulls back and cups my face with his hands, angling it toward him so he can meet my gaze. His affection washes over me like a flood of warm sunlight. "Just so we're absolutely clear, I have no regrets about how my life has turned out. Not a single part of me wishes I could set aside our bond to form one with this woman. I feel sorry for how Orion's meddling has affected her life and happiness, but that's already done, and I have my mate."

I wet my lips, and the fear that's been slowly building in the back of my mind spills out of me. "When we defeat Orion—when we destroy his false Heart... we expect all the magic he's cast with it to be destroyed too, don't we? The curses and everything else too. That means... when that happens, the bond that he created..." The possibility makes me so miserable I can't quite force the rest of the words out.

Corwin can follow my train of thought. It could be he's already thought that far ahead himself with his logical mind. He strokes his thumb over my cheek, his eyes still fixed on mine. "You will be my mate no matter what happens. I love you, and I'll still love you whether our souls are bound or not."

"But if we're no longer tied together, then you and Kara..."

His mouth sets in a tense line. "We can't know what will happen until we get to that point. None of us can predict how the Heart of the Mists will shine on us. But I can swear right now on my soul and my throne that I will not turn my back on you. I love you for so much more than the intimate understanding we share. *Nothing* can change that."

He doesn't have to turn his back on me for Kara to become a part of his life. I have more than one mate, so there's no reason he shouldn't be allowed to do the same… as much as the idea makes me prickle with unfair jealousy. Especially if it happens because I lose the most intimate part of our connection and she gains it instead.

The other factor that's occurred to me brings a lump into my throat. "She'd be able to give you a true-blooded heir like you should—"

Corwin cuts off that comment with the press of his lips to mine and a wave of bittersweet emotion that rushes from him into me—sweet because of the love radiating through it, bitter because off the loss we've suffered. He kisses me firmly but tenderly, moving from my mouth to my cheek and my jaw, dappling my face with increasing gentleness. The adoration conveyed with each brush of his lips lights up something inside me despite my worries.

"I cherish you, my soul," he murmurs between kisses. "And I will cherish any child you bring into our family. You are *more* than just my soul. You showed me how to open myself up to my feelings, how to trust my judgment. You made me see that past mistakes don't define us. You are twined with my heart and my mind and every other part of me, and I will not give you up for anything." He pauses, bowing his head over mine. His tone turns softly wry. "Of course, it might be easier for *you* to have one fewer mate to keep track of."

Every particle in my body rejects that suggestion.

"*No*," I say, more fervently than I realized the word would come out, and then I'm yanking his mouth back to mine.

I let the rest of my words travel to him silently so that I don't have to end this kiss. *You've made me feel like more than just your mate, like I really am your lady, your equal. You showed me how I could reach for all the happiness I can imagine regardless of what anyone else thinks. I love you so much. There's no part of my life that isn't better for having you in it.*

Then we're agreed, he replies, his hand caressing down my side. *No one and nothing will tear us apart.*

The emotions flaring in me and rippling between us through our bond are more than just affection now. I kiss Corwin harder, and he responds with equal ardor, easing me down on the bed. His wings continue to form a canopy over us as his tongue delves between my lips. The feathered tips curl in to stroke their soft surface along my arms, sending an eager shiver through me.

You are mine, he says as he teases his tongue into my mouth. *Mine, always.*

Yours, I agree. A fresh rush of needy heat washes over me, and all at once I need to be so much closer to him. To reaffirm our bond in every way I can.

I yank at his tunic, and Corwin pulls back from our kiss just long enough to toss it aside. As my fingers travel over the tattooed planes of his bronze skin, his chest reverberates with a pleased hum.

The desire rising in him turns me on even more. I can feel him reveling in my eagerness, in the curves of my body and the heat of my mouth, and his hunger sets me on fire.

He drops his head and tugs down the bodice of my dress. In one swift movement he's cupped one of my breasts and sucked the peak into his mouth. Pleasure races through me at the swipe of his tongue over my hardening nipple. My fingers tangle in his dark curls, a whimper escaping me.

Mine, he repeats through our bond like an incantation. *My soul. My love. My mate. Mine.*

His mouth worships every part of me: one breast and then the other, the lines of my collarbone, the arc of my rib cage, the slope of my stomach. He lingers just below my belly button, placing a curving line of the most delicate kisses there. A tendril of grief penetrates the lust that's gripped us.

There will be another, I tell him, willing it to be true. *If it could happen once, the one time we came together when I was fertile, it can't be too hard to make it happen again, right?*

Corwin looks up at me, his dark eyes fathomless. *I will wait as long as it takes, and should it never happen, I still wouldn't have a single regret about tying my life to yours.*

The lump comes back into my throat. Then he's peeling my dress the rest of the way off me and lowering his mouth to my sex, and there's no room left in me for anything but a surge of bliss.

I gasp, my hips lifting to meet his lips. He grazes his teeth over the sensitive spot above and then teases his tongue over my opening, and I outright moan. At the same moment, his wings sweep down to stroke across my shoulders and chest. The texture of the feathers sparks all kinds of delight in my already sensitized breasts.

Corwin picks up on every tremor of pleasure and adjust his position to heighten the sensations even more. I tip my head back into the pillow, rocking with the movements of his mouth, totally adrift on ecstasy. It only takes one sharper suck on that sensitive nub to have me careening over the edge of my release.

He laps at me again as if he isn't done devouring me, but I need so much more of him. I tug at his shoulders, and he eases up over me, anticipation thrumming through him alongside his joy at seeing me so satisfied.

I reach for him, curling my fingers around his rigid shaft. The bliss that jolts through him at my touch only makes me wetter down below. I pump my hand around him experimentally, but the groan that escapes him shatters what's left of my self-control. I push my hips up to meet him, and he sinks into me as if we were made to fit together this way.

Maybe we were. Maybe this is right even if it isn't exactly how fate would have intended it. How could it feel so perfect if it wasn't?

Corwin plunges in and out of me, taking me higher and higher as the pleasure builds again. Then he rolls us over so I'm on top, straddling him.

I brace my hands against his chest and ride him with all I have in me, taking him deeper, my breath stuttering as he hits that special giddying place within. Impressions of me through his eyes flit into my awareness—I soar over him, my hair flying wild and my face alight with happiness, as if I'm as much a raven as he is.

I can't hold on very long. The feeling of him thrusting so deep inside me has me racing toward my second release in a matter of seconds. Corwin grasps my hips and adjusts my angle just slightly, and then a sharper flare of delight sizzles through both of us. Our lust feeds off each other's pleasure until I can't tell which sensations belong to me and which to him.

I clutch his shoulders, he slams up into me, and it's as if my whole body shatters with bliss. I cry out, every muscle shaking. Corwin lets out a choked sound as he spills himself in me.

Staying impaled on his softening shaft, I lean down over him to sprawl against his chest. Corwin wraps his arms and his wings around me to nestle me in his embrace. Our sweat-damp skin clings together as if even it refuses to consider us ever being parted.

I wish I could believe our future is as certain as our passion is right now. I wish there was nothing to fear in the destruction of Orion's awful Heart. But none of us really chooses our fates. I've made my choices where I've been able to as well as I can, and there's nothing left to do but hope that those choices keep all my mates with me.

5

Sylas

s we come to a stop by the portal, Whitt frowns. "Are you absolutely sure you're going to insist on doing this alone?"

I inhale the thickly humid air of the fringelands, trying not to let thoughts of the invasion of Murk miles away distract me from my current purpose. "I need a clear show of trust and humility. Last time we miscalculated by having too many men on hand who were too eager for a battle. I can't think of a better demonstration of my intentions than presenting myself without any guards at all, can you?"

My older brother grimaces, but for all his strategic smarts, he has no answer for that. We've been debating my decision on and off from the moment I came to it.

The few guards we did bring along, more for our security on the way to the fringes than for my trip to the human world, stir restlessly on their feet where they're stationed by our carriage. Their gazes scan the hazy forest for any sign of the enemy Murk. I hope I've emphasized to them enough how important it is that they not treat the rat shifters who might return with me like anything other than allies.

If my word as arch-lord isn't enough to get through to my own people, there may be no hope of an alliance at all.

But the proof that it is possible stands right next to me. Madoc considers the portal with his heavy-lidded eyes and then nods to me. "It is a risk, but I don't think Delta or her people have any interest in slaughtering an arch-lord. And she'll be intrigued."

"And I have you to call on to support my claims," I say, my tone going slightly wry. A Seelie arch-lord and the once right-hand man of the Murk king certainly make an odd pairing. Perhaps that will intrigue the sorceress too.

For now, though, I'm going in utterly alone to get my message across as emphatically as possible from the start.

I murmur a word to test the loose spell that temporarily ties Madoc to me so that I can quickly alert him when I need his presence on the other side of the portal. Then I tip my head to both him and Whitt. "We need this, or I wouldn't be taking the risk at all. Wish me luck."

"Heart help you," Whitt mutters, but there isn't much argument left in his voice. I think he was coming to respect Madoc's input even before the Murk man proved just how far he'd go for our mate.

Squaring my shoulders, I step into the wavering

surface of the portal. A rush like a chilly wind whips over me, the uncomfortable smell of salt fills my nose, and I find myself standing at the edge of the secluded ocean bay that was the site of our first disastrous meeting with the Murk sorceress.

Delta has evidently been waiting for me, drawn by the message we sent ahead of my arrival but still wary. Rather than coming right down the low rocky cliff that circles the beach, she merely eases up to the top of it from where she was perched behind the craggy ridge. She grips the rough stone tightly, her eyes narrowed as she takes me in.

I can't see them, but I have no doubt that a full force of her warriors is poised just out of view, ready should she give them a signal. Why wouldn't they be after the way our last meeting played out?

I've only taken a couple of steps from the portal. I could dive back through it in an instant if the thought of those Murk warriors worried me too much. That would mean giving up all hope of even having a conversation, though. I hold myself rigidly still, letting her look me over.

"Arch-lord," Delta says after a minute, in a voice that's not exactly sneering but definitely skeptical. She flips her burgundy curls back from her golden-brown shoulders. "Am I supposed to consider this an honor after the reception we got at our last meeting?"

The pride in me wants to point out that the reception her people offered mine wasn't much friendlier. I rein in the impulse and duck my head. Talia encouraged me to be humble, and I can do that when the fate of my entire people rests in the balance.

"We acted in haste and unfairly," I say. "The first gesture I wanted to make on seeing you again was to apologize for how sorely we misjudged you. The fact that you've come at all shows your generosity. I hope that you're willing to hear me now that I'm prepared to lay out my proposal properly. As you can see, I've brought no guards with me. I've put my faith in your good will, as I should have before."

Delta hums under her breath. At a flick of her hand, my wolfish ears catch rasps of movement from beyond the rocky ridge. Her people must be taking steps to confirm I haven't brought any warriors with me who are concealed. They may also be surrounding me. I do my best to tamp down on the apprehension prickling over my skin.

Instead, I lower myself to my knees. It's a position that makes me even more unsettled, but at the same time, I know it's necessary. I think of the stories Talia's told us of the horrors she witnessed done to the Murk—of the parents and children slashed apart by Seelie claws. My stomach knots, but not out of fear for myself.

"There's much more I should apologize for, as much as I can when it comes to the entirety of the fae of the seasons," I say, still keeping my head low. "We have mistreated you and all of your kind at every turn in monstrous ways I had the luxury of remaining partly ignorant of until now. There's no excuse for that or for the way we've demonized the Murk. Even as others like you are attacking my home now, I freely admit your hatred is understandable. I'm here to see if we can make enough amends to create a more peaceful future for both sides."

Delta makes a soft scoffing sound, but she adjusts her position to one that looks more relaxed, sitting on a small outcropping with her hands resting on her thighs. "How unsurprising that you come making this appeal while the entire Mists are under threat from those I'd say are very little like me other than in the most basic sense of our animal natures."

I raise my head to offer her a grim smile. "That's a fair distinction. I wouldn't be reaching out to you if I didn't believe that the Murk have as many facets as any other fae —and that you're very different from the one who calls himself king."

Her dark eyes continue to scrutinize me. "I'm listening, arch-lord. What is this proposal you're so desperate to make?"

The "desperate" comment rankles my pride again, but it isn't inaccurate. I straighten up so I can face her with more authority, so that it'll seem more likely that I can deliver on the promises I'm making.

"Both I and my colleagues understand that the greatest injury done to the Murk has been their all-but banishment from the Mists, which is the rightful home of all fae. We recognize the injustice of this situation and believe the first step toward a more cooperative relationship between our peoples is to give you back that home. If you'll take it, we have a domain within the summer realm where you could relocate your colony. Within its boundaries, it'd be yours to govern as you see fit."

"And outside its boundaries?" Delta asks, although I think I catch a glimmer of more intense interest in her eyes. "How will we be treated there?"

"As long as you do no harm to any of the Seelie, we will insist that you and your colony be treated like any of our packs." My smile turns crooked. "I can't promise every overture will be friendly. We deal with animosities and disputes amongst ourselves on a regular basis. But any sign that someone is targeting you because of your nature will be punished. I believe that simply being exposed to Murk who are living their lives normally will help my people come to accept you as equals."

"So, we're to be an experimental test case and a lesson in proper etiquette as well."

I restrain a wince at her interpretation. "Unfortunately, a certain amount of learning is going to be necessary. I've had to go through it myself. But I don't think it'll be only on our side, will it? Your people will also need time to adjust to the idea that you can exist among Seelie who won't attack or degrade you."

Delta blows at a stray curl that's slid across her forehead. "I suppose that's true. If we moved into the Mists, though, we would be taking a far greater risk, placing ourselves essentially at your mercy. What reason do I have to trust that this offer is genuine and not an attempt to knock out another major power among the Murk while Orion is thwarting your efforts to defeat him?"

This is a moment I expected to come. "I have someone who can join me who I believe can speak to that matter. If you'll allow me to summon him, he'll come alone as I did."

The sorceress hesitates for a second and then nods, but I notice her stance tenses again. This is how it will be for quite some time, I expect: a small gesture of trust followed by a small request, and then the same in return, until we're no longer so cautiously feeling each other out. I can't criticize her for her wariness.

I say the word to trigger the spell that'll alert Madoc and step more to the side of the portal. It's only a matter of seconds before he eases out onto the beach next to me, the ocean breeze ruffling his pale hair.

His posture is tense too, and it occurs to me on a deeper level than it did before that this is the first time he's revealed himself to any of his people since he committed to siding with the fae of the seasons. From what he's said, he has little past connection to Delta, so it's unlikely she'd take the betrayal anywhere near as personally as his king will, but that doesn't mean she'll be happy about it either.

He hasn't cast an illusion over himself like he did last time. He *has* unfurled his tail before arriving. He stands tall with the thinly furred appendage curving across the ground next to his feet, announcing what he is in a way more definitive than any words could manage.

"Hello, Delta," he says, gazing up at her. "We've never met before, but I know you have scouts throughout this world. Maybe they've kept you well enough informed that you can recognize me."

The Murk woman hasn't moved, but her eyes have widened. She speaks a few magic-laced words that I manage not to flinch at. From the way Madoc's posture turns even more rigid, it's a spell testing for any magic laid over him. She's ensuring his appearance isn't an illusion.

"You're one of that megalomaniac's so-called knights," she spits out, with more hostility than she aimed even at me. "What are you doing here?" Her gaze darts to me. "What are *you* doing with him?"

Madoc answers, his voice going dry. "It seems we need to work on acceptance not just between the fae peoples but within our own. Yes, I used to stand beside Orion. But I've come to see him for what he is, and now I oppose his methods whole-heartedly. I'm only trying to make sure he doesn't take too many others down with him."

Delta still looks skeptical. I raise my eyebrows at her. "I'm not sure if I should be offended that you apparently think I'm so dim-witted I'd ally myself with a supporter of the man currently trying to destroy my people."

She gives herself a little shake, and for the first time, a smile crosses her own lips. The glint in her eyes is more mischievous than anything now. I suppose that will always be part of the Murk's nature no matter how nicely they promise to play.

"Fascinating," she says, studying Madoc for a little longer. "And *you* believe that our best chance at not being ruined by the mad dictator lies with types like this?" She motions haphazardly toward me.

Madoc's mouth curls into a smirk I decide not to be offended by either. "I think that for all Orion's power and fury, he's going to have trouble completely wiping the Mists clean of other fae. And I think I'd rather not live in a society of Murk founded on so much death—on both sides—if there's a better way. If we're not exterminating them all, then the only way to coexist with the fae of the seasons on the lands we deserve is to find a way to work with them. But I haven't been letting them off easy."

"And you'll vouch that the offer they're making is genuine? They truly have lands they'd give to my colony without any hidden demands?"

Madoc shrugs. "This one definitely means it. We also have a major advocate in the human woman who's been the cure for their curse. She holds plenty of sway among the fae of the seasons and has forced them into plenty of other compromises they might not have agreed to without proper motivation."

He hasn't mentioned his newfound connection to the Heart of the Mists. From what he's said, Delta and her colony have never completely lost their own connection since they never fell in with Orion to bind themselves to his false Heart. We'll save that appeal for the Murk king's followers.

Delta hums again and returns her attention to me. "What exactly are the lands you'd offer us? I have no interest in the swamps or scrubby forests along the fringes."

I open my mouth to tell her about the spot Whitt and I picked out that my fellow arch-lords agreed to, a well-sized stretch of fields and forest about halfway between the fringes and the Heart that's not terribly close to any pack we feared might be particularly hostile. But something stops me.

Through my deadened eye, the ghostly impression comes of another version of Delta's face overlying the one before me. It's tipped to a stream of sunlight that dapples her cheeks with a pattern so familiar my breath catches in my chest.

Understanding comes to me like a spark flaring in the back of my mind. The place we chose is good *enough*, but it's hardly impressive. It's not much of a show of dedication to an alliance. I'm only going to get one chance to pitch this, and I'm getting the sense that Delta is going to need more.

I'm speaking before I give myself the chance to second-guess the impulse. "I'd say it's an excellent domain, but I may be biased. Until very recently, it was mine."

Madoc's head twitches as if he's caught himself from jerking around to stare at me. He knows I've diverted from our plans.

Delta's eyebrows jump up. "Yours?"

"Yes," I push onward. "I founded a domain in a bountiful forest not far from the Heart, one I called Hearthshire. It has plenty of space and natural resources, and you can make use of the buildings already there if you wish—or replace them with your own. It was my pride and joy for decades, and I only left it when I had to move my pack with my appointment as arch-lord. I couldn't offer a better home to anyone."

The Murk sorceress is silent for a long moment. I can't tell whether it's a good silence or a bad one. She rubs her hand across her mouth and another flicker of a smile touches her lips. It's then that I really start to hope.

"I recognize the generosity of your proposal," she says. "But I do still feel the need for some caution, as I'd imagine you can understand. I'll send a small envoy of my people to inspect this domain and observe how your people respond to their presence for a few days before reporting back to me. If I'm satisfied with their report, we can discuss the possibilities further."

I incline my head to her. "Thank you for hearing me and for giving this alliance a chance."

Delta chuckles lightly. "Let's hope you prove that it's worth my while."

6

Talia

The huge, round room in the center of the Bastion of the Heart is packed fuller than I've ever seen it. Seelie men and women swarm around the three thrones of their arch-lords. Sunlight beams over them from the high windows and catches on the veins of gold that stream through the sandstone walls. Sylas, Celia, and Donovan have drawn their grand seats together at one end of the room so they can speak in unison to the many lords and ladies who've gathered from domains all over the summer realm.

At the moment, though, they're only talking among themselves—in hushed voices in the small alcove formed behind the thrones. I can hear them because I'm perched on the arm of Sylas's throne, leaning close with August at my side.

"Offering Hearthshire was not what we agreed on," Celia says.

"I realize that," Sylas replies, keeping his voice even. "But it allowed me to give a more personal touch to the offer, and I think that's what persuaded Delta to trust me. As with the other spot we'd spoken about, there aren't any near neighbors who should cause major issues."

Donovan cocks his head with a pensive air. "It is prime territory, though. We've already gotten a few requests from emerging lords looking to set up a new pack there. The fact that it was established by a lord who went on to your esteemed position only makes it more appealing."

"Well, we'll just have to inform those lords that it's no longer available." Sylas glances around at his colleagues. "What's more important—ensuring our alliance with the Murk who aren't actively at war with us or gaining the favor of some minor lord who should be loyal to us regardless? There's plenty of land to go around, as you well know. The fact that this land is special is exactly why it made a good offering."

I can't help speaking up. "Arranging peace with the Murk isn't going to happen unless you can treat them like equals. Why shouldn't Delta and her colony deserve Hearthshire as much as any of the Seelie?"

"It's not entirely about *deserving*," Celia starts, but then she doesn't seem to know how to explain what else it'd be about. She sighs, and I can see that she's resigned herself. "Well, we can hardly go back on what you promised now without having her question the entire arrangement. I hope you've sent your own pack-kin to help her envoys settle in?"

"We expect them to arrive later today, and yes, I've already assigned two of my people as well as my cadre-chosen Astrid to overseeing the initial transition." Sylas motions to the horde of gathered fae waiting for the larger meeting. "Shall we get on with planning our next steps? Even if Delta decides to throw in her lot with us, that hardly wins us the war."

"Yes, yes." Celia moves to come around the thrones to take her seat, and the two men follow. I slip off the arm of Sylas's throne as he sinks onto it, but he catches my hand with a quick squeeze. August and Whitt stay close by, and Madoc draws up close behind me. My men are still particularly wary of any new attacks the Murk might attempt on me now that Orion's horrible curse has been foiled.

A lot of the gazes in the crowd linger on Madoc even in his sheltered position by the throne. The fae might have heard about his role in healing me and be overjoyed that I've survived, but I don't think all the lords are totally happy to see a rat shifter standing so close to their arch-lords.

My eyes snag on a few figures *I'd* rather have never seen again. My pulse lurches as I yank my gaze away.

Aerik and his two cadre-chosen, icy-haired Cole and the burly man whose name I've never bothered to learn, are standing near the thrones, waiting for the meeting to start. It's not surprising that the lord who murdered my parents, savaged my brother, and stole me from the human world is here when pretty much every lord in the summer realm is. I just hadn't thought about the fact that I might have to face my former captor.

August squeezes my shoulder. I nod to show I'm okay, even as concern flits into me from Corwin across the border after he's picked up on my momentary distress.

It was months ago that I helped my Seelie mates defeat Aerik and his cadre and sever any claim they had on me. They hold no power over my life. I won't let them shake my strength or distract me from what's really important.

"Let's come to order, please," Celia calls out from the central throne, and the voices echoing off the vaulted ceiling fade. Everyone turns to face the arch-lords.

Donovan raises his voice next. "We need to come to a consensus on our next course of action against the Murk forces that've captured domains on both sides of the border. Since this war requires all of your aid, we feel it's only right that you have a say in the course we take. So far, we've managed to hold off further incursion, but haven't been able to displace the rat shifters and their king from the lands they've taken."

"We're open to hearing any suggestions and offers of resources that might help us turn the tide," Sylas adds. "We *can* overcome them, but only with all of us working together."

Someone speaks up from the middle of the crowd. "What's this about Murk being invited to take up homes here in the summer realm? Why are we bringing them into our midst?"

The disgruntled murmur that follows those questions

sends a chill over my skin. We won't be able to work out any kind of alliance with Delta if too many of the fae object to her presence.

Sylas sits up a little taller in his throne. "As should have been explained to all of you, we've come to recognize that our understanding of the Murk is flawed. Many of them don't support this war or the king who's launched it, or only support it because they fear that we'll wipe them out completely if they don't strike back, which I have to say is a reasonable concern given our past aggression toward them. We'll stand a much better chance of ending this conflict with few lives lost if we can find a common ground with those who'd rather not be our enemies."

"But after all the ways they've attacked *us* over the years—and this curse—" someone else starts.

Donovan cuts him off, speaking just as firmly as Sylas did. "The curse was the doing of the Murk king. And I can't say that the Murk have attacked us more than we've even attacked each other. We're all fae, and we all belong to the Mists."

"I can assure you that every precaution is being taken to see to the safety of all our people as the Murk move among us," Celia puts in, with an imperious glower at the crowd that seems to dare anyone to accuse her of being careless. I have to admit that sometimes her authoritarian air works in our favor.

"I think we're ignoring another very obvious factor," a voice rings out, and my previous chill sinks right through to my bones.

It's Aerik speaking, in the same cool, bored tone he

often took when instructing his cadre about how to deal with me. When my gaze darts to where I spotted him before, I find he's staring right at me. It's all I can do not to cringe against August as if I can hide in my mate's embrace.

I can't contain a shiver. August sets his hand on my shoulder with a reassuring grip, his lips drawing back with a hint of a snarl. From behind me, Madoc strokes a comforting hand down my back. He knows who Aerik is too, I remember. He watched over the lord's domain while Aerik held me captive, waiting to see how Orion's plan would play out.

Celia's eyes have narrowed. She may not be as warm to me as the other two Seelie arch-lords, but I don't think she cares for Aerik's tendency toward cruelty either. "And what factor is that, Lord Aerik?"

He lifts his chin toward me before turning to her. "The human girl. Our supposed cure. She's a tool of this Murk king, isn't she? Who's to say he isn't still weakening us and the Heart through her?"

I stiffen at the accusation, my heart thumping hard enough to dizzy me.

Menace glints in Sylas's eyes as he stares Aerik down. "I'll remind you once that you're speaking not just about the woman who's protected us from the curse for years but also my mate. We've found no indication that Orion is continuing to work any magic through her or that she presents any direct threat to the Mists."

Aerik doesn't shy from the arch-lord's glare. "All her relationship with you means is that you're hardly an unbiased judge of the danger she poses to us. The Murk king recently attempted to kill her, didn't he, as a way to distract you? We're also ignoring her value as bait or a bargaining chip. She means something to him, and we can use that against him as he tried to use her against us."

The sounds passing through the crowd now sound like protests, which should reassure me, but I'm still struggling just to hold myself together with Aerik's sharp words resonating in my ears. My breath has started to come short. I grope for the tricks I've learned to deal with the spells of panic that used to come on me much more frequently.

Whitt leans close, his breath grazing my ear alongside his voice. "He's nothing, mighty one, and you're so much more. We won't let him lay a finger on you."

His resolve steadies me. I focus on his assurance, on the warmth of August's and Madoc's hands, on the solid floor beneath me.

This man has taken too much from me. I *refuse* to give him any power over me.

Someone else raises their voice in the crowd. "We can't let any harm come to Lady Talia. She's the only one still holding back the Murk's curse."

"But will we even need her temporary cure if using her means we could conquer him completely and end all this?" Aerik's gaze snaps back to me. "If she's so concerned for all of us, perhaps she should offer that sacrifice of her own accord."

Maybe that's what he hoped to get at all along. He couldn't really have expected that his fellow Seelie would support throwing me to the rats, could he? Unless he's blocked out all the support that's been growing for the woman he treated so awfully. Or he honestly can't imagine that any of the fae could truly respect me as an equal and assumes they'd toss me aside for their own benefit if that was the easiest way to save themselves.

But I could see him scheming up some way to provoke my sense of responsibility and guilt, to push me toward giving myself up regardless of what the rest of the fae think.

From anyone else, that gambit might have had a chance of working. I might believe they really were concerned about finding a way to save all of their people —I might see myself as selfish for not being willing to offer up my life to save so many others.

But from this man, I know he's the selfish one. I doubt he's thinking about anyone other than himself, to keep him and his pack out of the fighting. As if his family won't have played at least as big a role in driving the Murk's resentment of the other fae as anyone else in this room. As if the war isn't their responsibility too.

Anger starts to stir inside me, burning away the quivers of panic. My hands clench at my sides.

"We've seen no reason to believe that Lady Talia would have that significant an impact on the outcome of the war," Donovan says.

"And we certainly aren't going to throw *any* of our people to our enemies to shield the rest of us, especially not one who's already given so much for all of the fae," Sylas adds with a growl.

Aerik shrugs with an air as if he feels they're all taking his suggestion with far too much offense. "Why not let her make that decision? Or does she no longer need to speak for herself now that she has an arch-lord and his cadre to hide behind?"

His gaze seeks me out again. I stare back at him, my skin tightening around my body. I feel like I might crack, but maybe not in a bad way.

He treated me like a helpless animal for years. He used me to advance his standing while leaving me in filth and breaking my body, and now he thinks he can use me again. How can I stand here and let him get away with it?

My chest constricts, but I step forward anyway, tugging free from August's grasp. My mate makes a discomforted sound, but he doesn't pull me back.

The fae between me and Aerik draw to the sides as if trying to steer clear of whatever's about to go down between us. I'm not sure whether they're at all intimidated by me or only worried about his response, but it gives me a clear view of the man who ripped my childhood and my family apart.

"I can speak," I say, my voice trembling but coming out loud enough to carry. "But I'm not sure you should be asking me to, when there's so much I can say. How can anyone trust your opinion about me after the way you had me living all those years you held me captive? Do they all know that you kept me in a cage so small I couldn't even stand up? That you barely gave me enough food to keep me alive? That you let your cadre bruise and batter me as if I were a punching bag for their amusement?"

The color starts to drain from Aerik's already sallow face. Apparently he didn't think I'd ever challenge him this openly. The hisses of disgust in the crowd make him stiffen.

"You fought us," he snaps. "You tried to break free. We needed you. No one should blame us for doing what we had to in order to hold on to our cure."

"And yet somehow the moment I joined Sylas's pack, I didn't need any cages to hold me or to be starved so I'd be too weak to move." I motion toward the arch-lord's throne, my gaze still fixed on Aerik, pain and fury searing up my throat. How dare he? How *dare* he still treat me like I'm nothing more than a tool? "Because I'm a thinking, feeling person, and I *wanted* to help the fae when I found out about the curse. You never even gave me a choice. So, I don't give a damn about your opinions now, especially when it comes to how I can 'help' you. I'd be happiest if I never had to see your face or hear your voice again."

None of the arch-lords interrupt, watching to see how the confrontation plays out. Aerik's gaze flicks to them as if he expects them to intervene on his behalf. I don't risk looking away from him, but from the clenching of his jaw, none of their expressions give him the support he was searching for.

Madoc steps up beside me, his head held high. He pitches his voice to bounce through the vast room, his tone scathing. "If anyone needs proof that spiteful and malicious behavior isn't confined to the Murk, they can look no further than this man. How strange that some of you would paint all of my kind as villains when monsters like him exist among the Seelie."

The rumbling of the other assembled lords is taking on a fiercer tone. A few lean close to Aerik with words that must be harsh given the way his face twitches. He motions to his cadre, and suddenly they're weaving away through the crowd toward the exits.

A strange sensation of lightness comes over me. He didn't acknowledge anything I said, didn't bother to say a word in response, but I'm glad I said it anyway. He might not care that he hurt me, but an awful lot of the fae around me do, and he cares what *they* think. That's good enough for me.

As the angry muttering starts to die down, Madoc raises his voice again, more calmly this time. "If we can get back to discussing strategy, I may be able to help. We've given Orion's army time to realize that taking the Mists will hardly be easy, and we've begun making overtures to the Murk who don't stand with him. I think it's time for me to reveal myself to the king's followers and show them there's another way."

My pulse hiccups. Presenting himself to Orion's forces means tipping Orion off to the fact that he survived—and I have no doubt at all that the Murk king will be baying for his former knight's blood the second he finds out.

I grope for Madoc's hand. "Are you sure?" I ask quietly.

He aims a tight smile at me. "It's what I'm here for. The sooner I speak up, the more of them I may be able to save."

7

Madoc

As the defensive wall of magic comes into view up ahead, the carriage slows. My heart thuds faster as if to make up for the change.

As far as I can see in both directions, hundreds of Seelie are gathered along the wall, maintaining the shield against Orion's army. The magical barrier is mostly transparent, but I can't make out all that much of the Murk forces on the other side. They've left a stretch of grassy field turned cracked and muddy by the fray as a buffer between them and the Seelie. As I watch, a few spots on the wall spark where an aggressive spell must have hit it.

The breeze that wraps around me is warm and increasingly humid this close to the fringes, the late afternoon sun overhead beaming brightly, but neither of those elements touch the cold, clammy sensation in my gut. I told Talia I was ready to face my people and reveal the full extent of my betrayal, but I don't feel totally prepared now.

I wish I could be sure I'll be able to convince any of them my desertion wasn't a betrayal but an act meant with their future in mind too. How can I explain to them that the Seelie don't have to be our enemies? That Orion poses a greater threat to their lives than most of the fae of the seasons do?

I'm still not completely sure how true that is myself. No one's approached me with any overt hostility since my resurrection by the Heart of the Mists, but my reception from most of the fae here hasn't exactly been joyful either. I trust Talia, and I'm going to trust her men, but I can't shake the niggling worry that their influence might not be enough.

It doesn't matter, though. Even if we end up struggling against the Seelie and Unseelie in one way or another, I *am* sure that the war Orion's leading so many Murk into will only make things worse. His dreams of grandeur weren't particularly accurate. He wasn't able to storm right through the realms and topple the fae of the seasons like dominos. Even if he can win, it'll be a drawn-out, brutal victory in which more Murk die than survive.

The carriage comes to a complete stop at the camp where some of the warriors are getting a break from the standoff while digging into a meal. I forced down a little food at the start of the journey to keep my energy up, and it sits heavy in my stomach. The smell of the hearty stew makes me a bit queasy.

Sylas comes up beside me where I'm still poised by the bow of the carriage. The fae who came with us, mostly pack-kin of his who are switching off with those who've been on the front for a while now, are already disembarking.

"We'll keep a shield around you the entire time," he says. "As long as you don't stray too far from the wall, you should be able to get back behind its protection quickly enough if they attack."

I nod. I'm going to have to step through the barrier in order to convey my message to my people. I have tricks up my sleeve to do it somewhat safely, but it's still going to be a dangerous task.

Sylas pauses and looks me up and down, his pale, blind eye seeming to see as much as his darkly alert one. Talia told me he got that injury from a Murk woman's spell. I never really know what to say to him with all his lordly airs.

He loves Talia, and he's accepted me because of the sacrifice I made for her. I have no idea what he makes of me beyond that.

"If you need a moment to ground yourself, there's no sense in rushing into it," he says. "You're doing a valiant thing here today, and I defy any of my fellow fae to claim otherwise."

My skin prickles with the suggestion that I've been some kind of hero. I don't feel like it.

"I'm doing it for them," I say, tipping my head toward the Murk in the distance. "Because I want them to have the best lives they can."

The corner of his mouth quirks upward just slightly. "I'm not going to criticize you for that. Why shouldn't they be your first priority? My kin are mine."

"Well, I hope your kin prove me right that this is the best course of action."

Sylas's expression turns serious again. He glances along the front at all the Seelie who've joined the fight, and for the first time, I can really see the burden of his role weighing on him. This is a man who's been through a lot and who's discovered that no plan is ever truly cut and dried, that you can always lose something no matter how well you think you've prepared.

I never saw that kind of gravity in Orion. He treated his rule like both a divine right and a game. I doubt my king ever questioned whether one cruel whim or another was justified.

And that's why I'm here, isn't it? In some ways, my people are as trapped as Talia once was, caged by flames of hatred that Orion is determined to fan past the point of no return.

"There will almost certainly be more turmoil ahead," Sylas says, "but after everything we've already weathered and all the changes for the better Talia's brought about, I have faith that it'll come out right in the end. For all of us." He glances at me again. "I can only imagine how difficult taking this step toward bridging the gap between our people's will be for you. If there's any other way I can help, don't hesitate to say so."

"For Talia's sake?" I can't help asking, my tone going dry.

Sylas considers me. "I hope you don't actually believe that's true. It may have been a fraught journey getting to this point, but you're family now and a colleague besides. You've shown who you are at heart, and I admire that man quite a lot. Your king may not support you, but you have plenty of others who will now."

I hadn't expected a response anything like that. My stomach flips over, startled but also weirdly pleased. In that moment, for the first time, it hits me that I could be a full part of Talia's odd family and not just a hanger-on grudgingly accepted.

I open my mouth and close it again, abruptly awkward with the knowledge of how skeptical I've been about his intentions. "Thank you," I say finally. "I might not always be the best at keeping my snarky remarks to myself, but I do appreciate your trust and respect all the same."

Sylas turns toward the wall, his gaze fixing on the Murk. "They should extend the same. But it'll likely be a slow process." He moves to the edge of the carriage. "Give us a signal when you're ready to cross."

I'd been wavering, but something about the conversation has solidified my resolve. I may as well take advantage of my confidence while I have it.

"I'll go now," I say, hopping to the ground on the other side.

Sylas waves a few other Seelie over, and the four of them weave a shielding spell around me to protect me from any sudden attacks. As their magic tingles over me, I intone several words of my own, constructing the spell I'll put into action as soon as I've passed through the wall. I may not be much of a warrior, but illusions can get you pretty far when you're not looking to do damage, only to avoid it.

When the Seelie are finished building their protections around me, they escort me over to the wall and open a small section of the barrier so I can walk through. I know they'll keep it open the entire time so I have an escape route and so they can bolster their spells on me if they need to.

The landscape on the other side is exactly the same, even though at this point it feels like it should be a different world. I inhale the humid air deeply, restraining a grimace at the sour tang of hostile magic that hangs in it now after all the fighting, and focus my attention on the Murk forces about a mile away across the beat-up field.

With a few more quick words and energy directed with all my concentration, I project an illusion of myself across the distance to stand on a low lump of earth I've picked out. All at once, the swarm of Murk come into sharper focus, many of them startling at my sudden arrival and swiveling to face me. I can see them and hear their uneasy murmurs as if I really were standing just fifty feet away, with a jarring awareness of the spot where I'm projecting the image of myself superimposed over my real surroundings.

"My friends and comrades," I say, flicking my tail to the side to make sure it's fully in view. "I think many of you will recognize me. I've fought and worked alongside you for decades. I've given my all to support you and work toward the future we deserve in every way I can, so please, give me your ears now. I have something incredibly important to tell you."

My voice and the small gestures I make are echoed into the illusion just as the sights and sounds facing that conjured version of me echo back to my real eyes and ears. Several of the Murk have raised their hands with weapons or in preparation to cast spells, but someone else calls out, "It's Madoc! He's alive." The others gathered around outside the pack village they took over stir on their feet, restless with uncertainty.

I wish I could reach all of the Murk who are stationed across this realm and the winter side, but the best I can do is hope that my message sticks well enough that at least a few who believe me will pass it on. "That's right," I say. "I was Orion's knight, and I helped you all prepare for this war. But I've discovered that there's another way. A way we can have our home and not just that, but the power of the Heart of the Mists as well."

"How do we know it's really him?" a skeptical voice calls out of the crowd. "Maybe this is just a trick from the Seelie who killed him."

I train my illusionary eyes as well as I can on the figures in front of me. My vision is slightly blurred as it travels across the distance to the real me, but I can still identify a few fae whose names I remember.

"Dani," I say, nodding to one woman, "I found a space for your new home in the Refuge when you arrived with your son and got you set up in the weapons workshop." My gaze slides to an older man. "Cullen, I was always grateful for your scavenging runs because you'd find the freshest meats, as I thanked you for more than once." And to another man. "Lucah, I hope your leg isn't troubling you anymore after that clash we had with the Unseelie sentry in Stadtpark."

I *have* been there for my people, and I can tell from the widening eyes and the shift in the tone of their murmurings that they at least believe that I'm *me* now.

I pitch my voice to carry even farther. "Many of the fae of the seasons have savaged us over the years. We will not forgive the ones who carried out those crimes. But as I've spied on their leaders, I've come to realize that they aren't all the monsters we think of them as any more than we're all the vermin they've made us out to be. There are fae among them who can see reason and hold sway over the rest of their people. Even as I speak, the first Murk colony is taking up residence in the summer realm with no blood shed on either side and full autonomy to live as they please."

I catch a few gasps from the crowd. "You can't be serious," someone says. "The fucking wolves and ravens would never—"

"They would," I interrupt, raising my hands. "How do you think I'm here at all? I've been able to gain their trust and persuade them toward the future we deserve. And it's not just the fae on our side. The Heart of the Mists itself has welcomed me."

I tug open my shirt, revealing the multiple true-name marks that've formed on my chest and shoulders. An awed hush falls at the crowd's first glimpse, followed by a chorus of excited chattering.

"You could all find your way back to the true Heart with the full extent of its power too," I say. "I'll help guide you. You only need to step away from this war and join me in building a home for ourselves here without the slaughter. I swear on my soul and my magic that if you come to the fae of the seasons peacefully and call on my name, they'll bring you to me unharmed. The more of us stand together, the more we can win for ourselves without any more of us needing to die."

"Like you died," a crisp voice rings out. A shudder travels down my back at the sound of it before I even see the speaker.

Orion pushes through the crowd. I wonder how far away he was when he must have gotten word, how quickly he had to rush to get here to confront me. He steps a couple of steps ahead of the rest of his army, his arms folded over his chest, his yellow eyes narrowed, the sharp white tufts of his hair looking even more vicious than usual. The splotch of a magical burn marks his chin. He hasn't shied from the actual fighting, but then, I wouldn't have expected him to.

The sight of my king makes part of me want to turn tail and duck back through the wall. Ghosts of old pains wake up in the scars that crisscross my body between the true-name marks. But I hold firm, facing him, willing my stance to remain steady.

He might rule our people, but he isn't the leader they need. If Delta can dismiss him, then so can I.

"Yes," I say before he can go on. "I died. I died by my own free will saving the woman who's already given up so much herself to advance our cause, because *you* decided to repay her for her help with a torturous death. But the Heart of the Mists has touched her, and it brought me back to life when I saved her. Even your magic couldn't defy its will."

Orion's lips pull back in a sneer. "You think you know so much." He gestures carelessly at the crowd. "Don't listen to this traitor. I sent him to his death because his mind had gotten weak and his dedication shaky. He's nothing but a wolf in rat's clothing now."

"You sent me?" I retort. "You wanted me to torment her and her mates even more—"

His gaze snaps back to me. "Did you think I was so distracted I wouldn't notice how your loyalties were shifting? I only told you the cure because it ought to have been an easy way to get rid of you while she still met the same fate." He tuts with his tongue. "But of course the meddling Heart managed to get in the way of what should have been. It won't overshadow my power for much longer."

His words pierce my chest with a spear of ice. He noticed? He *meant* for me to sacrifice myself for Talia, as some kind of punishment for the loyalties he threw away more than I discarded?

I was playing into his plan all along.

For a second, I rock on my feet as the revelation sinks in. But it's chased by a certainty that steadies me again.

I *didn't* play into his plan—because he was wrong about me. He thought I'd die needlessly, and that Talia would follow me; he thought my cure wouldn't work.

He assumed I was only delusional in imagining I loved her.

It isn't surprising, really. I doubt Orion is capable of that kind of feeling for anything outside of himself and his sadistic games. How could he wrap his head around anyone else truly being that devoted to another being?

I square my shoulders. "You're wrong. You're wrong now and you were wrong then. The Heart didn't save Talia—I did, because I love her. Just as I love my people, in a way you could never be capable of. If they let themselves admit it, everyone here knows that you care more about seeing blood spilled and pain dealt out than bringing anyone happiness. I can lead the way to a future that's *joyful* rather than—"

Before I can get any farther, Orion whips a spell toward me with a flick of his hand. It's so fast I barely have time to react—so fast that if I really were standing right in front of him, it'd likely kill me.

Instead, the searing, stabbing agony only grazes my real flesh before I'm yanking away from the shattered illusion. A holler goes up far away across the plain as my former king must be rallying his troops.

I don't stop to see what fate he has in store for me next. I leap through the gap in the Seelie's wall. The guards waiting there hastily speak the words to seal it again, just as a barrage of hostile magic batters the surface and the ground all around where I was standing a moment ago.

Sylas has stayed nearby in anticipation of my return too. He meets my eyes with a respectful dip of his head. "You spoke well."

I let out a shaky laugh I can't contain. "I hope so. The proof will be in how many of my people really took in my words."

We wait, joining the soldiers in their dinner despite my churning stomach. The blue of the sky deepens into evening and then night. The Murk continue bombarding the wall for hours before finally taking a break. They might have thought their efforts were futile, but the warriors along the wall breathe a sigh of relief, exhausted from reinforcing its magic.

We're just about to head back to the Heart when a wolfish messenger lopes past the warriors to Sylas. He straightens up into the form of a man, his expression an odd mix of eagerness and apprehension.

"My lord," he says. "We've had a few Murk cross over just now, asking for Madoc. Should we let them through?"

A smile stretches across my face as hope unfurls in my chest stronger than ever before.

"I think we should," I answer for the arch-lord. "I'll go talk to them right now."

8

Talia

I can't help thinking that the Unseelie who built this halfway house of sorts could have used more welcoming materials. The walls are a dark, chilly metal, the floor a lighter gray stone. They included one window, but it's so small it almost makes the room feel darker in contrast with the wintry sunlight outside. At least Zelpha was able to conjure a lantern orb to cast a warmer glow over the small space.

Five Murk are huddled together on the lightly padded bench that stretches along the far end of the room. They look ready to shift into rat form and bolt for the nearest hidey hole at the slightest suspicious move. I finally convinced the guards to hang back outside the doorway while I came in to talk to them, although Zelpha told me there was no way they weren't going to keep protective spells shielding me the whole time.

I guess it's possible that this bunch of Murk might decide killing me would help them somehow, but they don't look like malicious schemers. They look scared. And why not, when they've essentially thrown themselves on the mercy of the fae who've slaughtered so many of their kind in the past?

But they believe in Madoc. They came for him. That knowledge lights up a glow of fondness and pride in my chest.

I step toward them now, stopping in the middle of the room under the lantern. "Hi," I say. "I'm not sure—do you know who I am?" A couple of them look vaguely familiar, but I can't remember whether I crossed paths with them in the Refuge or not.

One of the women offers a tentative nod. "You're Orion's human. The one he tied into the curse."

I've heard that phrasing enough that I don't bristle, even though it makes me feel a little sick. "I don't belong to Orion. He worked magic on me that changed the course of my life, but I'm still my own person—which is why I came back to the Mists rather than staying and letting him use me to hurt the fae of the seasons. But I want to protect fae like *you* too. I've been working with Madoc to ensure you'll be treated fairly."

"Where is Madoc?" asks the man at the end of the bench.

"He's coming," I assure them. "We've had several Murk come over on the summer side, and he's been helping them get settled in. Arch-Lord Corwin—my soul-twined mate—has sent a messenger to him, and I'm sure he'll come as soon as he can. He's grateful for every one of you who've decided to try for peace instead of war. So am I."

The second woman shudders. "There are fae of the seasons who've attacked us, but… Orion killed my brother in front of everyone in the Refuge, just for asking for an explanation about one of Orion's plans that wasn't clear. Orion *smiled* while he was doing it and then had the body chopped up and stuck in a forge. I never really understood why that had to happen."

A lump rises in my throat. "It didn't have to. That's the kind of world Madoc *doesn't* want you to end up in. We think all of the fae can share the Mists in harmony, without so much violence between us."

"And the Heart…" Another of the men glances toward the wall in the direction of the glowing mass he can't see from here but that he can obviously sense, even though he has no connection to it yet. "We could draw on it again?"

"I'm sure you could," I say. "It welcomed Madoc—I was there when it healed him." It feels too self-aggrandizing to mention that I was the one who badgered it into restoring his life. "I don't think… I don't think it ever totally turned its back on you. I'm not sure how it all works, but it belongs to all of you just as much as the Mists do."

The first woman tucks herself closer to the man next to her, who I'm guessing is her mate. "And the arch-lords—the Seelie and the Unseelie… They aren't going to punish us for helping with the invasion?"

"They've agreed not to," I say. "And some of them are

looking forward to finding a common ground. If anyone treats you harshly, tell me or Madoc or anyone who works for Arch-Lord Corwin or Arch-Lord Sylas. They'll make sure it doesn't happen again."

The second woman gazes out the window. "I've never been this far into the Mists before. It's… it's beautiful out here, even if it's cold."

A smile tugs at my lips. "Yes, it is."

I spend the next half hour telling them about my favorite spots in both realms, describing the scenery and other features in as much awed detail as I can give as I see their rapt attention. By the time the door opens behind me, I'm wrung out of stories, but the five Murk have relaxed their stances.

Their faces brighten at the sight of the figure who's just walked in. The first man springs to his feet. "Madoc! We—we heard about what you said to Orion. This war—it's only just started, and it's already nothing we'd have wanted."

Madoc comes up beside me and sets a gentle hand on my shoulder, giving it a squeeze. "I'm happy to see you all and glad that Talia could keep you occupied while you waited for me. Did you want to stay in the winter realm? We're building a small temporary village on the summer side not far from the Heart until we see how many Murk join us and can start to think about forming new colonies. I could have you join them, or we could set up something similar here." He glances at me.

I nod. "I'm sure Corwin would be able to make that happen. Do you want me to talk to him?" My impression of my soul-twined mate is vague at the moment—he's gone out to the front, and he tries to avoid distracting me with his observations of the ongoing battle as much as possible—but he expected to return soon.

"I think the summer realm sounds nice," the second woman pipes up. "After all that time in the subway tunnels, I could use some summer warmth."

The others chuckle and mutter in agreement, and Madoc shoots me a quick smile before leading them off toward the border. I follow them out and stop by Zelpha where she's stayed with the guards.

"See," I say to Corwin's youngest coterie member. "They weren't interested in hurting me."

She clucks her tongue at me. "Can't be too careful. And I'd say that same about any Unseelie I didn't know too, just to be clear. We've had enough trouble from some of the ones we *do* know." She flicks her gaze not all that subtly toward Laoni's domain.

I can't really argue with her there.

I stretch my arms in front of me, and my gaze veers to the vast camp set up nearby, at the base of the plateau. "I think I'll go talk with the fae in the camp and see if there's anything I can do to make things easier for them. Unless there was something else you needed to get to?" My mates' insistence that I always have at least a couple of guards monitoring me does mean a few restrictions on my activities. I understand the need, but it can still be frustrating.

Thankfully, Zelpha shakes her head and sweeps her

arm toward the camp. "Let's see what our assorted warriors are up to."

I head across the fields in my limping way, the thin layer of frost crunching under my boots, and Zelpha matches my slow pace without complaint. But before I've quite made it to the assorted buildings dotting the terrain, a slim figure with mottled maroon and burgundy hair slips around the nearest structures to walk over to join us.

My pulse stutters when I recognize the young woman as Kara—the true-blooded woman who pointed to Corwin as her supposed soul-twined mate.

I stop, waiting for her to reach us, my stomach twisting. I have no doubt about Corwin's dedication to me, especially after our interlude together where he affirmed his love so many times and I did the same for him. But that doesn't make this situation any simpler or less stressful.

What can Kara want to talk to me about? I have no idea what to say to her. I've essentially stolen her mate, though, so the least I can do is give her a little of my time and see what she wants.

Zelpha and the guard she brought with us hang back a few steps to give the fae woman and me a little space for our conversation. As Kara reaches me, her gaze darts to them and then back. She bobs her head in a meek gesture that contrasts with her almost regal lady-like bearing.

Part of me can't help thinking about how she'd look much more fitting at Corwin's side than I do. She was born into true-blooded fae royalty, even if only a small fringeland flock. This is her heritage. I was meant to be an ordinary human living my life with no idea that the fae even exist.

But we're here with things as they are now, and there's no turning back time to change any of it.

"Hi," I say awkwardly. "Was there something you needed?"

"I was just—" She hesitates and wets her lips, and I get the sense she's equally uncertain about how to have this conversion. That impression eases my nerves a little, although she's the one who sought me out, so I have no idea how to encourage her.

She glances at my guards again, and her mouth slants at a pained angle. "Could we… speak privately? Since really, our association is around a private matter."

I guess that's a fair statement. I know Zelpha isn't going to agree, though. When I check with her, she's frowning.

"You can cast a spell to keep us from hearing what you're saying," the coterie woman says. "But Lady Talia will stay close by and in our view. Arch-Lords' orders."

Kara's lips purse, and for the first time a hint of annoyance touches her expression. But she doesn't argue, just murmurs a few words that make the air hum and then go totally silent around us.

Her hands flit beside her body as if she isn't sure what to do with them. She settles for clasping them in front of her. "You were there—you know what Arch-Lord Corwin is to me."

I swallow hard. "Yes. I'm so sorry. I can't imagine how difficult it is to be in your position."

"Yes. Well." She unclasps her hands and fidgets with the skirt of her plum-purple dress. Her eyes narrow slightly as she considers me. "I was thinking, though, that if it was outside magic that created your bond with Arch-Lord Corwin, then it should be easier to dispel than an actual soul-twined bond."

My stomach starts to sink. "Maybe," I say. "But neither of us wants to dispel it. Corwin and I have bonded in many ways other than just through magic. There's more to being someone's mate than just having the internal connection." I should know, since I don't have any magical bond with the other four men who've worked their way into my heart.

"But the internal connection is what takes it beyond a regular mate-bond," Kara says. "I *should* have that connection with him. I can't have it with anyone else." She pauses. "And you have other mates as well, from what I've heard."

There's a faint derisive note in her tone that brings my hackles up despite my sympathy for her. "It just happened that way. I'm fully dedicated to all of them."

She hums to herself. "I heard you were generous, that you're always looking out for the fae and doing what you can to help us. Wouldn't you step out of the way of the soul-twined bond I was supposed to have?"

Her gaze turns so beseeching that guilt clamps around my gut, but I don't know any other way to answer her. "Corwin and I have already sworn our loyalty and love to each other. I don't know what's going to happen with the magical part of our bond as we continue to fight with the

Murk, but the rest isn't going anywhere. I *am* incredibly sorry that it worked out this way, but there's no way to undo what we already feel for each other."

Something flares in the fae woman's eyes. Her voice sharpens. "Then you're stealing him from me. Stealing another woman's destined mate. How can you even look me in the face when you're ruining my life?"

My jaw goes slack at her abrupt transformation, even though I saw hints of her animosity before. "I—it's not like that," I stammer, but she barely seems to listen.

"It's exactly like that," she says, stepping closer so she can loom over me with her greater height. "You know he's meant to be mine, but you'll happily keep him wound around your finger. A *human*. A human full of Murk magic. He deserves so much better than you. If I could—"

The silencing spell around us fractures as Zelpha bursts through it, clamping her hand on my arm and positioning herself partly between me and Kara. She's a few inches shorter than the true-blooded woman, but she glares up at Kara with a flex of her muscles that gets a clear threat across. "You'll step away from Lady Talia and calm yourself," she says in a taut voice. "And you won't be having any more private conversations with her, that's for sure."

"*Lady* Talia," Kara says with a scoff, but she spins on her heel and marches off without another word.

I deflate a little in Zelpha's grasp. The coterie woman whirls toward me. "Are you all right? What did she say to you?"

"Nothing I can't understand, even if she was harsh

about it," I say quietly, and hug myself. The words still ringing in my ears aren't about what I've done or what's done to me but the most fundamental piece of who I am: *A human.* Spoken with such disdain.

I'm more than that. I'm worth just as much as Kara or any other fae is. But it's hard to hold on to my certainty in that knowledge with her scorn still echoing through me.

9

Talia

"This really isn't necessary," Corwin assures me for what might be the fiftieth time. He's stayed close to me on the carriage for the entire journey out to the winter realm's front, poised by the side of the vehicle next to the bench where I'm perched. He hasn't expressed his worries for me any more overtly out loud, but his concern radiates through our bond.

I reach to grasp his hand. "I know. But we've seen how everyone—especially the Unseelie—has responded to me since I started curing the curse. I don't feel like a savior exactly, but if it lifts their spirits to see that I've come out to encourage them, then I think that's worth something." *More than sitting around back at the castle not knowing how else to contribute*, I add silently.

You've already given more than anyone could have asked, Corwin replies in the same way, his fingers tightening around mine. But he doesn't argue about my insistence on joining him on today's foray to the front again.

"I can always tell when you're talking in your heads," Madoc says from where he's sitting at my other side, in a tone that's more wry than offended.

I bump my shoulder against his. "It's just Corwin being his usual protective self."

"Hmm. That does seem to be a common theme." Madoc isn't yet comfortable making any obvious shows of physical affection in front of the other fae, but his tail tucks around my waist in a loose embrace. He's coming along for similar reasons to me, although by speaking up to the Murk on this side of the border, he's got a lot more chance of accomplishing something useful than I do.

The winter fringelands are basically the opposite of the summer ones, which I suppose makes sense. I can tell we're getting closer as the temperature dips from refreshingly crisp to bitingly cold and the limited vegetation vanishes completely, giving way to long stretches of jagged rock and ice. The only similarity is the growing haziness of the sky overhead, dulling the sunlight. On the summer side, that effect ramps up the humidity. Here, it deepens the chill.

I let go of Corwin's hand to wrap my arms around myself. I'm wearing a hooded wool coat over my Unseelie-style dress, with warming charms in both pieces of clothing as well as my boots, but the frigid air still makes me shiver. It's hard to imagine anyone wanting to live out here, but I guess that's why it's only less prominent lords who end up settling their flocks this far from the Heart.

Maybe there are some minor benefits to being so close to the human world… when the Murk aren't launching an attack from that direction, anyway.

The squadron of warriors around us has mostly been sitting in quiet conversation for the trip, occasionally calling over to the several other carriages arriving with us. When one man suddenly leaps to his feet, I can't help startling.

"Something's wrong," he says, pointing toward the distant horizon.

My human eyes can't make out whatever he's seeing, but the second Corwin's head has jerked around to follow the man's gesture, his posture stiffens. He mutters a curse in his head that only I can hear and motions to the warriors around us, pitching his voice to carry to the nearest carriages. "It looks like the Murk have pressed forward with a fresh attack, and our people may be struggling. Push on as quickly as you can and prepare to enter the fray as soon as we arrive."

He shoots a frantic look my way. I tug my coat even tighter around myself and offer him a wavering smile. *We knew it was possible this would happen. You have to join them—we can't turn back now.*

I can't lose you either, he replies firmly. *I'll stop this carriage farther back and ensure every possible protection is placed around it.* He pauses. *I suppose our soldiers may need your encouragement now more than ever.*

I wish that were a happier thought.

Madoc stands so he can take a closer look. The carriage soars ahead so quickly the wind starts to whistle against its sides. I peer through the crystalline windshield that stops the air from stinging my eyes too much, and the scene that disturbed the Unseelie around me so much swims into view.

Light is flickering all along the horizon like tiny streaks of lightning. Conjured attacks, I have to assume. And they're flashing against a nearby castle of pale stone. My stomach knots.

Before, the front was well away from any domains other than the ones the Murk had already taken over. They've driven their offensive all the way to at least one that's deeper into the winter realm. How many more flock folk are dying right now?

A fae in raven form dives from the sky to land on human-like feet in an open spot in our carriage, her wings still out.

"My lord," the woman says in a rasp. "We hadn't been able to send word, we've been so busy. The Murk struck out at us unexpectedly less than an hour ago. We had to fall back or they'd have managed to surround us and slaughtered us all. We're trying to hold Silverspun, but— With the tricks of the Murk magic, it's hard to keep up with them."

Corwin's mouth sets in a grim line. Madoc raises his hand to catch the woman's attention. "What exactly are the Murk doing?"

She hesitates for a second but answers at Corwin's nod. "They used an illusion to give the impression that they were launching an attack farther along the front. As soon as we'd diverted significant manpower that way, they actually pressed forward in a spot no longer so well-defended. Quite a few managed to burrow into the earth far below the wall in rat form, which allowed them to come at us from both sides. And they've been manipulating the thick ice out here to their advantage: melting it beneath us, propelling it up into blades... We lost quite a few people as it was, even pulling back. The wall shattered, and we haven't had a chance to focus on rebuilding it, we've had to put so much effort into fending them off."

"We'll lend our strength to yours, of course," Corwin says. "I'll join the battle myself. I don't want to see them taking any more ground."

"We're trying our best."

"When their forces are on the move, always strike out at a few of them to test them before assuming anything you see is real," Madoc puts in.

The woman dips her head. "We've been doing that. But they had enough real fighters among the illusions that it was convincing." She grimaces. "We now think they had spells on them to draw any magical attacks toward the real figures rather than the illusionary ones."

Some of the Murk volunteered—or were bullied into —taking on a suicide mission. I wince inwardly.

We speed the rest of the short distance to the new line of fighting. Corwin motions the other carriages to form a barrier ahead of ours and has the warriors around him join him in constructing a swift but potent shield around this specific vehicle. "Stay here," he tells me. "If things take an even worse turn, we may need to leave in a hurry."

I nod reluctantly. There's nothing I can offer from back here, still nearly half a mile distant from the real fighting. But it's not as if the Unseelie army has time to really take in any encouraging words right now. They're caught up in a fight for their lives.

"I'll stay with her," Madoc says, running his fingers gently over my hair. "I won't be able to speak to my people properly while they're in the middle of a rampage. If you can temporarily subdue them, call me in."

"Thank you," Corwin says, and with a flurry of wings, he and the dozens of Unseelie around us soar off to meet our enemies.

I move to the bow of the carriage, but even from there, I can't make out much of the fighting. My gut has balled into a knot as hard as a stone. My men worry about me so much, but I have plenty of reasons to worry about them too.

"Will the Murk target Corwin specifically?" I ask Madoc without looking back. "Will they recognize that he's an arch-lord?"

"In the middle of the fray when they're all fighting as hard as they can? I doubt it." Madoc joins me, slipping his arm around me and pressing a careful kiss to my head now that we're alone. "I won't lie to you and say he isn't in danger, though. You know how fiercely the Murk are willing to fight for what a lot of them see as their only chance at real freedom."

"Yeah." I lean into him, an ache expanding through my chest. In that moment, the war ahead of us feels endless.

It seems as if the front is moving closer to us rather than farther away, meaning the Murk are still making headway. I'm racking my brain for anything I could do that might make a difference when an odd chorus of shouts goes up, loud enough for my ears to pick up on them even across the distance.

"What's going on?" I ask, straining my eyes. Corwin has blocked me out so I don't have to feel more than vague impressions of the danger he's facing.

Madoc leaps onto the edge of the carriage for a higher vantage point and murmurs a few words that must enhance his vision. His stance goes rigid. "Damn it, Orion." The words come out ragged.

My heart lurches. "*What?*"

Madoc is grappling with so much fury it takes a few moments before he manages to answer. "He's brought out children. All the Murk kids he could round up from the orphanages and wherever else, from the looks of it. He's pushing them ahead of the real warriors."

My stomach plummets. There's no way that choice won't end badly for us. Either the Unseelie will balk at attacking while the children are in the way, in which case the Murk can press on even farther… or the Unseelie will cut them down like other Murk children have fallen to the fae of the seasons in the past, and their deaths will only fuel the other rat shifters' hatred.

If they take the latter route, I'm not sure there'll be any winning this war at all—not the way I hoped to see it end. The Murk won't be able to believe that any Unseelie would ever treat them with respect or kindness.

Before I can really think about it, I'm already scrambling out of the carriage. *Corwin*, I call out, as firmly as I dare for fear of distracting him at a bad moment. My voice hits the barrier in our bond, but I hope he can hear me at least a little. *Don't let anyone hurt the kids. Please. There has to be a way—*

Madoc catches me by the arm before I've made it more than a few limping steps toward the front. "Where are you going?" he asks, his face taut with panic.

I motion desperately toward the line of fighting. "I have to say something—I can't let them screw this up. If they start attacking the Murk children…"

We're doing our best, Corwin replies in a strained tone, and I catch a glimpse of the battle through his eyes: kids who look no older than five or six in human years scattered among older ones, all of them cringing while spells fly over their heads. Then he shuts me out again.

Madoc's mouth twists. "They aren't going to fall back all the way across the realm. At some point, Orion will force their hand."

"Isn't there something we can do to counteract this approach?" I ask. "Could you talk to the kids, convince them to retreat…?"

Even as I say it, hopelessness rushes through me. I doubt the kids want to be there anyway. If they had a real choice, they wouldn't be in the fray to begin with.

Madoc sucks in a rough breath, and then a glimmer of inspiration lights in his eyes. "Maybe not with words, but —our children are more sensitive to materials like iron and salt because they're not fully connected to Orion's

Heart yet. If I could quickly slip through a portal farther down the fringes and bring back a sizeable amount—we could set up a different sort of protective boundary that the kids couldn't cross. The Unseelie couldn't either, but it'd at least force a stopping point."

"Yes," I say. "Go—as fast as you can." And then, when he hesitates, "I'll be fine. I won't get any closer until you come back."

He gives me a quick kiss and leaps into the carriage. Thankfully, my other mates taught him how to work their vehicles. They wanted to be sure he could quickly get me out of danger in a situation like this, but I think this use is just as important.

In a blink, the carriage vanishes from my view. He's cast an illusion over it. I slink close to the backs of the other carriages and duck down on the icy ground, praying for a safe and swift journey.

Of course, Madoc bringing back whatever he's able to quickly grab won't be enough of a strategy on its own. We have to get the materials onto the ground between the Unseelie and Murk armies somehow. Madoc will be able to handle a little with his reduced sensitivity while he's still forging his new bond with the Heart of the Mists, and I can help some if the fae shield me while I'm in range of our enemies, but will that be enough?

Corwin has picked up on our planning and opened the connection between us just enough to communicate. I can feel the strain behind his words. *What are you doing? Where's Madoc gone?*

I explain our tentative plan as succinctly as I can and

then ask, *Are there other Murk who've come over to our side with the Unseelie now? Or any human servants who could help?*

My mate's reluctance to see *me* helping carries through, but he doesn't voice it. *I believe at least a few of the lords sent human servants to help with things like the meal preparation. I'll see if we can gather them and get ready to clear a strip of land where you can work. We won't be able to save this domain today.*

Then maybe that's our answer. If there's no way to push the Murk far enough back anyway, get ready to fall back yourselves, and we'll lay down the protections just outside the flock's village.

He replies with a sense of sorrowful agreement. I give him an affectionate mental nudge. *It's horrible, but it could be so much worse. Send any humans around back to the carriages.. I'll get them ready to act.*

It takes what feels like ages before the first figures peel away from the crowd of Unseelie and hurry over to me. The sight of the dazed expressions on the several men and women who end up joining me makes me shudder inside, but I don't have time right now to badger the fae about their policies for human servants. I talk my new allies through the basics of what we're going to do—throwing down materials that'll ward off our enemies—and they seem to grasp enough of what's going on that I think they'll participate.

A crackling explosion sounds from over by the fighting. One of the turrets on the stone castle crumbles away amid sputters of flaring magic. I flinch.

Despair has just started creeping over me again when Madoc's carriage blinks into view right next to us. He's standing at the very front, as far from the sacks heaped at the back of the vehicle as he can get, but his face has turned a sickly shade.

"I didn't consider that *I* don't have the Murk Heart easing my reactions now either," he says, almost tumbling off the bow and staggering a little on the landing. "I had to 'convince' some humans into carrying the salt over... and the trip back wasn't exactly enjoyable."

"But you made it," I say with a rush of relief. "We can handle the rest." At least, we'd better be able to.

I beckon the other humans over and have everyone heave a sack over their shoulder. There's a tab at one end where we can rip them open. Sending word to Corwin that we've got our supplies, we hustle toward the fray.

Several Unseelie warriors hurry to meet us. One of them is Corwin's coterie member Olander, who was out here helping guide the battle before we arrived. Wings unfurled, they scoop us up in their arms with just a grunt at being so close to the noxious substance. "We'll make sure you spread it widely enough and quickly enough," Olander says in a terse voice, holding me carefully. "Corwin's orchestrating the rest of the plan."

We whip across the rest of the terrain so quickly I barely have time to think about what I'm doing. Searing energy sizzles through the air around us and smacks against shields suddenly thrown up. Just as we jar to a halt, the rest of the Unseelie army surges backward around us at a call from voices throughout the crowd.

"Now," Olander says, and I echo his command to my fellow humans as I tear open the bag.

Salt spills all across the frozen ground, the grains sparkling in the muted sunlight. A hiss goes up through the Murk nearby. With his breath rasping painfully as he flaps his wings, Olander sweeps us along the boundary they've chosen, spilling a thin layer of salt all the way across. The other warriors who hefted us do the same with their charges.

More voices shout out words of magic on both sides. A splinter of flame pierces a shield and slices across my temple. I ignore the pain, focusing on pouring out the salt steadily.

And then the sack goes limp in my hands. Olander hauls me away from the jeering Murk forces, but as we spin, I catch a glimpse of the rat shifters at the front of the fray. The children have fled backward, as we hoped. The others can't use them as a shield without drawing farther away themselves.

I don't know how long our gambit will hold, but as Olander sets me back on my feet at the back of the swarm of Unseelie warriors where Madoc is waiting, a new sense of conviction grips me.

There *is* more I can do in this war, more than had ever occurred to me. And now that I know it, I'm not backing down.

10

Whitt

I study my mate where she's perched in one of the chairs in my study, her legs drawn up next to her and her bright eyes even more alert than usual. Sometimes I find it difficult to wrap my head around what the woman I love is capable of.

"That was a crazy plan," I tell her. "Literally salting the earth? Sending the most vulnerable beings among us to the front of the battle? But somehow you pulled it off."

"We had the Unseelie protecting us the whole time," she points out in her typically stubborn way. "And it only worked temporarily. The Murk still gained ground. I was hoping you'd have some ideas for ways we can use similar strategies."

I lean back against my desk and raise my eyebrows at her. "We want to start seasoning the rats some more? Hold a barbeque, perhaps?"

Talia's lips twitch with a hint of a smile, and she rolls her eyes at me playfully. "No. The whole point is to try to *avoid* anyone getting barbequed unless it's totally necessary. Especially those kids."

A little shudder runs down her body that sends a pang through my chest. If Orion cared even a fraction as much about our people as she still does about his, we wouldn't be in this situation.

"It made me realize how much the humans who've been living among the fae can help," Talia goes on. "The Murk who're drawing their power from the false Heart might not be as sensitive to the usual materials as the rest of you, but it does bother them, especially over time. If we could find ways to expose them and weaken them, then it'd be easier to reclaim the territory they've taken over and stop them from taking more."

"But the only way we can use those materials is if we have people who aren't affected by them to carry out the hands-on work," I fill in. It's a clever approach, one I'm ashamed to say never occurred to me. For all I admire the woman in front of me, I often forget how human she is— and that the others like her may have nearly as much to offer. "Very sly. The difficult part will be how to expose the Murk to salt or iron or both without them catching our human allies first and destroying them."

"Yes." Talia's mouth slants at a pained angle. "I haven't figured that out yet. I decided that coming to the resident strategist was my best bet." She tips her head in a beseeching way that makes her look particularly lovely.

I decide there's no point in ignoring my desires while

we have this conversation. I walk over, scoop her up, and flop down on the chair with her in my lap. A snort escapes her as my arms wrap around her, and she leans her head onto my shoulder. "A better position for thinking?"

"Much better." I nuzzle her soft hair. "Makes me even more inspired than usual to determine how to *not* put your neck on the line any more than we can possibly help."

Talia exhales slowly, her gaze going distant with thought even as she cuddles closer to me. "I guess there isn't any easy way to propel the materials toward the Murk forces, right? If the fae tried to cast their magic directly at the salt or iron, it'd affect them too badly for them to get very far."

I nod. "And somehow I can't picture you humans, as mighty as some of you are, managing to fling handfuls of salt far enough with just your muscles to make much of an impact. We'll need to rely at least partly on stealth."

"I don't think even Madoc could create a spell that would hide us well enough for us to walk right among the Murk without them catching on."

"No. And as soon as you started laying your trap, they'd sense it and attack you." I frown, my thoughts starting to whirl with possibilities. "Perhaps if you were in carriages, some kind of vehicle we could quickly yank back out of their range…"

"That did occur to me too," Talia says. "Raining it down on them from above somehow. If we were high enough up, would that work?"

"Perhaps. It still feels very risky to me. And there's a

high chance of them being able to deflect falling materials toward *us* instead, which could even make it difficult for us to retrieve your carriages." Even the breeze could work against us in its temperamental state near the fringes.

"The Unseelie carried us while flying yesterday." Talia's brow knits. "But it was hard for them even only a couple of feet off the ground, being so close to the salt we were carrying. That would probably be dangerous too."

"Yes, I wouldn't consider that a reliable method." But the cogs in my mind are spinning toward a sense of eagerness I'm happy to be familiar with. I'm on the verge of something. If not from above, then...

The idea clicks together in my mind so abruptly and perfectly that it's hard to believe I wasn't planning it out all along. A grin stretches my lips. "We take the opposite tactic, then. Turn their own scheming around on them. They've tunneled toward us before, so why can't we do the same with them?"

"Tunnels?" Talia repeats.

"Larger ones than required to fit a rat," I say, adjusting her against me. "We have our barrier against the Murk army extending well into the ground now, so they'll have had to give up on that tactic for themselves. We can conjure tunnels beneath their camps. I don't think we could bring *our* whole army at them that way, but just a few here and there to lay the trap... Yes, it could work. Then you and the other humans carry the materials in and lay them down. The effect would gradually creep up over the rats through the soil. They shouldn't realize what's happening until they're already weakened, and then we can drive them back."

Talia's face brightens. "I like the sound of that. Do you think all the arch-lords will agree? We'd want to strike out all along the front at the same time, wouldn't we?"

"I'd imagine so. Once we've used the tactic once, we're not likely to get away with it again, so we need to give it our all the first time out. And what's there for the arch-lords *not* to like about getting their domains back?" I give her a quick hug and a peck to her forehead. "Clearly we're an excellent strategizing team."

"Well…" Talia pauses, her body tensing a little against mine. "I should be there with the other humans, helping prepare them ahead of time and guiding as many as I can when we go through with the plan. I'm the only human in the Mists who has much idea what's even going on. And I have one condition before I'll agree to take on that role."

"What's that, mite?" I ask, though I can already guess.

She peers up at me. "You know that before the war started, I was pushing for better treatment for the human servants here. If I'm going to help the fae win this war—if all the humans in the Mists are going to put their lives on the line like that—I want the arch-lords to vow that they'll give their servants more freedom of choice once the war with the Murk is over and ask the other lords to do the same. No more drugging them into obedience. No more controlling them through magic. No more preventing them from going home if that's what they want. I don't think the arch-lords are going to be very happy about that —well, some of them."

"I expect you'll have the full support of at least two," I say wryly, and consider the rest. "There's meant to be another meeting of the full host of arch-lords not long from now. I can propose the scheme—and your conditions—to them then. I think your request is perfectly reasonable… and I don't deserve my job title if I can't convince them of that too."

"They aren't always the most agreeable," Talia mutters.

"No, they aren't." I rub my jaw. "Why don't you sit this meeting out and let me handle it all myself. I suspect it'll go over better coming from me rather than them feeling like you're ordering them all around directly. And you deserve a break from all their squabbling."

Talia looks hesitant, but then she sighs. "Maybe you're right." She relaxes into me a tad more, and an ache wraps around my heart.

She's been through so much in her time in the Mists, and worse calamities than ever in the past month. I don't know what to do or say that could make up for what she's lost or the pain she's experienced.

But maybe there is no making up for it. There's only moving forward and showing her that we're there for her every step of the way.

"Go visit that dress-making friend of yours," I suggest, setting her on her feet so I can stand up. "I think she's getting restless with so much of the pack gone to join the fighting."

I'm not looking forward to this conversation with the arch-lords, but it's best dealt with quickly and cleanly. As Talia heads out, I let Sylas know I've got something to say to the bunch of them, and he gives me the go-ahead with a glint of amused anticipation in his dark eye. He can obviously tell from my energy that I'm ready to go on the offensive.

When the eight leaders have gathered around the long table in our meeting room with their associates nearby, most of them looking predictably gloomy, I don't give them any chance to get started on their own business. I step up to the table, rap my foot against the floor, and peer around at all of them. "Lady Talia and I have come up with a strategy to win back the territory we've lost from the Murk. But it's going to require some cooperation from the lot of you."

I'm met with a mix of curiosity and apprehension, the latter mostly from Corwin's Unseelie arch-lords. "Where is Lady Talia?" Laoni asks, as if that factors into what I said.

"Getting some much-needed rest after all the running around she's been doing on our behalf," I say. "This is ultimately my plan, but she's fully ready to participate. And her participation will be required for it to work. But if we want to go ahead with it, there's a condition you need to agree to."

Uzziah coughs. "Asking for our agreement before we've even heard the plan?"

I narrow my eyes at him even as I smile. "I can give you the gist. We all know—you ravens more than anyone, I'd suppose—how your human servants contributed to pushing back the Murk and undermining their efforts to unnerve us with horrible tactics yesterday. Talia led that charge. She's willing to lead another one, one that will involve every human in the Mists who's able to take up the cause—and I believe this effort could win us back a significant portion of the ground we've lost."

"I'm waiting for the 'but' to come," Celia says, but her tone is more dry than cool.

I tip my head to her and let my gaze skim over the assembled arch-lords again. "You also know Talia's feelings about how the humans in our realms have been treated—stripped of free will and often of most of their minds as well. My lord and I and her other mates agree with her stance. If she's going to lead them in risking their lives to fend off the Murk, she wants you all to swear a vow that once Orion has fallen, the chemical and magical manipulations will end, and those humans will be given free choice about whether to continue serving you. Both your own servants and you'll also ask it of the rest of the lords."

The air of restrained outrage that emanates from our regular opponents doesn't surprise me at all. "And you'd let her get away with this kind of blackmail?" Laoni demands. "We're in the middle of the war—it's not time to be negotiating amongst ourselves when so many lives are at stake."

Sylas speaks up. "I'd imagine it's lives Talia is concerned about—the lives of all the humans in the Mists that many of us have treated so carelessly. This isn't *their* war. Why should they put themselves in danger on our behalf if we aren't even willing to give them their basic freedoms?"

"I'll agree to it," Donovan says easily, but then, he'd

already essentially agreed to work with Talia on this subject before our concerns were diverted by the Murk.

"Our influence over the humans is how it's always been," Terisse says, looking torn.

"This demand is ridiculous," Uzziah mutters.

Oh, he doesn't like ridiculousness, does he? The feather-brained ravens take so much pride in their supposed reason. My spirits lift as I see the exact way to skewer that pride.

"What am I supposed to make of all these arguments?" I say, arching my eyebrows at the Unseelie crew in particular. "Here I thought the ravens had complete faith in their ability to rule. Are you so incapable of handling your flocks that you can't believe any of these human servants of yours would stick around unless you were forcing them to?" I tut under my breath.

Laoni's face flushes into a blotchy complexion. "It isn't about capability," she snaps, but then seems to realize she isn't doing herself any favors with her show of temper. She pauses for a moment to gather herself.

I take the opportunity to drive the point deeper home. "If you're not incapable, then it shouldn't be a problem. Unless it's actually that you're lazy, preferring to take shortcuts rather than put in real effort to maintain your authority."

The Unseelie arch-lord glares at me. Her voice comes out thinner than before. "Hardly. It's simply that we rely on them, and such a huge change would be a big adjustment."

"So would living under the Murk's tyranny, I'd

imagine," Celia says, to my surprise. I'd expected her to resist too. She leans back in her seat with a resigned air. "It's an understandable request, and after all we've seen that Lady *Talia* is capable of… perhaps it's been too long coming."

Corwin nods. "Yes, I quite agree."

Uzziah shoots him a glare as if to say, *Of course you would,* but his animosity has deflated. "She's not exactly an average example of her kind," he says in one last-ditch attempt to hold on to his slaves.

"How would you know?" I ask mildly. "Have you ever given them the opportunity to show just how much they're capable of? That smacks of not just inability and laziness but a failure to embrace your subjects' full potential as well. I really thought the winter fae were much more diligent than that."

His jaw flexes. "We didn't need more from them."

"Ah, but a truly efficient ruler should allow everyone within their domain to contribute to the best of their abilities, I should think. Forgive me if I'm wrong."

He frowns at me, and I gaze steadily back at him, keeping my expression affable. "I suppose we would manage," he grumbles, with a sideways glance at Laoni. "And perhaps we may have missed a few possible benefits."

The self-appointed head of the Unseelie arch-lords sighs. "Fine. It isn't as if we're so dependent on having a few humans around to clean and cook. Now let's hear the rest of this plan."

The corners of my lips curl upward with a sense of triumph I mostly hold inside. "It'll be my pleasure."

11

Talia

The temporary Murk settlement not far beyond Hearth-by-the-Heart's borders has such a peaceful atmosphere that I feel my nerves unwind as I sit at the base of an oak in its midst. More tall trees loom over the several wooden houses that've been constructed there, the breeze whispering softly through their leaves. Streams of golden sunlight pool on the grassy ground from the gaps between the branches. A delicate floral scent drifts from the wildflowers dotting the edges of the clearing.

Do the Murk find this atmosphere as peaceful as I do after so many years living in whatever underground or otherwise hidden spaces they could make their own in the human world?

The ones Madoc is talking to right now keep gazing around them with an expression somewhere between awe and terror. I wouldn't blame them if they're still afraid that the fae of the seasons might descend on them at any moment with claws and talons out.

"I can feel it," says a young man named Flynn, whose scruffy brown hair nearly hides his pale hazel eyes. "I know it's there. But the energy isn't coming right inside me."

Madoc gives him a reassuring pat on the shoulder. "It'll take time for you to learn how to open yourself up to the Heart of the Mists and for it to accept you. I… took a pretty extreme route to getting there quickly, which I don't recommend trying on your own. But if it welcomed me, I'm sure it'll reach out to all of you in time. You just need to show you're willing to meet it halfway."

"And you've already taken a big step in that direction by coming to us at all," I pipe up.

The woman next to Flynn, whose name I haven't caught, is swaying a little with the breeze. "They're really going to just let us have all of this?"

Madoc nods. "The fae of the seasons have become increasingly committed to making cooperation between willing Murk and themselves work. And you can be sure I'm taking them to task whenever they balk." He grins, though his stance looks a bit awkward. "Have you gotten totally settled in? If there's anything else you need in your homes for now, I can arrange it. This won't be your permanent village—we're still working out the details of how the resettlement is going to work with the colonies so disrupted."

As he walks off with the woman and a couple of the

other Murk, who start asking him questions about the nearby trees, Harper scoots closer to me from where she was poised under a neighboring tree. After we'd spent a little time discussing the state of the fae world and her latest fashion projects earlier today, I mentioned I wanted to see how the newest arrivals were fitting in, and she asked to come along.

"They really are a lot like us, aren't they?" she says now, her over-large eyes even wider than usual as she takes in the temporary settlement.

"More like you than I am," I remind her. "They're still fae. The relations between the groups have just gotten very… twisted and bitter over the centuries. I guess the same thing might have happened between summer and winter eventually if that conflict had kept going for a lot longer."

Harper sucks her lower lip under her teeth to worry at it for a moment. "I wonder how everything soured to begin with. There must have been some kind of falling out or dispute like there was between the Seelie and Unseelie."

"It's probably impossible to know now. And it doesn't really matter. No one involved would still be alive. Trying to figure it out would just give all the fae an excuse to point fingers at each other again."

"And we do seem to love doing that, don't we?" Flynn says in a flippant tone, sinking onto the grass near us. He studies me for a moment. "I know you're the human with the cure." His gaze slides to Harper. "But who are you?"

Harper sits up a little straighter, her mouth twitching

as if she doesn't know how to take the question. "I'm Talia's friend," she says stiffly. "Harper of Hearth-by-the-Heart—that's Arch-Lord Sylas's pack."

"Oh, I've figured out *that* much." Flynn leans back on his hands casually. "So, you just came to gawk, then?"

Harper's mouth opens and closes before she answers. "No! I—Talia said she was going to visit. I thought there might be something I could do to help." She pauses, and I decide it's better to let her choose if she wants to say more rather than jumping in. She wets her lips. "I can imagine it must be hard leaving behind your home—I mean, even though the Mists should be your home. I'm sorry if any of the other Seelie have been rude to you."

Flynn snorts. "Rude? That's hardly what I'm worried about." But his shoulders have relaxed, a defensiveness seeping out of his posture that I hadn't noticed until now as it fades. "Well, thank you for saying that. What do you think of us so far?" With a flicker of movement, his tail swings into view as if trying to provoke her.

I'm proud to see that Harper appears not at all fazed by that aspect of him. "I don't know what to think. I haven't really gotten to know any of you. But I can see that Talia's right and the Murk aren't all bad."

"Managed to make a good impression, did I?"

A tiny smile curves her lips. "A little. You could still do some work on it."

A laugh sputters out of Flynn, and then Harper and I are giggling too. It's a relief to find humor in the situation instead of the tension that's been weighing on us for so long.

"Maybe I'll swing by your fancy arch-lord domain sometime and you can give me the tour," Flynn says. "Really test your hospitality."

"Any time," Harper retorts, responding like it's a challenge, but I think I see a hint of a blush in her cheeks. Interesting.

Madoc ambles back over to us. He tips his head to Flynn. "I heard you're decently handy when it comes to food prep. Do you want me to walk you through the local flora and fauna it's easiest to make use of? I had to rely on that knowledge a lot during my missions while I was still spying for Orion."

"Sure." Flynn jumps up, but he aims a wink at Harper before he saunters over to the edge of the clearing with Madoc.

I look at Harper. "I think you made a new friend. And apparently he cooks. That's definitely a plus."

She makes a face at me. "We were just chatting a bit. I wanted him to feel welcome." But there was definitely a bantering tone to their conversation that I haven't really heard from Harper before—and her gaze follows him for a few seconds before she jerks it back to me.

It isn't long before Madoc rejoins us, and we hop in the carriage that's been waiting with two of Sylas's guards keeping watch over me. Madoc's expression has turned pensive, but I'm not sure what to say to him with the others around. He might be trusting the fae of the seasons more, but I doubt he'd want to share anything all that personal with relative strangers just yet.

He may not want to share what's on his mind even with me.

When we reach the pack village, I give Harper a quick hug before she heads off to her house. I might have gone to see what news Whitt has on the plan we're hoping to launch tomorrow, but my attention comes back to Madoc.

He's adrift here among the fae he spent so long hating. I don't want to leave him to work through whatever uneasiness he's dealing with alone.

"Hey," I say as he helps me out of the carriage. "You haven't really seen much of the border castle yet, have you? Other than the common rooms and, um, my bedroom." And the room of his own that my other mates furnished for him. I can't imagine it really feels like *his* to him yet.

Madoc gives me a crooked smile. "Is there more I've been missing out on?"

"Oh, yes. Come on, I'll show you."

Inside the border castle, the guards drift away and it's just the two of us. But I really did want to show Madoc that there's more for him here than responsibilities and expectations. I lead him down to the basement where August and Sylas have re-located their entertainment room now that we're spending at least as much time living here as in their castle back in Hearth-by-the-Heart. *And you never know,* August had teased as we brought his electronics over. *Maybe I'll even convince Corwin to have a go at a video game someday.*

It's admittedly hard to picture my Unseelie mate getting caught up in a digitized race or fighting match, but Madoc is more familiar with human entertainments than any of my other men. When we walk into the room, which is on the summer side with a wooden floor and walls that give off a light birch-y scent, he takes in the TV and game system and lets out a low whistle.

"Okay, another reminder that I misjudged your taste in men. Which of them lowers themselves to indulging in human pastimes like this?"

I swat his arm and walk over to the leather sofa. Its well-worn surface hugs my body as I sit down on it. "August's the main gamer, but Sylas joins in now and then. The movies are his."

Madoc takes in the DVDs on their built-in shelves at the other end of the room and chuckles.

"And you can use whatever you want down here too," I add. "The entertainment room is for all of us to share."

Madoc sinks down next to me. He tucks his hand around mine. "Is that why you wanted to show me this part of the castle—you're looking to challenge me to a gaming battle?"

I gaze up at him, taking in the heavy-lidded eyes and slightly crooked nose that make his handsome face particularly distinctive. We're still really feeling our way out with each other. Our lives have been chaos since the day we first committed to each other as mates, so there hasn't been much time for settling into any kind of new normal.

But I want that with him. I want us to have the same certainty and ease that's developed with my other mates over time.

"I thought it might be nice to have some time to

ourselves to talk," I say. "You seemed like you had a lot on your mind after we visited with the Murk village. Do you think they're doing all right? Have any problems come up?"

"No, nothing like that." He gazes at the wall for a moment, seeing something in his mind's eye. "They're not totally convinced that I haven't roped them into some batshit scheme, but they're giving it a shot, and the Seelie have been… decent so far. That's what matters."

"It's going well, then."

"As well as I could have hoped." His attention slides back to me. "I don't have any specific concerns. It's just all a little much, I guess. I never—I gave orders on Orion's behalf, but he was always the one in charge. And now the Murk who've come over are looking to me as the ultimate authority on how we'll get by among the fae of the seasons, and I don't feel like any kind of supreme expert. I hardly know how I fit in yet. I just hope I don't lead them down the wrong path."

A rush of affection sweeps through me. I push myself up on my knees so I can more easily look him right in the eyes, bringing my hand to his cheek at the same time. "I know you won't, because you care about them even more than you care about yourself. You're doing everything you can to make their lives better for them. It might still be hard, but they're better off here than if they were still under Orion's rule."

Madoc brushes his fingers over my hair, meeting my gaze with a look so adoring it melts me. "At least I'll always have you on my side, my bright one."

The nickname sends a giddy quiver through me. "It's not just me," I say firmly. "Sylas and Corwin and the others will be standing with you the whole way too. You're part of our family now, on the same footing as them. We're all in this together."

In an attempt to emphasize that sentiment, I lean in and press my mouth to his.

Madoc lets out an approving hum and grasps my waist, tugging me to him. In a moment, I'm straddling him, my dress riding up my thighs, our chests pressed together in perfect cohesion. Madoc kisses me deep and slow, savoring my mouth until it's all I can do not to squirm against him to relieve the pressure forming between my legs.

"I don't know how I got this lucky," he says in his lightly hoarse voice, teasing his fingertips right over my scalp. "Not just to live beyond death but to have you as well."

We haven't really gotten to "have" each other all that much so far. I dip my head so my nose grazes his. My voice comes out in a sultry tone I'm not used to. "How do you want to have me right now?"

A strangled sound of need escapes Madoc's throat, and then he's pulling my mouth back to his. This kiss is more urgent but still tender, his tongue slipping between my lips to twine with my own. His hands circle my waist to rock me gently against him. When my core brushes the growing hardness behind his trousers, a whimper spills out of me.

"I want you," he murmurs between kisses, "every

way… I can possibly have you." He pauses and peers up at me, his dark gray eyes lit with a glow of desire. "I imagined this, dreamed of this. You coming to me, wanting *me*. I never believed it could be real."

"We had a long way to go to find each other properly," I say. "Both of us." I yank at his shirt, and he lets me peel it off so I can trace the lines of the new true names now marked on his chest. "And I'm not the only thing you found your way to."

"No, but you're the most important."

My throat constricts with so much love I don't know how to put it into words. A memory rises up of a time when I had dreams I never expected to see fulfilled of my own, and Whitt showed me just how enjoyable it could be to have them made real.

I lean forward and press a soft kiss to Madoc's jaw, marking a path along it to just below his ear. "What did I do in your dreams?"

His throat bobs. "Usually I was lying out on the grass in the sun, and you'd kneel over me, and…" He traces a finger along the neckline of my dress. "And offer yourself to me, I guess you could say."

I can do that without any hesitation at all. I pull my dress up over my head and toss it over the arm of the sofa. As Madoc's gaze darkens with hunger, I nudge him around until he's lying on the cushions with me braced over him in only my panties. "Like this?" I murmur.

"Damn close," he says roughly.

I ease forward, kissing him eagerly as my naked breasts

sway against his chest. With a growl, he brings his hands to them, caressing the soft curves. When he swivels his palms against my nipples in unison, I gasp at the shock of pleasure that races through me.

Crawling a little forward, I offer my breasts to his skillful mouth. Madoc grins and pushes up on his elbow to slick his tongue over one pebbled tip. As he works it over, I have to swallow a moan. My body starts to rock again, my panties dampening with my desire.

Madoc doesn't leave me hanging. A narrow line of pressure teases across my leg, and I realize he's brought his tail out to play. He flicks it all the way up to the apex of my thighs, and I hiss at the swell of pleasure as he sucks my breast deeper into his mouth at the same time as he caresses me between my legs.

"I love the sounds you make," he mutters as he moves to claim my other breast with his lips and tongue. "I love the way your body moves with mine. I love *you*."

For a second, I choke up. I grip his hair, arching with the quickening strokes over my sex, but not too lost in the haze of bliss that I can't reply, "I love you too. So much."

With a rough sound, he pushes his body up and flips us over so I'm under him now. As he tugs at my panties, I lift my hips to help him along and then fumble with the clasp of the fae trousers that've replaced his old jeans.

His tail lashes from the air above us and then coils alongside me. As he grazes his shaft over the slickness of my sex, the thinly furred length flicks over my nipples and traces around my belly button.

I'm panting with longing now. Madoc captures my mouth for one more passionate kiss and slides inside me, filling me until I'm quivering with the delight of the sensation. He thrusts in and out the same way he first kissed me, slow and savoring, like the most delicious sort of torture. I gasp and let out a very undignified whine that makes his gaze spark hotter.

"You'll have everything you could possibly need," he says like a promise. As he hefts my hips off the cushions, his tail slips beneath me and settles into the spot it offered so much pleasure the first time we came together. It rubs across my other opening as if I'm about to be penetrated in a way I've only ever experienced before with two men. Giddy heat blazes through me from both sides.

I moan and clutch the back of Madoc's neck. He bows over me, his breaths turning ragged, his thrusts speeding up in tandem with the rhythm of his tail between my cheeks. "Come for me," he whispers. "I want to see you come so hard that in that moment, there's nothing else."

His heated words send me careening over the edge. My head jerks back against the cushions; a tremor of ecstasy runs through my entire body, making me clench around him.

Madoc groans, watching me as he continues bucking inside me. With a few more erratic thrusts and a hitch of his chest, he floods my sex with his own release.

He eases down over me, covering me like a blanket but holding himself so he doesn't crush me with his weight. After he steals another kiss, he murmurs, "That's one sort of entertainment."

A laugh tumbles out of me, but I have to say, "Not just entertainment. It'll always be an act of love too."

"Yes." He lowers onto his side and wraps me in his embrace and his thunderstorm scent. "No matter what comes. Always."

12

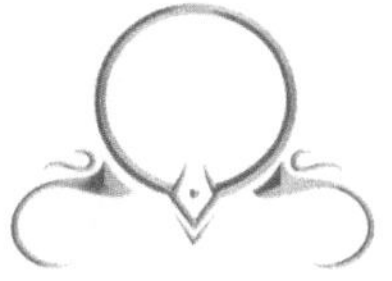

Talia

’m the first human to enter the tunnels. The fae skilled with earth and stone have been working for hours constructing passages from well behind the current battlefront to out beneath the current Murk camp.

We realized pretty early on that we weren't likely to drive the Murk out of the Mists completely, since if the Seelie and Unseelie linger too long in the areas where we've laid our trap, they'll weaken too. There's too much distance to cover. But we have hope we'll at least take back the domains the Murk most recently stole and shake their resolve.

After the initial influx of Murk crossing the border to speak to Madoc, no more have joined us. There are fewer than twenty living in the temporary settlement. I hope the setback we're going to create now will convince more of

Orion's followers that their king isn't their best chance at a better life. Delta is bringing her colony to Hearthshire later today if all goes well, but I don't think she'll turn the tide. We need more than that.

Astrid descends into the tunnel with me, standing off to the side as I peer through the network of passages that veer off in several directions from the common starting point. The initial tunnel is broad, with enough room for maybe a couple dozen people to squeeze in together, but the rest are much narrower. Having seen them mapped out on paper before the construction began, I know they branch out even more at various points, ending in over a hundred different key spots where we'll place our materials.

The Unseelie have made a similar construction on the other side of the border. I've already talked with the humans on that side and given as much guidance as I can. Madoc will be overseeing them, since I can't be in both places at once.

I rest my hand against the earthen wall, finding it solid and cool but not unpleasantly so. Lantern orbs light up the tunnels off into the distance, but their amber glow gives the narrow spaces an atmosphere that's more eerie than comforting. We're far enough down to block out any sound from above, so there's nothing but silence and the faint wisp of our breaths.

Once we reach the end of these tunnels, we'll be right beneath the Murk most eager to slaughter us all. The fae who constructed the passages did their best to ensure we shouldn't be noticed before we can withdraw, but they can't protect us completely.

"All good?" Astrid asks, leaning against the wall opposite me.

"I think so." I inhale the air thick with the scent of disturbed soil and restrain a shiver. "I hope none of the humans who'll be helping turn out to be claustrophobic."

She hums to herself. "I believe Whitt and some of the others who helped prepare them checked for that possibility."

Right. I should have realized Whitt would think to take that factor into consideration.

"I guess there really isn't anything more to do except give it our best shot," I say, and then pause, studying the warrior's wiry form in the magical glow for a moment. She's lived a long time—more than a century—and knows her people way better than I do. I can't help asking, "Do you think this effort will make any difference? To how the fae see people like me, I mean? Or are they just going to think of it as servants doing their job?"

Astrid sighs and cocks her head. "I don't know. I've certainly been impressed seeing how the humans you've brought together have risen to the task, even though they don't totally understand it and most of them are still feeling some effect from drugs or magic or both. And *you've* proven how much strength and smarts a human can have. But we fae tend to be pretty stuck in our ways. It's at least a step in the right direction."

"Yeah." I glance toward the narrower tunnels again. "We're doing something none of the fae can. This might be the moment that turns the tide of the war in our favor. That should count for something."

"I think it will." Astrid grins. "Besides, you got all their vows to start treating humans right whether they think they deserve it or not. What they do matters more than what they're thinking for now."

I'd like to change both, but she has a point. I square my shoulders and turn back toward the earthen stairs that lead up to the surface. "All right. Let's get started."

The crowd of assembled human servants stands in a semi-circle near the opening. Most of the fae warriors are still in position along the front and throughout their camp, ready to make their move when the Murk show signs of faltering, but several have drawn closer to watch our plan play out. My Seelie mates and Donovan have been walking around the gathered humans, answering any questions and reminding them of the task ahead.

None of the fae gets too close to the inner part of the semi-circle, though. There lies a huge heap of bags of salt and iron filings. Madoc was able to persuade some of the rebel Murk to help him gather it. I can't sense anything from it, but the fae who come within several feet of the stash wince and start to pale before immediately retreating.

To make the materials as easy to carry as possible, my fellow humans and I spent much of the morning pouring them from their original containers into backpack-like sacks. Each holds a mix of salt and iron, as much as we could stuff them with before they got so heavy it'd be hard to carry the loads for miles beneath the surface. Thankfully we don't have to rely on only our physical strength for that.

"Has everyone received their quickening spells?" I ask.

Whitt nods, coming over to join me. "You're the only one left," he says. "Shall I do the honors?"

"Please." I hold myself still as he chants a few soft words. A tingle spreads over my feet. I test the spell the way he explained earlier, digging my heel into the ground to push off, and one step carries me several feet.

I land with a puff of air and a short laugh. "This must be what walking on the moon is like. Have they all tried it out?" I glance at my human companions.

"Yes, with varying degrees of success. We kept at it until we were sure they could all navigate well enough once they're in the tunnels. They have their badges with their numbers." He motions to a nearby woman who has a bracelet marked 73 on her wrist. The fae labeled the tunnels so everyone would know which passage they're supposed to end up in. "Do you want to give them their last pep talk, mighty one?"

"Of course." I drag in a breath and rub my own bracelet, the bronze one that connects me to my brother back in the human realm. Maybe when all this is over, I'll be able to properly reach out to him and find some place in his life. Then I step forward to where all the assembled humans will be able to see me.

"Hi, everyone!" I call out in as upbeat a tone as I can manage. "We're going to do an amazing thing today. It is going to be dangerous as well, so please keep in mind your instructions. I'll be right down there with you. Watch the numbers on the tunnels and walk to the one you've been assigned as fast as possible using your quickening spell. As soon as you get there, open your backpack and pour the contents along the trough near the ceiling—there'll be a ledge to stand on so you can reach it easily. As soon as you've done that, hurry back here and come back above ground. We should all be in and out in less than an hour. Is anyone confused?"

The expressions around the semi-circle do look dazed, but no one raises any concerns. My stomach knots.

I couldn't ask the fae to totally free their servants right away, because we couldn't predict how they might act otherwise, and if they make the wrong move during this operation, they could get themselves and all the others killed. I have to believe the trade-off is worth it. If I hadn't suggested this course of action, I wouldn't have had any bargaining chip to get the arch-lords' cooperation for afterward.

"Let's go, then!" I say, and heft my own pack over my shoulders. The other humans move without hesitation to grab theirs. With a little direction from the fae who are careful not to get too close, they assemble into a line two across. We tramp down the steps into the tunnels.

Once I'm inside, I slip into the corner where Astrid stood before to watch everyone go by and make sure no one seems uncertain. The others stream past me, pausing only to glance at the numbers marked by each passage. I even see several already pushing off and taking advantage of the spell attached to their feet. We have miles of territory to cover—and I want everyone back fast enough that they can stay safe.

When the last of them has marched by me, I set off for my own tunnel, which is the farthest of the bunch. I bound along through the glow of the orbs, the feeling of being momentarily in flight giddying but also disorienting. The straps of the pack start to dig into my shoulders. I hope none of the others are too uncomfortable.

Before the tunnels finish splitting off, I cross paths with a few of my fellow humans who are already on their way back to the Seelie camp. They don't look particularly triumphant, but they match the smiles I shoot them, which eases the knot of guilt inside me a little.

Those ones got out okay. The Murk clearly haven't noticed anything unusual yet.

Several minutes later, I reach the end of my passage. It's not even a room, just a dead end with the ledge I was expecting and a high trough built into the earth just over the level of my head. I hop up on the ledge, wobbling on my bad foot, and heave off the pack. In a matter of seconds, I've loosened the ties holding it shut. The mixture of salt and iron filings hisses out into the dark space.

The trough is still about five feet beneath the ground the Murk are walking on. It'll take time for the effects to seep through, but with so many of these toxic pockets spread out beneath them, we think the effect should be significant within a few hours.

In case it starts creeping over them sooner than that

and they catch on, I hurry back the way I came, faster now without my load weighing me down.

I catch up with more of the other humans on my way out. "Thank you for your help," I say to them, urging them along. "We couldn't have done this without you." And the fae above had better keep that in mind going forward.

When I finally clamber back out into the fresh air above ground, the humid atmosphere near the fringes tastes extraordinarily fresh. I want to flop down on the grass and absorb the sunlight for a little while, but this isn't the time or place for that.

Carriages are already soaring off, conveying our human helpers back to their packs. The last of them are climbing into a few more vehicles that've been waiting for them. The Seelie warriors are all poised along the edge of their camp now, several of them sending out periodic murmurs of magic words. They're checking for any signs of weakening among the Murk across from us.

August must be in the middle of the army, ready to lead our pack's warriors in the coming battle, but Whitt spots me and hustles over. "We should get you out of here," he says.

I shake my head. I suspected my men would try to insist on my leaving. "No. It was partly my idea. I want to see how it goes. Obviously I'm not going to run in there and join the fighting, but I'd like the fae to know their cure is standing with them."

His mouth twitches, and I can't tell whether he's

suppressed a smile or a frown. "Somehow I suspected you'd say that. Let me arrange a safe vantage point."

In the end, I find myself with Astrid again, sitting on a low knoll just beyond the camp. The terrain around us gives off a thrum from all the protective magic cast there, but I can't really argue about the necessity for that precaution.

"You don't mind having to play babysitter while the rest of them fight?" I ask the wizened warrior.

She shrugs. "I've had plenty of battles in my time. These old bones don't object to getting a break when there's other work to be done and plenty to take up swords in my place."

As the last words fall from her lips, her body goes still. She stares into the distance, her brow furrowing. "I think it's starting."

I peer across the landscape with my less acute sight. I can't make anything out clearly, but there does appear to be a little more movement—and more erratic movement —among the Murk forces in the distance. The Seelie are stirring too, probably gearing up for their charge.

And then it happens. Someone must give the word, because all the Seelie surge forward as one being, some in the form of men gripping swords and lances, others dashing in their midst as wolves. They've used the same quickening spell they offered us, racing across the no man's land between the camps in a matter of seconds.

My heart starts thudding so hard my ribs seem to shudder with it. My fingers curl into the grass as if I need them to hold me steady.

The Murk appear to rally against the coming onslaught, but with less precision and cohesion than the force rushing at them has. Flares of magic shoot out on both sides; the ground cracks in one place and heaves up in another. Rumbles fill the air. A tremor races through the earth all the way to where I'm sitting.

Tension grips my body. Every second matters. Every second the Seelie are fighting, the salt and iron will start to wear down their strength too. And there's nothing more I can do now to help them.

I'm not sure how long I sit there watching the battle from afar, my gut clenching harder with every passing minute, my fingernails now digging into my palms. But then there's a shift in the currents of movement. The Murk fall back, a little at first and then in a flood, pulling away from the attacking Seelie as quickly as they can.

Relief washes over me. I blink back tears that spring to my eyes with the wave of emotion. I still don't know how many of our own people have fallen, whether my men are okay—but we won. We forced them back. Seelie are already swarming into the nearest pack village to reclaim it.

I'm just getting to my feet, wanting to head down to meet the first messengers to report back the moment they arrive, when a voice I know far too well echoes across the landscape, amplified by some sort of spell.

"You're proving just as tricky as the Murk you call villains, my pet," Orion says from wherever he's projecting his words. A shiver travels down my back, knowing he's addressing *me*. "Don't delude yourself into thinking we're beaten. You'll soon regret turning your back on the one who made you—and I suspect those who've taken you in will regret it too."

With those chilling words, his voice falls silent. I have no idea what he means or whether it's an empty threat, but abruptly my heart is thudding hard all over again.

Astrid reaches me and grasps my elbow. "We won't let him hurt you," she says firmly.

I believe she means that, but I also know that Orion has found many ways to hurt me in the past that none of my friends or mates could protect me from.

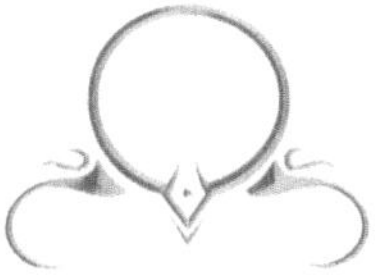

13

August

As the carriage passes through the entryway to Hearthshire's castle and the surrounding village, Madoc peers up at the immense, arching trees. "So, this was *your* home once upon a time, was it?"

I can't tell from the rat shifter's mild tone whether he's impressed or amused. But ever since I tackled him on the verge of saving our mate and nearly prevented him from making the sacrifice Talia needed, I've committed myself to giving him the benefit of the doubt.

Even if he is amused, so what? I'd imagine the grand entrance and the lush landscape in the clearing beyond it does seem a little over the top to someone whose last home was a subway station.

"Yes," I say. "Although not for all that long. I was here for a few decades with Sylas before we were banished to a fringe domain, and it was only a matter of weeks after we had Hearthshire restored to us that he was chosen as a new arch-lord." I pause. "There's a lot of complicated history there."

Madoc chuckles, but at least he doesn't sound mocking. "Talia has filled me in on a little of that. Is it strange, handing the place over to a bunch of rats?"

I'm not sure if there's a good way to answer that. I grapple with my words for a few moments before saying, "It would be strange seeing *anyone* take the place over. Sylas founded the domain—we encouraged the growth of the forests, built the castle from the ground up… And I guess it is particularly strange to have the new residents be Murk. I mean, it isn't as if we've had any Murk living among us at all for a long time—not openly, anyway."

"Fair." Madoc leans against the inner hull of the carriage as it comes to a stop several paces from the nearest homes and inhales deeply. The flicker of appreciation that crosses his face convinces me that he does actually admire the setting, even if he's not being effusive about his appreciation.

Regardless of what I said, my first look at the Murk slipping from the old houses, which they've mostly left as is, makes my skin crawl until I tamp down on my instinctive reaction. The rat shifters don't look so different from Seelie exactly, but they're still wearing the layers of worn clothing that seems to be the preferred style in Delta's colony, and they move with a stealthy, slinking quality rather than typical fae confidence. Or, typical *summer* fae confidence, I should call it. Since they're as much fae as I am.

A bunch of them stop near the edge of the village to study me, unspeaking. Then Delta strides out of the castle with no lack of assurance in *her* stride. Several more of her people emerge behind her and arrange themselves at her flanks.

"The arch-lord himself couldn't come?" she says, raising her eyebrows at me.

I will myself not to bristle. "He is a little busy with the current war," I point out. *I* was very busy with that war less than a day ago, rushing in on the weakened Murk forces and sending them running. If I twist at the waist too quickly, my side still stings a bit where I took a hard magical blow, but it was worth it. We recovered three of the domains the Murk had stolen. We've had to rebuild our defensive wall and spent hours neutralizing the salt and iron that's now on our land, but it was worth it.

Orion hasn't shown any sign of giving up, though. That's part of the reason I'm here, although I don't think Delta will appreciate me leading with that subject.

She doesn't appear to be overly offended by the fact that I've come instead of Sylas. "Well, I guess an arch-lord's… what do they call you? Cadre? Is a great honor in itself." Her tone is lightly teasing, but her smile is warm enough that it doesn't rankle. "Did you come to check up on us?"

"Yes," I say. "If there's anything you've had a problem with or resources you need help finding, or if any of the other Seelie have hassled you at all, we'll deal with the issue as quickly as we can."

"Hmm." She glances behind her at the castle. "Your

lord isn't going to mind if we start rearranging the rooms and all that, is he? I assume he's relinquished all claim on this castle."

The thought of the kitchen I spent so many happy hours in being dismantled niggles at my heart, but I ignore the sensation. Between Hearth-by-the-Heart and the border castle, I have *two* very nice kitchens in my new home.

I sweep my arm in what I hope is a gesture of generosity. "This entire domain is yours now. It's up to you what you do with it. As long as nothing you do adversely affects any of your neighbors, of course."

"Of course," Delta says dryly. Her gaze flicks to Madoc. "How long do you think it's going to take before they stop feeling they have to remind us not to be a menace?"

Madoc's mouth twitches into a smile. "I'd give it at least a few decades."

She shrugs. "We have been a bit of a menace, so as long as they don't mind us reacting the same way to them, I suppose it doesn't matter." There's a gleam of mischief in her eyes when she meets my gaze again.

If she's trying to get a rise out of me, it won't work. I have my temper well in hand these days, if not quite as controlled as my older brothers can manage. "I'm sorry for phrasing it that way," I say. "It will probably take a while for old habits to die. And also, my lord wouldn't be very happy with me if I misrepresented expectations."

Delta laughs. "No doubt he wouldn't. Well, you could be some help, come to think of it. I can tell your pack had magical protections set up along the boundaries of the domain—warning signals and wards and the like. There are traces of the spells left, but not enough for me to work with. And I'm not used to dealing with quite so much plant life. Maybe we could take a stroll through the forest, and you could advise me on some typical techniques." She glances at Madoc again. "And you've spent quite a while adapting your magic to the Mists, haven't you? You might have some useful insights too."

"I'll do my best to provide them," Madoc replies.

We set off, still with the retinue of what I've now counted as eight other Murk trailing behind us. I'm not sure whether Delta wants them to learn whatever we end up teaching her too, or if she has them along because of her concerns about how menacing *we* might become.

She picks her way through the brush like it's an obstacle course, springing onto logs and skirting shrubs more nimbly than I bother with. Her sharp eyes dart across the terrain, and I don't think she misses very much. I'm impressed that she even picked up the traces of those protective spells that haven't been bolstered in months.

"I have to admit I'm pleasantly surprised," she says after a few minutes. "The guards Arch-Lord Sylas had escort us from the fringes kept any hostile thoughts they were harboring to themselves. I wouldn't say they were outright friendly, but no one came to blows, even though my people can be rather… cheeky at times." She flashes a grin at me that suggests it's not just her underlings who have that inclination.

Sylas was very strict with the pack-kin he chose for

that job, and he selected them carefully based on their self-discipline as well as their open-mindedness. I think it's better not to mention how concerned he was about the proceedings, though.

"We're working hard at making a new balance between our peoples feasible," I say instead. "It might take time for everyone to come around, but I think we've made a good start of it."

Delta cocks her head at me. "You're still not totally convinced we won't turn around and attempt to murder you all in your sleep."

She doesn't sound offended with the comment, but I lose my hold on my tongue for a second anyway. "I—I'm not totally sure I'd blame you for trying, considering how many of the Murk the Seelie have murdered, often without real cause. It shames me that I didn't realize the full extent of our cruelty earlier."

It's hard to tell what Delta makes of my remark. She gambols onward, turning to Madoc now. "And you've been right in the thick of it. Have you managed to convert many of Orion's believers?"

"A small number so far," Madoc says. More crossed the border yesterday, and I know he was integrating them into their temporary lodgings well into the night. "Not enough to put a real dent in his forces, but we're whittling away at them."

Delta sighs. "He's going to drive them all to their deaths, and who will benefit for that other than him and his sadistic inclinations?"

Madoc grimaces. "Unfortunately, I've come to agree

with that assessment. Maybe the reason I've found I can get along with the wolfish louts is that I have plenty of my own regrets." He shoots a wry glance my way.

The Murk man has grown in confidence since he first ventured openly into our midst. It's hard to connect the man ambling along beside me with the one who crouched defensively amid the magical cell Celia's guards had conjured around him the first time I met him. But then, the reception he's gotten has improved quite a bit too.

The more time I spend around Madoc, the more I can see how he earned Talia's affections. There is a kindness and honorableness to him despite his past associations, qualities she spotted much sooner than the rest of us did. But of course she would, when those are the features that call to her spirit so strongly.

I'm still getting used to the idea of the rat shifter being part of our collective of mates, but I can't say I resent his presence. I might even be coming to appreciate it.

Delta comes to a stop by a vine-laden tree. "This is one spot where I can still sense the wards, but I can't quite get a grip on how they were constructed. They feel more potent than what I'd typically conjure—especially when they've held on so long after you left."

Ah. It makes sense to me immediately why the practiced sorceress had trouble here. I step closer and pat my hand against the trunk of the tree. "This is a bracewood, with its typical begone vine around it. They have a special symbiosis where the vine gives off an aura that deflects pests from the tree and the tree offers some of the nourishment its leaves take from the sun to the vine here in the shadows. Where they're native to the land, it's typical for us to draw on their essence in creating our spells."

Delta examines the tree. "And how exactly does one do that? I'm not getting a sense of much energy off it."

"To really make use of the effect, you need to learn the vine's true name," I say, and pause. I know it myself. While Sylas is the plant expert among us, anything defensive falls into my purview as well. But something this specialized can't be taught as easily as passing on a true name—and it might not work for Delta if she doesn't come to it more naturally.

I can offer a tip I picked up on my own journey to earning that true name, though. "You can learn it faster if you—carefully—wrap some of the vine around yourself and meditate within its hold."

The Murk sorceress raises her eyebrows, but she doesn't scoff at the idea. She strokes her fingers over one of the leaves with a thoughtful air. "That's useful to know. Thank you."

Maybe now would be a good time to bring up the favor I'm supposed to ask of her. But I can't quite figure out how to broach the subject. Whitt should be here doing this. Except *I'm* the military leader.

As I waffle internally, Delta crosses her arms over her chest. "If there's something else on your mind, wolf, you should simply spit it out."

Yes, definitely they should have sent Whitt, who rarely gives away what he's feeling even when it isn't any great secret. I let out my breath in a rush and look at Madoc, who makes a bemused gesture. He knows what I'm supposed to ask, but he isn't going to bail me out. Really, he shouldn't.

"You should know this is a request, not an order, and your answer has no effect on your being welcome here," I start, figuring I should get that part out of the way upfront.

"Duly noted."

I can't see any way to continue other than barreling right onward. "We've made some good progress in pushing Orion's forces back, but he's been difficult to completely displace. You clearly don't like what he's doing any more than we do, even if it's for different reasons. If you or your colony would be willing to contribute at all to our efforts against him, whether in the fighting or simply suggesting strategies or spellwork… The more of us are working together on this, the faster we'll be able to defeat him."

"Ah." Delta's eyes narrow in a way that doesn't seem all that promising. But then she adds, "I've been expecting this. I should give you points for not leading with it."

I don't know if that means she's on board or not. I wait, trying not to look too beseeching. Madoc gives off the impression that he's restraining a smirk.

"I think," the Murk woman goes on after a long pause, "that we should take a little more time to get our bearings here before throwing our lot in too much with the Seelie. I don't mean that as an insult to you or your lord. But I have to look out for my people's safety first. I'm sure you can understand that."

My heart sinks, but I dip my head. "Of course I do. I'll just say that if you do think of anything that might improve our chances, we'd be immensely grateful if you let us know."

Delta smiles, and in that moment, my failure doesn't feel like quite so much of a loss. "Because you took my refusal so well, you can count on me doing that," she says. "Now let's see about another spot in these woods that's confounded me, and maybe I'll come up with some inspiration along the way."

14

Talia

From a high window in the border castle, I spot August and Madoc's carriage returning. By limping across the fields around Hearth-by-the-Heart, I reach them just after they've disembarked. Sylas has already joined them, his expression intent.

"Was the sorceress willing to offer any kind of aid?" he asks.

August's mouth slants at an awkward angle. "Not exactly. She isn't ready to put her people in the line of fire right now. But she didn't seem totally against the idea, and I think she was genuine when she said she'd do some thinking on tactics we might take against him."

"She was," Madoc says without preamble. "You might associate the Murk mainly with lying, but when we say a thing that plainly, we generally mean it. If she'd wanted to lie to get something out of you, she'd have made more of a show of what she was supposedly going to offer in return."

One corner of Sylas's mouth crooks upward. "And that's why I'm glad I sent you along too. We'll be meeting with the other arch-lords later this afternoon. I'd hoped we'd be able to bring Delta to the table as well, but if she needs more time, I—"

My attention is yanked from his words to my wrist by a quiver of the bronze bracelet that grips my skin. As I stare at the gleaming band, the quiver intensifies to an all-out shudder. Prickles of heat race into my flesh.

My mouth goes dry. "My bracelet," I croak. "It's connected to Jamie—it's supposed to warn me—I think something must be happening to him."

August and Sylas spring to my side in an instant. August touches the bracelet he enchanted, and his stance tenses. "Something's definitely wrong."

"Jamie?" Madoc says, and then understanding clicks in his expression. "Your brother. He's still in the human world, isn't he?"

As I nod, his eyes turn stormy. For a second, I can't speak through the constricting of my throat.

"It's Orion," I say. "It's got to be. He warned me, and now—"

"We don't know that for sure," August says quickly. "And the spell is meant to detect extreme emotional distress as well as physical. He isn't necessarily hurt. It could simply be something happened that upset him a lot."

It's sad that his reminder gives me some relief. Maybe

the bracelet is alerting me because it's *only* that Jamie's girlfriend broke up with him in some horrible way, or our aunt and uncle kicked him out of their house, or he's found out he's failing all his classes. But any of those would be better than having him fall into Orion's hands.

I hadn't known Orion was even aware that Jamie existed, but it's not surprising that he would. His people have been keeping watch over me since I was an infant and he embedded his spells in my body. Madoc may even have reported to his king that I discovered my brother was still living.

I meet his gaze, and I can tell the Murk man has restrained a wince. "I didn't know your brother was alive until you told me," he says, as if he can guess what I'm thinking. "I did report to Orion about your abrupt interest in something in the human world when I noticed your travels there, but I didn't follow you, and I didn't know what you'd found. He'll have had other spies in the human world, though."

Clenching my hands, I pull myself together as well as I can. "It doesn't matter. What matters is protecting Jamie now. How quickly can we get to him? Is there any way we can defend him using the connection through the bracelet?"

August shakes his head. "Not at this distance, not when we have no idea what's happening to him. The portal that leads to his town isn't in the Murk's area of occupation, so we could go to it—at our fastest, it'd take a couple of hours, but that's unavoidable." He looks at his lord.

Sylas is frowning, but he nods. "You take her. I'll have Whitt join you. I should stay to continue the discussions around the war with the Murk." He touches my cheek. "I'm sorry, my love. If I thought my coming would make a significant difference, I'd be with you no matter what."

"It's all right," I say, meaning it. "If Orion *has* done something, then figuring out how to beat him will help Jamie too."

"I'll go as well," Madoc says. "The arch-lords have already heard everything useful I've had to say lately. I might be able to help interpret the signs if Orion's people have been involved with whatever happened."

Corwin's voice peals into my head, full of urgency. *What's the matter, my soul? What's upset you?*

Something's happened to Jamie, I reply as I scramble into the carriage that just returned from Hearthshire. *We're going to find out what. Sylas is staying back for the meeting with the other arch-lords, and you should too. No matter what Orion's done, the most important thing is defeating him.*

Corwin's anguish travels through our bond, but he can't argue with my reasoning. *Let me send Zelpha so you have additional support if you run into any danger out there. She can be with you in a minute.*

All right, I say, and a chill seeps through my skin. I was so worried about Jamie that I didn't even consider what might happen to *me* on the other side of that portal.

Is this more than just an attempt to hurt me through my brother? Is Orion laying a trap? I'm not sure if he could know that I'd be warned so quickly about Jamie's situation, but it's always possible. We'll have to hurry but also go carefully. My stomach twists in on itself.

As Whitt hustles out of the castle at Sylas's summons, his eyes wide with worry, Zelpha drops out of the sky in raven form. August speaks the word to set the carriage in motion. In an instant, it's racing forward across the fields and down the forest path toward the fringes.

As the howl of the wind rises with the speed of our journey, August tugs me down into the lowest part of the carriage's floor. Whitt takes over steering, shooting concerned glances my way. Zelpha perches by the stern, keeping watch from there, and Madoc sinks down across from me, close enough that his raised knees lean against mine.

The sensations emanating from my bracelet fade away. It lies cool and still against my wrist. I touch it, swallowing hard. "I can't feel anything now. Does that mean—?"

"The worst of his distress might have passed, leaving him perfectly fine," August assures me. "Or he could have been knocked out."

Madoc rubs a comforting hand over my calf. "He'll still be alive. I know this much about Orion—if he's involved, he wouldn't waste a useful bargaining chip by destroying it right away." He grimaces. "Forgive my phrasing. That's only how he'd see it."

"I know." I stare up at the stark blue of the sky and try not to let my worries overwhelm me. There's no way to find out what's happened to my little brother until we get to his home… Even then, it might not be obvious. I have no idea where he even was when the bracelet activated. For all I know, the family went on a last-minute trip. He could be halfway around the world, as unlikely as that is.

I'll be able to help him better if I'm clear-headed and focused. Panicking is only going to make figuring out the problem and dealing with it harder.

I take slow, even breaths, girding myself as well as I can for whatever we might discover. August rubs my shoulders, and Madoc leaves his hand resting on my leg, his touch reassuring.

I'm not alone. My men and Zelpha will do whatever they can to protect Jamie too.

We just have to get to him.

The traces of humidity in the air can't thicken quickly enough. As the sky hazes overhead with the now-familiar fog, my heart thuds faster. It's all I can do to keep sitting on the floor of the carriage while Whitt guides it the last short distance to the right portal. Its slowing speed makes my muscles itch with restlessness.

When Whitt finally halts the carriage, we leap out and stop just long enough for him and Madoc to cast concealing spells over all of us. We're not only keeping ourselves out of view of the regular citizens of the human world now but any of Orion's lackeys who might be lurking around too. Then Zelpha takes a quick prowl around the portal while August and Whitt conduct a hasty magical search for any sign of Murk presence.

Zelpha returns to us with her brow knit. "I can't see any evidence that Murk are here now, but I thought I caught a whiff of rat over in the trees nearby. Someone may have come through this area recently."

We can't know if that had anything to do with my brother or if it was simply part of their ongoing war efforts. Biting my lip, I join the fae at the portal. August takes my hand and tugs me through with him.

In the park on the other side, my legs ache to run straight to Jamie's house. My men insist that we hold off for just a few minutes so they can check for Murk on this side too. When they don't turn up any sign of a waiting ambush, we hurry through the streets under what looks to be the thin light of early dawn. It's always a different time of day here than in the fae realm I've left.

The neighborhood where my aunt and uncle live is so peaceful at this hour that my nerves start to settle despite my uncertainty. It's hard to believe anything all that bad could happen here. My bracelet hasn't stirred again since that first warning signal.

Maybe it really was just a particularly bad emotional spell that Jamie's worked through. Maybe the alert misfired, and nothing's been wrong at all.

Then we come around the corner onto the block where their house is, and my legs stall.

Two police cars are parked outside my aunt and uncle's house. A couple of officers are just walking back to their car, one of them shaking his head, his expression somber. My heart plummets.

The next thing I know, I'm running over in my limping way. My fae companions hurry after me, but they don't try to pull me back. They trust me not to do anything that'd reveal us.

All I can think of is finding out what's happened. I

pause, panting, by the front porch. My aunt is talking to a police officer who's paused in the doorway. "I don't know what could have happened or what that could mean," she's saying in a wavery voice. "It doesn't make any sense. You didn't see any signs that he's been hurt?"

"There's no indication that there was a struggle or that he was injured in the room," the officer says. "It could be it's some kind of odd prank that he's in on?"

"He's never been the type to do anything like that."

The officer shrugs. "Teenagers. They can be unpredictable. I should know—I have two of my own. You can be assured we'll follow up on every lead, but take heart that there's a decent chance he'll turn up before the end of the day."

In the room, he said. Jamie's bedroom? I rush on around the side of the house to the window that looks into my brother's one private space in the house.

I stumble to a stop in front of it and whirl to peer inside, gripping the window frame. When my eyes catch on the scene inside, my head jerks forward so fast my nose bangs the glass.

Now I understand what my aunt was saying about "what that could mean." There's a message scrawled on the wall of Jamie's room over his bed in thin but deep gouge marks I can already imagine one of the Murk carving with their razor-sharp claws.

He'll be returned when you return to me, the ragged letters spell out.

Of course my aunt wouldn't know what that's talking about. The message isn't meant for her. It's for me.

My fae companions have gathered around me. August lets out a growl, and Madoc makes a strained sound in his throat.

Whitt sucks a harsh breath through gritted teeth. He's the one who speaks first. "He isn't having you."

"He has Jamie," I say faintly. I sway on my feet, and August and Zelpha catch my elbows on either side, steadying me.

"Orion wouldn't bring him back even if you went to him," Madoc says, gently but firmly. "He'd *enjoy* showing you that he doesn't have to keep his end of the deal. It'd be his punishment for you running away from him in the first place."

"Jamie has nothing to do with this." A sob clogs my throat. "He never should have been dragged into the war at all." The fae have already slashed up his face and left who knows how many other scars on his body, stolen his family from him as surely as they have from me. And after all the work he's done to rebuild his life, they'd smashed it apart all over again.

A vicious emotion flares deep inside me. In that moment I want to raze it all to the ground—every inch of the Murk colonies and the Mists too, until there's no one left who could torment people like me and my brother.

It's only for an instant, and then I come back to myself feeling even more helpless than before. I don't really want all the fae to die. I just want the horrors of my life to be behind me, not multiplying at every turn.

I glance at Madoc. "Is there any way of telling where he's brought Jamie?"

The Murk man shakes his head. "They'll have traveled through multiple portals. That's our standard tactic for muddying our tracks. They had at least a couple of hours head start on us. They could be anywhere by now."

"The Refuge…?"

He hesitates. "I don't think so. Orion knows I'm with you now, and I'm familiar with all the tricks for getting in there."

Whitt slips his arm around my shoulders. "Let's go back to the Mists. We have scouts we can send to sniff out whatever trail there is to be found. You're vulnerable here—we aren't much of a force to protect you if it comes to that."

I don't want to leave without knowing how to help my brother, but I can see I'm not going to get the answers yet. Feeling like I'm trudging through a fog, I walk with them back to the portal.

Partway there, August scoops me into his arms like he's so fond of doing and cradles me against his chest. I press my face to his shoulder, tears welling in my eyes. I long to soak in the comfort he's offering, but at the same time, it's hard to believe I deserve it.

I brought this on my little brother, just like I did nine years ago that night when Aerik and his cadre tore through my family.

The cloud of despair sinks over me so thickly that I barely notice when we reach the portal. August carries me through. All of the fae around me stay in solemn silence as we march the short distance back to the carriage.

It isn't long after we've left the humidity and the haze

of the fringelands behind when Whitt draws the carriage to an unexpected stop. Another, smaller vehicle is racing toward us with a single Seelie woman at the helm.

"I'm glad I caught you," she says in a rush as she swings around beside us. "Arch-Lord Sylas said you'd be traveling through this way. The Murk have launched another attack, and they're gaining ground. We need everyone who can come at the front, now."

15

Talia

 know how bad it is from the fact that Sylas doesn't assign any of the warriors to stay back with me as guards. All of my companions, even Madoc, leap out of the carriage the second we reach the battlefield with hasty instructions for me to stay there out of sight. I crouch on the floor near the bow, peeking up over the side of the vehicle and across the tops of the other carriages that've brought a renewed wave of warriors to the front.

From what the messenger who caught us reported, we've lost the domains we recovered yesterday. The Murk have already pushed forward beyond their previous gains. I'm not sure how they managed to overwhelm the Seelie this time—the woman didn't explain before she rushed back to rejoin the fighting—but whatever tactics they used, those were clearly effective.

Grunts, clangs, and cries ring out from where the fae

are struggling against each other just a hundred feet away. Magic like lightning crackles across the sky. More sizzles back and forth between the warriors. The ground shudders. All I can make out is a mass of bodies swinging and twisting this way and that, some of them as men, some of them wolves.

The Seelie army must be trying to raise a new barrier to at least stop the Murk from advancing any further. I catch a shimmer in the air above the battlefield—but it's shattered apart a few seconds later by a blast of magical energy. A few slivers of the hostile spell fall to the ground around me like fragments of shooting stars. One hisses across the bow, leaving a burnt mark in its wake.

I scramble to the stern, putting a little more distance between me and the fighting. I think my men cast protective spells over the interior of the carriage, but I'm not sure how well those are holding. I can't blame them for rushing when there'll be no one to protect me at all if the Murk tear through the Seelie forces completely.

Slivers of similar urgency flash through my bond with Corwin. I'm guessing that as before, the Murk have launched their new offensive on both sides of the border. I'm afraid to reach out to my Unseelie mate to ask what's going on. He probably needs all his concentration to ensure he and his people survive.

Guilt winds around my gut and squeezes tight. What can *I* do to protect any of them? I've been held up like a savior for the cure I could offer for their curse, but now that the war has shifted to overt combat, I'm a liability, a weak link that needs to be defended.

No, that's not totally true. I managed to get the other humans involved to offer a strategy that turned the tables on the Murk for a little while. It obviously wasn't enough, though. And no humans can wade into this fray to lend a hand. We'd be cut down in a matter of seconds.

Is there anything I could do from a distance? I strain my mind, but nothing occurs to me. Even if I had some on hand, flinging salt or iron around wouldn't do any good when the two sides are in such close combat. I'd hurt my own people more than Orion's.

I can't save my men or the rest of the fae, and I can't save my brother either. I wrap my arms around myself, but I can't hug the growing despair out of me.

No matter what I do, Orion has always found some new way to torment me—and the people I care about. Maybe in some ways, Aerik was right. My connection to the Murk king makes me a threat to everyone else. As long as I'm with the fae of the seasons, I'm a liability not just because of my physical and magical weakness but because of how much two of their arch-lords and others besides care about me. Because of how well Orion can hurt them through me.

As I worry at my lip with my teeth, an image flickers across the thin haze of clouds overhead. At first I don't even look up, assuming it's only more spells for the attack. But then I catch a glimpse of the shapes from the corner of my eye, and my gaze snaps upward.

It's Jamie. The Murk have cast a conjured projection onto the clouds—not just here, but at other intervals all along the front. They must be hoping I'll see it but unsure of where exactly I am.

I don't know how real the image is. It shows Jamie crouched in a corner with his knees drawn up to his chest, an angry scratch on his forearm and a bruise on his forehead, his eyes wide with confusion. I don't see any bracelet on his wrists. My hand shoots to my own, which is still inactive.

Is that because this picture they've conjured isn't real or because they took his off him, breaking the connection?

Maybe it doesn't matter whether this shows him as he really is right now. I know that the Murk took him. I know they aren't going to be kind to him. If he isn't huddled like this, he's in a similar position, experiencing similar emotions.

As I watch with horror clamping around my stomach, a shadowy figure moves at the edge of the projection. It kicks Jamie in the side, and he falls to the ground with a flinch. My posture jerks straighter, as if I could leap up into the sky to stop what they're doing to him.

But I can't. He's not really there. I have no idea where he even is.

A horrible understanding creeps up through my mind. I know it's true that Orion will have made a false promise. There's no way he'll free Jamie unless he's forced to. But that doesn't mean that me giving myself up to him would be pointless. He won't have any reason to torture Jamie if I've accepted his demands.

I can't put myself in the Murk king's control, of course. He'd only torture me to upset my mates and their people. But there was a time when I considered ending my life so that Orion couldn't use me any further. If I got close enough for his people to see and then went through with it… He wouldn't be able to hurt anyone else through me anymore. He wouldn't have any reason to hold on to Jamie.

I grapple with the idea for several minutes. The clash of magic is sending an increasingly acrid scent into the air. It mingles with a meaty, metallic odor I know is from all the blood being spilled.

How could I even give myself up if I decided that would be the best thing I have left to offer? I ease up on my knees to take in the view of the battlefield again, my body tensed to duck if I need to.

The battle is raging on. I think the Seelie have been pushed back a little closer to the carriages than they were the last time I took in the scene. The fray is so chaotic I can't tell where their forces end and the Murk's begin.

Is Orion himself anywhere near here, or is he overseeing the charge from some other point along the front?

There aren't exactly any gaps in the fighting where I could slip through. And as my gaze slides over the warriors, a more potent emotion rises up through my hopelessness.

The fae before me are throwing themselves into the battle with everything they have. I see blood streaming from wounds and flesh blackened from magical fire, yes. I see bodies fallen amid their comrades, limp and torn. But I also catch glimpses of the faces of those still living, their expressions taut with determination and defiance, their teeth pulled back in snarls as they refuse to back down.

They're fighting to the limits of their strength to hold on to their homes and defend their families. There's a certain desperation in it, but it's fierce and unrelenting. They won't give up unless the Murk completely overwhelm them, and they're putting every particle of energy they have into ensuring that doesn't happen.

There has to be more I can give, more I can do, than handing myself over. I'm not done yet, am I? There's so much more I wanted to have in this life.

And giving up might mean saving Jamie from further torture… but it might mean giving up on him too. Do I really believe it's impossible that we could manage to save him without my sacrificing myself, which might mean sacrificing him too anyway?

I have to protect my own family. I have to insist that the arch-lords lend people to help rescue Jamie as soon as we can stave off the most immediate threat to the entire Mists. I wish there was something I could do right now that would spare my brother any further pain, but there *isn't*. Not even losing my life would guarantee that outcome.

Orion might even torment Jamie more out of frustration that he didn't get to decide my fate after all.

But maybe there is a little something I can do even now for all the fae who're fighting for our home. I wanted to come out to the front and encourage them before. Here I am now. I need to make sure none of them succumb to the same despair that nearly dragged me under just minutes ago.

Ignoring the jittering of my nerves, I scramble back across the carriage to the bow. There, I pull myself onto the lip of the hull, which is just wide enough for me to steady my feet on it. Staying crouched for the time being, I cup my hands in front of my chest and close my eyes.

Joy. I need to summon all the joy I can find and create an image of my own to send out there.

My mind slips back to my interlude with Madoc in the basement lounge the other day. To Whitt's eagerness as we came up with our plan together. To Corwin's promises of unending love. To all the affection my mates have showered on me, all the promises we've made. To seeing Jamie happy with his girlfriend and his new family.

There'll come a time when that's all we have, when our worst troubles are so much smaller than our joys. I have to keep believing that.

The true name for light spills over my lips with a rush of energy. *"Sole-un-straw!"*

As I push myself upright, a golden glow blazes out from my hands. I raise them up to the sky and then stretch them to either side of me, casting the light all around me. Even this far from the Heart of the Mists, its power is with me. And I'm with the fae who are fighting for it.

"We can do this!" I call out, willing my voice to travel. "We can push them back. We can protect what's ours. This world belongs to the Heart, and the Heart shines through me and over all of you. Feel it in you now. Let it fend off those who want to break us."

I'm not sure how much sense I'm even making, the words tumbling out of me without much thought. But all through the fray, fae glance toward me and throw themselves back into the fight with what looks like renewed energy. More magic sings through the air from our side. More voices holler and growl. A surge of power hums through the air around me and through our army, and in that moment, I see the Murk start to falter.

"For the Heart!" a voice calls out, and I spot August raising his fist in the midst of the battle.

"For the Heart!" the chant rises up. "For the Heart!" More and more voices join in with each iteration.

More of the Seelie call out, casting their magic together, and a blast of wind knocks much of the Murk army backward. Before they can recover, the earth heaves up to topple more of them. They spit out their own spells, but the Seelie have managed to buy enough time to hastily build a new wall that deflects those first, less focused attacks. By the time the Murk are heaving the full force of their magic at us again, the barrier is thick enough to hold firm.

I sink back into the base of the carriage, my breath ragged and my head throbbing a bit from the amount of magic I managed to pull through me. This isn't a victory, but we held off a total loss, and that's enough for me —for now.

I only hope I can do the same for Jamie.

Madoc

The Seelie lord twists his hands together where he's standing at one end of his castle's meeting room. I suspect he didn't expect his complaint to be answered by both an arch-lord and one of the sort of fae he's complaining about.

Sylas has folded his arms over his broad chest. His voice stays even, but he doesn't bother to smooth a trace of annoyance from it. "If I'm hearing you correctly, you can't say there's anything specific that the Murk colony has done to disrupt your pack or your domain."

The lord grimaces. "No, not *yet*. But I—there's an energy to their presence—it's clear to me that they have suspicious intentions."

I raise my eyebrows at him. "I'd say your intentions are much more suspicious, considering you called us out here in the middle of a war with nothing to show for it except your impressions of 'energy.' You're the one who took your sentries close to the colony, aren't you? The Murk inhabitants haven't been near your domain?"

Something flashes in the lord's eyes. He definitely doesn't like being talked to that way by a rat. He turns to Sylas as if I haven't spoken. "You understand that given the history I needed to take precautions…"

Sylas lets out a skeptical rumble. "Given the history between the Seelie and the Murk, I think it's understandable that Delta's colony may not be giving off the friendliest impression. They're vastly outnumbered among us here, and they're fully aware that they're on precarious ground. When they haven't committed any actual crime, I ask that you leave them be."

"And if you start inventing crimes, you'd better believe we'll figure out who's really to blame," I add.

The lord's gaze flicks back to me. "Is that a threat?"

I offer him a thin smile. "No, it's just a statement of fact. I know about the animosities people like you hold toward people like me better than anyone, and I'm giving this peace my best shot for all our sakes."

"And I hope that you can look beyond your prejudices to work toward the same future peace, which all of your arch-lords wish for," Sylas puts in.

The lord hems and haws a bit but doesn't make any further complaints. I wait until he's seen us back to our carriage and we're well out of hearing before I say anything to Sylas.

"Do you think he's going to cause problems for the colony?"

The Seelie arch-lord sighs. I could pick up on his frustration with the unnecessary visit while he spoke to the lord, but it's a relief to see that wasn't just for show. He really does feel the prick was wasting our time.

"We'll keep a close watch," he says. "We anticipated that some of the packs might harass their new Murk neighbors. I suppose we can be thankful that he doesn't have enough manpower to make much of a strike, with so many of his warriors out at the front."

"Small blessings," I mutter.

Sylas tips his head to me. "You spoke well in spite of his attitude toward you. The more they see that the Murk can be both firm and reasonable, the harder it'll be for them to justify the idea that you're somehow less than us. It's simply going to take time to get there."

His praise warms me more than I'd have expected it to. I nod. "I know. I was prepared to never get there at all, so that one thing is going well. Now if only Orion wasn't continuing to be such a menace…"

"We have had another influx of Murk refugees from his army since the clash yesterday," Sylas points out. "While you're helping them adjust, perhaps you can find out something useful from them about his next plans, or the situation with Talia's brother—or any other factor we'd want to know about."

My heart aches at the thought of the latest attack Orion has made on Talia's happiness. The moment we returned from the front yesterday, she demanded that the arch-lords take action to rescue her brother—that at least a few pack members be spared to search for him and determine a viable plan. There was a lot of grumbling from some of the others, and I can tell she knows it isn't likely to happen quickly. Orion's giving us far too many other things to worry about at the same time.

"I'll see what I can get out of them," I say. "The Murk who've come over from Orion are particularly wary, and they see even me as a potential enemy because I've sided with the rest of you. Most of them aren't coming over out of any grand dream of peace but because they're getting the idea that they might be on the losing side. I'll freely admit we can't trust them not to switch back if the tide turns too far in Orion's favor."

"I'm not surprised to hear that, but I appreciate your candor."

He'd probably appreciate it more if I was able to honestly say something more optimistic, but I can't be too snarky about the man even in my thoughts. He's committed to this course of cooperating with as many of the Murk as will take us up on the offer, and he's seeing it through to the best of his ability.

It's a short trip back to the Heart, where no doubt the arch-lord is due to discuss our next steps with his colleagues any moment now. Corwin has come over to the summer side of the border castle in anticipation of our arrival. He glances from Sylas to me, aiming his question at both of us—a recognition I didn't know *I'd* appreciate until just now.

"We aren't facing yet another calamity, are we?" he says.

Sylas's mouth curves into a crooked smile. "No

absolute disasters so far. One of the Seelie lords is getting restless about having a Murk colony a few domains over, trying to stir up doubts about them. The two of us were able to put him in his place solidly enough that I don't think he'll take any action, at least not while the war is still raging."

"I suppose that's some comfort," Corwin mutters, and sweeps his hand back through his blue-black curls. He pauses and focuses on me again. "I hope he wasn't too disrespectful to you."

I shrug, startled that the Unseelie arch-lord even bothered to ask, though maybe I shouldn't be. "I've had worse treatment. Mostly he tried to ignore me. I made that difficult for him."

A hint of a smile touches Corwin's lips. He catches Sylas's eye, and I have the sense that some unspoken communication passes between them, maybe something they've already discussed.

Sylas clears his throat. "It's obviously not an ideal time for making any major changes here while our people are stretched so thin, but something we will need to raise with our colleagues before too long—the Murk will need representatives here by the Heart. Whether you decide to call them arch-lords or some other title of your choosing."

"Not king," I grumble, and Corwin's mouth twitches again.

"That'll be up to the Murk," he says. "But we thought —at least three leaders would make for a good start. With three, you always have a tiebreaker. And it may be enough

—the three Seelie arch-lords have held their own against the five of us ravens."

"That makes sense," I agree. "If you want me to watch for possible candidates among the refugees, I'll keep it in mind, but I don't think any of them are quite up to the task yet. They're barely up to coexisting with the Seelie at this early stage. Of course, there's Delta, if she's willing."

The two arch-lords exchange another look, one that makes the back of my neck prickle with apprehension. But then Sylas says, in a subdued tone that doesn't quite disguise a hint of amusement, "Yes, Delta would be an obvious one to ask. But we were first thinking of *you*."

Oh. *Oh.* I blink, startled much more deeply than before and embarrassingly so. It takes me a few moments to gather my words. "I—I hadn't really thought about setting myself up as some sort of figurehead—"

"You'd hardly be just a figurehead," Corwin says softly. "You've been instrumental in coordinating the efforts to bridge the gap between our peoples since before we even fully accepted you as an ally. You have enough sway with your people that many of them are choosing to trust you over Orion. There's no one it'd make more sense to appoint when the time comes."

I'm not sure what to do with the chaotic mix of emotions that's flooding me. I can't even tell whether I'm more awed or disturbed by the suggestion.

Me, a ruler of all Murk kind? Even with two colleagues, that seems like a stretch. And it'd mean dealing with the leaders of the fae of the seasons constantly.

But then, I'm doing that right now anyway, aren't I?

And I know what Talia would say if I told her about this offer. She'd tell me that it's only natural they'd want me as a fellow arch-lord—or whatever—and that she's sure I'd be up to the task. My lovely mate with her unshakeable faith.

Thinking of her doesn't erase my doubts, but it does steady me enough for me to say, "I'm glad to know you see things that way, and even more glad I don't need to make any decisions on the subject just yet."

Sylas chuckles. "We felt it'd be good to mention it before relations between our peoples go much further." His gaze slides down the haze of the border to a spot somewhere beyond the gold-laced walls of the Seelie's Bastion. "Perhaps we'd build another border castle at the other side of the Heart, one the highest Murk leaders could call their own. Seeing as you don't belong to one specific season or another."

Suddenly I can see it—a towering structure created in the Murk style, multiple materials woven together into something odd but functional. A place where all of the rat shifters in the Mists would know that they can come and make an appeal if they run into trouble—know that the Murk who rule from there have just as much authority as their Seelie and Unseelie counterparts.

Yes, that would be a miraculous thing.

"Let's win this war first," I say. "Then we can have fun negotiating about new castles and Murk arch-lords with your colleagues."

Corwin gives me a wry smile. At the same moment, one of the sentries comes loping over in wolf form.

"We've had another small group of Murk arrive," he

says when he's straightened up as a man. "They've been escorted to the temporary settlement. They're asking for Madoc—don't want to speak or even be near any of the rest of us."

I won't blame my fellow Murk for feeling that way. "I'll head right over." I tip my head in an awkward goodbye to the arch-lords and set off for the settlement.

It's only once I've passed into the shelter of the first stretch of forest that I sink down into rat form and dash along that way. I still don't feel totally comfortable showing just how rat-like I am too blatantly among the other fae. I guess that's something I'll have to get over eventually… but there's plenty of time to reach that point.

The temporary sort-of colony has doubled in size in the past few days, and these new arrivals will expand it even more. I shift again at the edge of the makeshift village, where a few of the more established Murk are conjuring new dwellings. It's good to see them taking some initiative to help the newcomers settle in.

I can easily spot the five who've just arrived. They're standing close together in the middle of the space, their stances defensive and their gazes twitching between the few Seelie guards keeping an eye on the place. In theory, the wolves are mostly here to assist if the displaced Murk need it, but I'm sure that's not how most of my fellow rats take their presence. I make a mental note to ask them to keep their posts a little farther off, out of view unless the Murk actually call on them.

There's another Seelie in our midst. Talia's friend, the one she's told me made her most elaborate dresses, is standing tentatively at one edge of the settlement. She's talking with a few of the more established fae, including the young guy named Flynn who's a little too cocky for his own good.

From the way he's grinning at her and flourishing with his hand alongside some remark he's made, I suspect he's flirting his ass off. He'd better make sure the wolf girl doesn't hand it back to him. She might not look like a fighter, but they've all got fangs and claws.

I head straight to the clump of newcomers, who relax only slightly at the sight of me. I recognize a couple as regulars from the Refuge.

"I'm glad to have you join us," I say, and motion toward the houses the other Murk are constructing. "Did you want to lend a hand with your new homes?"

The bunch of them all look uncertain. "We didn't realize those were for us," one woman admits. "The Seelie just… let you all build more houses whenever you want?"

I expand my gesture to take in the field around us. "They've given us plenty of room to set up camp while we're still figuring out how this whole cooperative existence thing is going to work. You can ask any of the others who've been here longer—we haven't had any trouble from the wolves. They recognize that you've already proven a lot just by leaving Orion to seek us out."

"To seek *you* out," one of the men I recognize clarifies, with a penetrating look I square my shoulders against. "Things have… things have gotten pretty troublesome over with Orion, even if a lot of the rest don't want to admit it."

"It's hard for anyone to acknowledge they've been wrong, even to themselves," I say. "I've been there."

The remark seems to set them more at ease. We drift over toward the houses-in-progress, and a couple of the newcomers join in with the casting, met with welcoming nods from the Murk who were on the job. I shoot them a smile and make another mental note to find some way to thank them well later.

I have other concerns at the front of my mind right now, though. I glance at the man who spoke about the difficulties with Orion. "We could bring over so many more of our people sooner if Orion was toppled. You clearly know he isn't doing us any favors with this war."

The second man speaks up in a gruff voice. "He's keeping the pressure on the other fae. Maybe they wouldn't accept us like this if they didn't see they can't get away with cutting us all down on a whim anymore."

"We've had good reasons for being angry and wanting payback," the first man adds.

"Of course—I've wanted that too," I say. I'm going to have to walk a careful line here. "But they've seen that our actions have been justified now. And the longer this war is drawn out, the more of our own people are losing their lives. I wouldn't ask you to reveal anything you're uncomfortable talking about, but if you've found out details that could get us to the peace we all need sooner, I'd make sure the information is handled with proper care."

I won't let the Seelie run rabid with it, I'm trying to

convey. The other Murk don't appear particularly convinced.

"We weren't as high up with Orion as you were, not by a mile," the first man says, hedging.

"Well, if you think of anything," I say, knowing it's better not to push too hard in a first conversation, as impatient for a resolution as I am. "Even about an aspect that's not all that crucial to Orion's plans, like where he's stashed the human boy he's kidnapped. Either way, you can settle in here, and we'll—"

The second man's snort cuts me off. "There's no retrieving that kid."

My spine stiffens, but I try not to let my reaction show. "Why would you say that?"

He opens his mouth and then closes it again, with a glance at his companions. I must have won enough points to earn this much trust, though, because the first man spreads his hands in a helpless gesture.

"We heard he's got him shut away in some pit in an old iron mine. Tons of the ore still all around. It's hard enough for Orion's people to go in—no one connected to the Heart of the Mists is getting within half a mile of that place."

My spirits sink, but I don't let that show either. "I guess we'll see about that. Do you have any idea where exactly this mine is?"

17

Talia

"An iron mine," Celia repeats. She braces one elbow against the table in the border castle's meeting room and pinches the bridge of her nose as if Madoc's report has given her a headache.

"Why not?" Laoni mutters from where she's sitting at the other end of the table. She shakes her head as if we've purposefully conspired to make this situation as difficult as possible.

Terisse frowns. "Do we have any idea where this specific iron mine is?"

Madoc exhales slowly. "It was hard enough dragging even a little information out of the newest Murk arrivals. They're still getting a sense of how they're going to fit in here among the rest of you. And I'm not sure how many more details they actually know. It's quite possible they were telling the truth that they had no idea."

"Are there a lot of iron mines in the human world?" Donovan asks. "How easily could we narrow it down?"

"It'd be like looking for a needle in a haystack, unfortunately," Whitt puts in from where he's standing just behind Sylas's seat. "But if we can find other methods to bring to bear—"

"We shouldn't even be discussing this!" Uzziah sputters. "How can we focus on one—*human*—boy when both of our realms are under threat?"

My hackles rise. For the first time since this meeting started, I lean forward and let out some of the emotion churning inside me. "It's not 'just' one human boy. He's my brother, and he's already nearly died once so you could have your cure. If we can get him away from the Murk, then we'll have screwed up Orion's latest plan. The more we undermine him, the less faith his followers will have in him—the more of them we'll win over."

"Talia raises a good point," Corwin says with a tendril of reassurance he extends through our connection. "We've made relatively little progress fighting the Murk head-to-head—and I'll point out that the one major victory we accomplished was based on Talia's inspiration and only possible with the hard work of her and many other humans. The rat shifters have been beating us when it comes to trickery, so if we can undercut their tricks, we're taking away their main advantage."

Thank you, I say to him silently, and he shoots me a quick smile.

Celia stirs in her chair. "I don't see how we'd be able to get at the boy when we're much more affected by iron than

Orion's contingent of Murk is. We can hardly send a squadron of humans into this mine to face off against the rats alone."

I've already thought about that, and the knowledge sits heavy in my stomach. "We can't," I agree. "But if we could just take a little time to discuss the possibilities… Orion's managed to out-scheme us more than once. We should be able to challenge him on that level if we all put our minds together, right?"

"The first concern is obviously finding the correct mine," Sylas says. "We can't do anything for the boy if we don't know exactly where he is."

Donovan perks up. "We were able to track down Murk before using Talia's blood. She should have even stronger physical ties to her brother than to the rat shifters, shouldn't she? Could we make use of a similar strategy?"

Whitt, who masterminded the tracking spell, taps his forefinger against his lips. "Unfortunately, that spell worked on a localized level. We'd have to end up in approximately the right vicinity to have any hope of it picking up his presence. Without narrowing it down more, it'd be a fathomless task."

"We still have sentries attempting to monitor the Murk in the human world," Terisse says, glancing around the table. "Have any of them reported recent activity that might point us in the right direction?"

Laoni's mouth tightens. "One of mine never returned. I think she was caught by the Murk and killed. The other is due to report in tomorrow."

"I haven't heard anything useful from ours," Uzziah says grudgingly.

There's no guarantee any of the sentries who'll send back reports in the next few days will have discovered anything either, and with every passing hour, there's more chance that Orion will decide he doesn't need to keep Jamie alive.

I exhale sharply in frustration and run my fingers over my bronze bracelet. "It's too bad they took Jamie's bracelet off him. I had a connection to him that way even across the distance. Maybe it could have led us to him."

Whitt's eyebrows rise. "I hadn't thought about the specific magical approach August used with his spell. I'm not sure how easy it'd be to locate your brother in the physical world using similar means, but you *do* have strong blood ties to him. I think if we conducted magic through you the same way August charmed the bracelet to work, we could cast a spell to wherever he is. It might not be the most comfortable process…"

My spirits have already lifted. "I don't care. If it's a way to reach out to him, I can endure it. But… if the spell doesn't tell us where he is, what other magic could we cast that would help him?"

"The girl has more uses than that," a softly creaky voice says. It takes me a second to realize it's Neve, the elderly Unseelie arch-lord who seems to drift through most of these meetings without paying much attention to them. Her gaze has cleared a little, and it's fixed on me. "We can work metal, and she can handle iron."

Whitt claps his hands together. "Yes. You're right—that just might work."

Celia looks from one to the other, her expression as puzzled as I feel. "What do you mean?"

"Talia doesn't have any aversion to iron," Whitt says. "If we conduct metal-working magic *through* her, we may be able to manipulate the ore around her brother. With enough effort and expertise, I could see it being possible to create some kind of protective shell or similar around her brother that would shut out the Murk until we can get to him ourselves—until they're defeated and he's no longer guarded."

My heart leaps. "You really think so?"

He nods. "But we'll need the strongest metal-workers we've got. There's Sorling in our pack—he's very adept with bronze and copper. Metal tends to be more an interest of the Unseelie, though, isn't it? You birds and your eye for shiny objects." His own eyes twinkle with humor.

Laoni hesitates and then admits, "A skill with metals runs in my family. I can contribute."

I blink, startled that she'd offer, but maybe she realizes her colleagues would point her out if she didn't. She meets my gaze evenly. "I don't want this to take too much focus away from our other efforts, though," she adds.

"Of course not," I murmur.

"I'm sure we can round up a few more," Terisse says. "How quickly would you have the technique worked out?"

Sylas glances back at his strategist.

Whitt has started to pace the room. "I may be ready in

a matter of hours. Perhaps we should convene in Corwin's palace, since this is more wintry magic. Gather your people, and I'll send word when I'm ready to direct the attempt. I need to consult my books." He stalks out into the hall without another word.

Uzziah huffs as he gets up, but he doesn't argue about the situation. I follow Sylas and the other Seelie back to the summer realm, figuring I might be able to help Whitt sort through his books—or at the very least, it might be useful for him to have me there to test out bits of techniques on. My pulse is thumping hard with the prospect of doing something for Jamie so soon.

Celia strides ahead of the rest of us, heading toward her own domain—and a figure steps into view in the distance, by the forest closer to the Bastion. At the sight of the sunlight glancing off his dandelion-yellow hair, my feet jar to a stop.

It's Aerik. He looks like he's waiting to speak to Celia. What does he want now?

The other men follow my gaze. Sylas lets out a restrained snarl.

Whatever Aerik says when Celia reaches him, she doesn't appear to listen for very long. She makes a dismissive gesture and then sets her hands on her hips when he starts talking again. Finally, he slinks off between the trees.

Sylas marches over, and I hustle along as quickly as I can after him, Madoc keeping pace beside me. Celia sees us coming and waits for us to reach her.

"What was that about?" Sylas demands.

Celia's gaze settles on me with an unusual amount of sympathy. "Word has gotten around that we're concerned with your brother's predicament. Your former captor was urging me not to be distracted by such 'minor matters,' as he put it. You don't need to worry. I informed him I don't see it the same way." She sighs. "I'm sorry you had to spend any time under that man's power. He isn't what the Seelie should be."

Her words can't change the past, but the sentiment in them loosens a little of the old pain that's lodged inside me. "I'm glad that most aren't as bad as him," I say quietly.

She waves me off. "Go with your mates and see to this scheme. The faster it's done, the better for all of us."

It *is* only a few hours later that I find myself sitting cross-legged on the floor in one of the grand diamond rooms in the palace of Heart's Cadence with several fae poised around me. Whitt outdid himself with his research, flying from book to book and scribbling furious notes on whatever papers he could lay his hands on.

He sent our pack-kin who are still on hand at Hearth-by-the-Heart into the woods to gather up a couple of different plants that are supposed to help open me to the magic that's going to flow through me. The leafy stems are now draped across my shoulders and pooled in my lap. They give off a sharp herbal scent that itches my nose.

"So, I don't have to *do* anything?" I ask him as he circles me, making one final inspection.

"Just sit still and keep your emotions as calm and your mind as open as possible," Whitt says. "I'll stay with you to help you relax, since the actual magical talents required aren't in my main repertoire." He glances around at the gathered fae, mostly Unseelie, including Laoni. His sharp gaze might rest a little longer on the arch-lord. "I trust that you all are totally clear on what's expected of you, or that you'll speak up now if you're not?"

When no one raises any issues, he turns to Corwin, standing directly in front of me. "Are you ready to guide the process?"

Corwin inclines his head, offering me a waft of affection and hope at the same time. "Absolutely. We'll make this work."

Whitt sinks onto the floor behind me and eases his arms around my waist. "Lean back against me and breathe slowly and deeply," he murmurs by my ear. "I've got you. The spellwork might feel confusing or even painful, but I won't let anything really hurt you. Do you trust me?"

"Of course," I say automatically. It's true. As I let my weight sink into Whitt's solid frame, the worst of my anxiety subsides. He's the cleverest person I know. He wouldn't be going through with this attempt if he wasn't sure it had a good chance of working—and no chance of going horribly wrong.

If we can protect Jamie, just about anything is worth it.

I close my eyes, letting my awareness narrow down to the cool floor beneath me, the warmth of Whitt's embrace from behind me, and the softly murmuring voices of the fae around me that start to spill out into the air. They're speaking in true names and other words of magic, so I can't understand them anyway, but a quiver of energy runs over my skin.

After several seconds, the quiver digs deeper, expanding into a tremor that travels through me from my breastbone down to my gut. I have to restrain a gasp. Whitt picks up on the tensing of my muscles and strokes his fingers over my arms in a soothing gesture. I let him lull me back into a sort of peace as the flow of magic passing into me continues to grow.

In a matter of minutes, it feels as if I'm lying beneath a waterfall that's pummeling my chest with a chilly torrent —if that torrent would pass right through my skin and flesh and out the other side of me. It takes concentrated will to keep my breaths steady. My nerves are singing in harmony with the deluge, both exhilarating and unnerving.

Images begin to flash through my mind alongside the stream of energy, giving me something else to focus on. I see my brother crouched in a darkened room with walls of packed dirt and wooden posts. I taste the metal woven all through the soil around me. Particles of it jitter free from the earth, my nerves twitching with every movement, and course into a current that flows around him.

At the same time, a colder wash of magic sweeps through me into him. Jamie's eyes roll up, and his body sags. My pulse stutters, but I simply inhale another slow breath.

We talked about this ahead of time. To make sure my

brother doesn't starve to death or die of dehydration while locked away from Orion's malice, the fae are putting him into a sort of magical stasis. He won't be aware of anything, and his body will sustain itself without nourishment for days on end.

With luck, it won't be *too* many days before we can wake him up again.

As Jamie slumps onto the floor, the metal is already rippling across the ground beneath him. It coats the earth there with a thick layer and then rises up on every side of him.

Other impressions are trickling through the torrent of energy now. This work is putting a strain on all of the fae who are combining their talents. The feel of the iron at the other end of their casting nips and gnaws at them, gradually biting deeper. Twinges of pain echo into me.

I steer my mind away from those uneasy sensations toward the rhythm of Whitt's breaths against my back and his familiar scent, like sun-warmed sand. It doesn't matter if it hurts in the moment. I'm saving Jamie from so much more hurt. I can hold on for as long as it takes, just as the fae around me are.

In my mind's eye, I see the iron shield around my brother curve up over him and seal into a seamless structure. Then the fae summon more and more of the ore out of the earth to thicken the walls. We need them so sturdy and potent that not even Orion can throw enough magic at them to break them. We need to make sure it isn't worth it to him to try.

More discomfort radiates from the fae around me:

clenched jaws, fisted hands, ragged breaths. I do my best to ride out the wave, but my concentration starts to waver. One more layer of iron smooths into place around Jamie's shield—and then everything falls away.

The images of my brother, the pain, and the flood of energy wash away in an instant.

My eyes pop open. I sit up straighter, looking at the fae around me, my gaze coming to rest on Corwin. "Do you think it's enough? Will he be okay?"

My soul-twined mate offers me a tentative smile. His brown skin has grayed with the effort, but a healthy flush is already seeping back into his face. "I believe Orion will find it quite impossible to inflict any harm on your brother now."

I can't imagine what the Murk king will make of the situation when the guards check on Jamie and find him encased like that. Thinking of Orion frustrated should give me some satisfaction, but instead it only sends a shiver through my stomach.

The sense of dread doesn't leave me as Corwin invites us all to stay and have dinner in his palace to refresh ourselves. The food is delicious as always, but after just a few bites, my stomach is churning. I flinch at the simple scrape of chair legs against the floor.

It's done, I tell myself. *It's done.* And I've almost convinced myself to believe it when Verik bursts into the room.

"My lord," he says, "my lady—you're needed to heal the curse. It's a child."

18

Talia

s I reach the small group of Unseelie clustered together in the glow of the Heart, starker now as evening falls and the sky darkens, I can tell it won't take any work to summon the required tears. The sight of the small boy curled in the woman's arms is enough to bring a burn to the back of my eyes all on its own.

He doesn't look as if he could be more than two or three, however many years that translates into in fae terms. His body is already nearly blue from head to toe, his hair laced with frost, his fingers curled into rigid forms. It's hard to believe he's even alive.

The words tumble out of me in my horror. "Why did you wait so long to bring him?" The only fae I've seen this far gone with the curse have been suffering for at least a couple of days before they reached that point.

"We didn't," the woman says, her voice barely more

than a faint rasp. "It started less than an hour ago. We set off as soon as we noticed—it's come on him so quickly." There's a hitch in her chest like she's suppressed a sob.

My horror grips me harder, with icy fingers. The curse has gone from its first signs to nearly fatal in the space of an hour? It's never been anywhere near that potent before.

I don't have the bandwidth to wonder too hard about that, though. The boy needs my help. I turn away, letting the tears that've been welling up spill down my cheeks and hiding my face with my hands.

These poor parents. I have only the vaguest experience in losing a child—one I never saw or got to hold in my arms to become that much more attached—and I know how painful even that loss was. And for the fae, with their limited fertility, every child is so much more precious.

More tears than I'm sure I need trickle from my eyes. I swipe at them a few times before turning back toward the couple and the few flock folk who've come with them. I stroke my damp fingers over the little boy's terrifyingly frigid cheek, braced for bad news.

It takes a few moments. At first, he doesn't stir. Then the blue starts to fade from his skin, and the frost melts from his hair. A breath of relief rushes out of me as he twitches and presses his face against his mother's chest with a whimper.

I cured him in time. It was close, but he's safe now.

Corwin comes up behind me and rests his hands on my shoulders. A similar crash of emotions is whirling through him—thinking of this child nearly lost and our child who was. He dips his head to the couple. "May he live long in the Heart's light."

The couple stammer their thanks, the woman squeezing my hand briefly with her own eyes flooded with tears, and then they head back to their carriage. I take Corwin's hand and turn back toward his palace.

Verik has been waiting farther to the side. The graying coterie member turns to follow us and stops in his tracks, peering toward the edge of the plateau. "There's another carriage coming."

My legs stall. Corwin stays next to me as we watch the vehicle come closer, the light of the lantern orb attached to its windshield expanding larger with its swift approach. A sickly sensation coils in my belly.

It must be a coincidence. Fae have been coming and going a lot since the war began. The carriage will probably swing to the side and go down to the camp at the base of the plateau…

But it doesn't. As the cool evening breeze licks through my hair, the new carriage pulls right up to where we're standing by the Heart. My own heart sinks even more at the sight of the fae scrambling over the side.

It's Fina, the pregnant woman I've healed from the curse more than once now, except she's not pregnant anymore. The bulge of her belly has shrunk, and she has a small bundle wrapped in her arms.

She and her mate hustle over to us, so frantic they don't even remark on the fact that we're already here. Fina is shaking so badly she can't seem to get words out.

Her mate keeps his arm tight around her shoulders.

His voice comes out with a quaver too. "Please. I don't know if— It came on so quickly. She's so *cold*."

In that moment, I hate the playacting of the Unseelie cure, the fact that I have to go through the motions of not wanting to show my vulnerability for it to work. I want to spill tears right over the infant tucked against the fae woman's chest, her tiny face like ice when they peel back the blanket. But I need to turn away as the tears well up again, need to give them a moment to overflow, need to paw at them as if I want to get rid of them before returning my attention to the baby and tracing my fingers over the curve of her cheek.

She *feels* like ice as well as looking it. I have to restrain a shudder. It's hard to imagine there's any life left in the tiny body.

"We could feel her still breathing up until just before we reached here," the father babbles as if he can talk the possible tragedy away. "We pushed the carriage as fast as it would go."

Then the baby's lips part. A thin wail pierces the deepening dusk as the curse's chill releases it. Fina gasps and hugs her daughter even tighter. "Thank you," she says to me. "Thank you and thank the Heart."

My relief at seeing the cure work doesn't dislodge the dread that's thickened in my gut. I glance at Corwin, not wanting to say what I'm thinking out loud in front of them.

This couldn't be left over from her *curse. She'd have come down with it too. And for it to happen at almost the same time as another child...*

The same anguish twists through Corwin's silent words. *I think we should stay here by the Heart for a little longer. Just to be sure.*

I don't like the directions my thoughts go from there, but I have to say it. *Do you know how many Unseelie children there are in the realm right now? Which domains they're in?*

I know a few off the top of my head and could determine the rest with a quick glance at our records. But—if this is more than just a horrible coincidence—anyone else affected will already be on their way here. We can't go to any of them without missing all the others.

He's right. But as we watch Fina and her mate drift back to their carriage, I'm tormented by the fact that I can't do anything except wait and find out just how horrible this night is going to get.

A small flicker of hope has just lit in my chest when the sight of another traveling light in the distance douses it again. I grip Corwin's hand, my pulse thumping harder.

Other Unseelie are starting to gather in a loose ring around the Heart, coming over to see what's going on while giving us lots of space. They must have noticed the first two carriages and now this new one. Maybe sentries from the other arch-lords' domains who witnessed the two cursed children passed on word. I don't know what to say to them, so I stay silent.

This carriage is racing toward the plateau so quickly that its hull groans as it passes over the ridge. In the glow of the orb, I can make out mottled sections on the outer walls where bits appear to have fallen away in the driver's haste.

Four fae leap out, the man in the middle hefting a girl who looks around eight in his arms. Her limbs are folded at rigid angles. Her eyes are half-open, what I can see of them frosted over. Her hair has gone pure white with ice.

My throat closes up. She's dead. I can already see that.

But maybe Fina's baby was too, just not quite so far gone that my cure couldn't work. Maybe I can still heal this girl as well.

The man stumbles to me with a wildly desperate expression. "Please," he says raggedly.

I have to try.

I've vaguely aware of the crowd around us growing as I put on my performance of hiding my tears. They gush freely now, driven by grief and a deepening sense of helplessness. The second I think it's safe to turn back to the girl, I swivel and reach for her cheek.

The moisture from my fingers hardens into fresh trails of ice on her cheek. Her father bows his head over her body, murmuring prayers under his breath.

She doesn't move. She doesn't come back to life. We stand there as the seconds slip by torturously, and the girl remains solidly frozen. Her father clutches her tighter with a stifled groan.

Tears I can't use dribble down to my chin. I wipe at them with my sleeve, willing down the scream that wants to break from my throat. It isn't fair. It isn't *right*.

But in Orion's mind, this is probably a perfect sort of justice. I stole one child he wanted to victimize from him, so he twisted his curse to victimize who knows how many more.

I don't need any message carved in a wall to tell me that this is my punishment for protecting my brother. *My* punishment... that the Unseelie are having to bear much more than I am.

The carriages keep coming. Another and another, closer together as those from farther flung domains converge on the plateau. From the choked explanations a few of them manage to give Corwin, it sounds like the curse struck all the children at the same time. The two families who were close enough to the Heart to realize the urgency of the situation and make it here within an hour or so got lucky. The others...

I try to heal every one of those deathly cold bodies. I haven't totally stopped crying since the first I failed to revive, so it doesn't take any effort. At least not that part. With every child that stays still and stiff, with every parental face that crumples with the most hopeless sort of grief, it gets harder to push down the scream that's still clawing at my chest.

After the ninth child, the family returns to their carriage, and I can hear the mother attempting to muffle her weeping. An ache has crept through so much of my body that I think it might swallow me whole. There must be a couple hundred fae standing around the Heart in what's now full night, bearing solemn witness to this extended tragedy.

Corwin rubs my back. Agony thrums through all my impressions of his inner state too, both for me and for his people. I can feel how much he longs to wrap his arms around me and take comfort in my embrace while offering the same to me, but he doesn't want to show any weakness in front of the other fae.

We watch the horizon for more lantern lights. One minute slips by, and another. Despite the warming charms on my clothes, my fingertips are starting to go numb. We wait, and we wait… and no one else comes.

Nine children struck. Seven who didn't make it. Seven much, much too many.

Someone speaks up from the crowd. "The Murk did this, didn't they? We have to make them pay!"

A restless muttering spreads through the assembled fae. "Yes," someone else says. "Why are we trying to make any kind of peace with them? They're monsters—they should be slaughtered, all of them."

A figure steps close to the front of the crowd, and in my daze of grief, I realize it's Kara. She's wearing a cloak with a thick hood that shadows her face, but her gaze seems to pierce right through me.

"The rats sent their own children out with their army against us, I hear," she says in a voice that rings through the night. "We fell back to *save* those children. And now they couldn't make it clearer that they'll never extend the same compassion to us. While this human tries to tell us we should make friends with them!" She jabs her hand toward me.

Corwin's stance pulls even straighter than it already was. "Kara," he says, his tone rough but firm. "You don't know the full situation. Not all of the Murk agree with those tactics any more than all of the Unseelie share the exact same views."

She shrinks a little under his criticism, but the crowd has already been riled up by her words. "We can't show them any kindness."

"Tear them all apart like they deserve."

"What does a human know about how the fae really are, how they've always been?"

"We've let the rats get away with too much!"

The mass of fae falls silent at the arrival of two other arch-lords. Laoni and Terisse nod to Corwin, Laoni's expression exhausted and Terisse's miserable.

"We have more to speak about between us arch-lords," Laoni says, taking in the crowd. "The Murk will not get away with this crime—you can be sure of that. For now, please go back to your homes or your camps—and look after each other."

The other fae start to meander away, a few shooting glances at me that feel decidedly hostile. Now that I've failed to save the most treasured members of their society, I guess they don't see me as quite so much a savior. I'm not sure I can blame them for that.

I can't believe people like Madoc and Delta deserve to die simply for being Murk. But... what if Kara's a little right? What if I've been too soft, and we could have ended this war already otherwise?

If I hadn't protected my brother, would Orion have done this anyway just to hurt the Unseelie every way he could? Or is it all my fault?

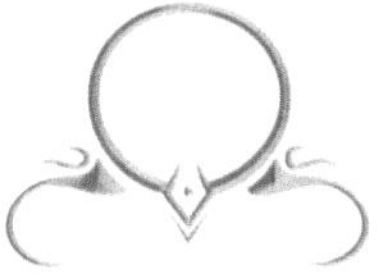

19

Whitt

’m a little surprised to find August alone in the border castle’s kitchen. I poke my head right through the doorway to get a better view of the room, but there’s no sign of Talia, even though I can tell from the mouth-watering scents in the air that this late breakfast is nearly done. He’s rarely without our mate as his helper on the mornings we’re here.

“Talia hasn’t come down?” I venture.

August shakes his head, his mouth twisting. “She’s still in bed. It took her a long time to get to sleep last night, so I was careful not to disturb her when I got up. I figured she needed the rest.”

I’d imagine she did—and not just physically. I can only imagine the emotional toll last night’s events in the winter realm took on her. Corwin himself was choked up, more emotional than I’ve ever seen him, as he told us what happened while holding Talia close as if he could protect her from the tragedy with the force of his affection. I doubt he'd have left her side if he'd had any choice, but the Unseelie arch-lords have a lot on their plate now.

Our mate's eyes were red-rimmed from crying, and she barely said anything on her way to her bedroom with August and Corwin. I wonder if she's still sleeping now or just having trouble facing the day ahead and all the fresh horrors it might bring.

"I'll check on her," I say. "She should get some food into her too."

I leave August to carry the plates over to the dining room and head upstairs, passing Sylas on the way. He tips his head to me in acknowledgment, clearly deciphering my intent. "Make sure she knows we all realize she did her best," he says.

My lips curl in a bittersweet smile. "I'll try." My mighty mite can be stubborn in many ways, not all of them to her benefit. She often has some trouble avoiding taking on more of a burden of responsibility than should really be hers.

I stop in the hall outside Talia's bedroom door and prick my ears. The rhythm of breaths I can make out tells me she's awake—and that she's been crying again. The pace is too rapid for sleep, with a soft hitch here and there as she struggles to get herself under control.

An ache squeezes my chest. I nudge open the door and walk over to the bed.

Talia is still bundled under the covers. She doesn't look up as I clamber onto the expansive mattress next to her, but when I tug her closer to me, she adjusts her position just slightly to nestle against me.

"Am I needed outside?" she asks in a tone that's trying so hard to be nothing but determined. "I can get dressed and come down."

"Right now, I'm not concerned about what anyone needs other than you," I inform her, nuzzling the back of her neck and breathing in her sap-sweet scent. "August has whipped up one of his masterpiece breakfasts. If you can't summon much enthusiasm for your own sake, think of how happy *he'll* be to see you enjoying it."

Talia lets out a grumble in response, but my ploy does work. She squirms out of my arms and slides off the bed. I track her movements through the room as she limps to the wardrobe and paws through it, noting the tension that appears to weigh on her limbs, as if she's pushing through sludge rather than air. Her face still looks worn with exhaustion, despite how long she's been in bed. When she turns to me after pulling on one of the Unseelie-style dresses Corwin has provided her with, the smile she offers me looks more pained than pleased.

The ache inside me digs deeper, but I don't know what to say to her to make this better. Maybe the best I can do is not focus on the horrible things at all but distract her with something totally different.

I prowl over to her and sweep her off the ground into my arms swiftly enough that she lets out a squeak of surprise. "What are you doing?" she demands, giving me a baleful look.

I press a peck to her forehead. "Auggie gets to cart you

around like this all the time. Why shouldn't I get to as well?"

She lets out a faint harumph, but the slightest bit of humor has crept into it. "I don't love it when he does it either."

"Hmm. Then I'll just have to improve on his technique."

"That's not—" She cuts herself off with a soft huff and lets her head lean against my shoulder as I carry her down the stairs. I glance toward the room we've set up for Madoc, but only silence emanates from within. He's often been leaving in the mornings to check in on the temporary Murk settlement. I'd imagine he has particular concerns about their safety after last night's offensive against the Unseelie.

Orion certainly has a knack for stirring up hatred against his people.

When we reach the dining room, Sylas and August are already there. August has taken the liberty of dishing out a small portion of each of the delicacies on offer onto a plate at Talia's usual spot. "You can have more of anything you want, of course," he says quickly as I set her down there.

"I'm sure this will be plenty," Talia says, looking at the meal as if it's a bowling ball she's being asked to swallow down. She picks up her fork but then simply holds it in the air, her gaze darting between the three of us taking our seats around the table. "You'd have heard from the winter realm—there haven't been any more children, have there?" Her jaw tightens as she braces herself.

Thankfully, Sylas can shake his head. "No further cases

of their curse have been reported," he says in the gentle voice I've only heard my lord and brother offer this one woman. "It appears that Orion was only able to amplify the curse in those nine victims."

"It must have taken an awful lot out of him even managing that," I say. "Up until now, he's ramped up the effects slowly, decreasing the time between victims and the speed they fell ill by tiny increments. To go from days to an hour or less in one go, and in not one but several fae… He's probably pushed himself to his limit. We may even see a respite from their curse for a week or more until it's recovered the energy he squeezed out of it."

Talia doesn't look as relieved by that suggestion as I'd have hoped. "It's still seven more children than should have died," she says faintly, staring at her plate.

"The Murk aren't the only ones who've crossed that line," Sylas says. "You've told us yourself about the fae who've slaughtered Murk children. I suppose they'd see it as fair turnabout."

"That doesn't make it better."

"No. But it does mean these sorts of things have happened through no influence of your own."

August jumps in. "For him to be able to put so much magic into the curse so quickly, he was probably already planning on using that strategy before you reached out to your brother. Maybe he sped up his timeline a little, but it was only a convenient excuse. You didn't *make* him do it."

"I know," Talia says, but she doesn't sound all that convinced. She stabs at a sausage patty and takes a bite.

Even her chewing seems sluggish, as if it's taking more effort than it should.

The rest of us start to eat too, but all of us pay more attention to how our mate is doing with her meal than to our own. She works her way through half of her plate before she pauses again and looks up at us.

"The Unseelie last night—the ones who came and saw what was happening—they weren't happy that I couldn't heal everyone. Or that I've been speaking up for the Murk. Do you think… They seemed to accept me before, but now that I've let them down, what if—"

"You haven't let them down," I break in, with a flare of irritation at the Unseelie. I tamp down on that emotion. "They'd just witnessed something terrible, and they weren't in their right minds. *Their* reaction has very little to do with you either."

"But maybe they shouldn't have put so much faith in me to begin with," Talia says. "I'm not a savior—I could only cure anyone because Orion wanted to use me against you—there's nothing all that special about me or my ideas."

August lets out a growl of denial, and a sharper pang shoots through my heart. But at the same moment, a spark of inspiration lights in my head. I push back my chair. "Come with me."

Talia blinks at me, startled. "What? Where?"

"You'll see." I motion for my brothers to join us. "I think this is more important than breakfast. As much as we appreciate your culinary efforts, August, we can come back to them later."

August doesn't argue, looking more hopeful than anything else. Sylas stands as well, trusting me to know what I'm doing. I'm sure they're as agonized over Talia's self-doubt as I am.

I wrap my hand around Talia's and match her uneven gait down the hall to the summer entrance and out into the pleasant late morning sunlight. The area right along the border is quiet for the moment, no other Seelie tending to business nearby. I lead my mate and my brothers across the open plain, veering away from the glow of the Heart itself to step through one of the entrances of the Bastion.

I glance around, dredging up the right path from my memory, and head for one specific staircase. It spirals up to a landing in one of the building's side towers, where a small arched window offers a view over Hearth-by-the-Heart.

Talia steps to the window, gazing out over the view, and then turns to look at me again. A soft light had come into her face that wasn't there before, and I know she recognizes the significance of this place.

"You remember what happened here," I say.

"I came up here during Sylas's coronation celebration," she says quietly. "I was—I was worried that you'd all take mates from the other fae now that you had even more prestige than you ever did before."

I stroke my hand over her hair. "And we found you here, and each of us swore to you that there was no one else we wanted more. It was here that we first agreed we'd make you our mate in every possible way, publicly and officially. It took longer than we'd anticipated to get to that point, but we did make it there in the end."

She bites her lip. "But why…"

I ease my arm all the way around her, tucking her against my chest. "I wanted to remind you of how much faith *we* have always had in you and still do. There's no one more special in our eyes in the whole of the fae world. And you trust our judgment, don't you?"

A hint of a smile touches her mouth, even though her eyes still look sad. "You might be a *little* biased."

Sylas chuckles and rests his hand on her shoulder. "You've proven again and again how much strength and insight you possess. You've guided us and opened our eyes in so many ways. Maybe your approach to the conflict with the Murk isn't absolutely perfect, but I'm sure none of the rest of us have perfect ideas either. That doesn't mean they aren't valuable. *You* are valuable, and any fae who tries to say you shouldn't be contributing is only proving that they're a dolt."

"But when it's kids…"

"No one else could save them either," August says. "You saved two that wouldn't have made it otherwise. Who else could offer that much? Who else even tried? If there's one thing I know about you, it's that you won't back down. You'll keep giving your all and doing whatever you can to help the rest of us, whether we deserve it or not."

Talia releases a shaky breath. "I'm sure the three of you deserve it."

"And you deserve everything we can offer you, mighty

one," I say, and draw her chin up so I can capture her mouth.

I mean it to be only a tender, reassuring kiss, but as she turns in my arms to embrace me more fully, a deeper heat stirs inside me. I pull her closer, reveling in the eager sound that carries from her chest, in the mix of softness and strength that flows all through her body.

She's our mate, and maybe what she needs more than anything right now is a full demonstration of how much we cherish her.

When Talia has melted into my arms, I draw out the kiss a little longer before bringing my mouth to her jaw and the side of her neck. Then I raise my head to glance at my brothers. "Perhaps we should ensure no one comes up this way to disturb us until we're done here."

A sly gleam has lit in Sylas's eyes. He and August murmur a few words to discourage any wanderers from venturing up this staircase, and I turn Talia in my arms so that she can receive more affection than I can offer on my own.

As I slide her hair to the side and nibble across the crook of her shoulder, August steps in to capture her lips. Talia keeps one hand clutched around a fold in my shirt and teases her other fingers into August's hair. Sylas moves in to complete our circle, trailing his fingers up from her belly to the neckline of her dress and along it, just above the swell of her breasts.

There was a time when I'd have felt jealous, seeing my brothers touch Talia this way. A time when I thought I couldn't have her because it would mean needing to share her like this. Those emotions couldn't be more distant now. Nothing but joy touches me at seeing the way she leans into Sylas's touch, hearing the whimper that escapes her as August deepens their kiss. Her body is made of heat against mine, pressed against my hardening cock like a brand, and I wouldn't have her any other way than so fully satisfied.

"I love you," I murmur by her ear, and nip her earlobe. "I'll always want you with me, want you sharing every idea that comes into your head. I can't imagine going without you."

Talia's grasp on my shirt tightens. She draws her mouth from August to kiss me again. Afterward, her voice comes out ragged, and not just with arousal. "I just want to be as good a mate as any fae could be."

August makes a rough sound. "You are that and more." He slips his fingers down over her bodice, provoking a gasp as his thumb skips over the peak of her breast.

"We couldn't have asked for a better mate," Sylas agrees. "*I* couldn't have asked for a better match while I rule as arch-lord. You're worthy of all the same awe our people offer me." He kisses her shoulder and starts to sink down to his knees. "But since they're not here, I'll offer all the worship I can—and happily."

When he eases up the skirt of her dress, Talia's eyelids flutter. She tips her head against my shoulder with a stuttered breath as Sylas's mouth grazes her sex through her panties. I know what a delight that experience is—and even if I'm not the one getting to enjoy her most potent flavor right now, I can make the moment even better for her.

I let her rest more weight against me as her body goes even more slack with the pleasure racing through her. As Sylas tugs down her panties and swipes his tongue right over her, skin to skin, a moan tumbles from her mouth. August leans in to drink the sound from her lips, and I dip my fingers under the neckline of her dress.

Her nipples have already stiffened beneath the fabric. I tease my fingertips in slow and then swifter flicks over one and then the other, until Talia is quivering against me, her hips rocking to meet Sylas's mouth, her breath coming in gasps. With a hasty motion, I loosen her dress and draw the cloth right down to bare her breast, cupping it in the same moment.

When I position it for him, August accepts my offer without hesitation. He lowers his head to suck the peak into his mouth. Talia's eyelids drift shut, nothing but a flush of bliss coloring her face now.

We're bringing her to these heights—the three of us, together. It feels like nothing short of a miracle.

My cock is straining against my slacks, but I do my best to tune its demands out until Talia gropes behind her, reaching for me. As her slim fingers close around my rigid shaft, a surge of pleasure flares from my groin. I can't hold back a groan.

She runs her hand up and down over me, her grip shaking with the eager tremors racking her body. Then she squeezes so hard I almost come just like that. A cry spills from her lips as she quakes and trembles with the force of the orgasm Sylas has brought her to.

It takes a moment for Talia to gather herself. Then she bends over in front of me, wrenching her skirt even higher with a glance over her shoulder.

I can't refuse her invitation. I yank my slacks open and run the head of my cock over her slick opening, reveling in the bliss of the motion, in the eager gasp that slips from her mouth. Sylas captures it with a kiss, and August kneels next to her, stroking her chest with his hands now.

My hunger for her grips me, and I can't hold back any longer. I plunge into her, the heat and the quiver of her channel around me flooding me with the headiest of pleasures.

Talia lets out a sound like a mewl. Then she's fumbling with my brothers' pants, taking Sylas into her mouth, August with her hand, switching between them as they both groan.

Even with the need for release blazing through me, I want to make her second peak even better than the first. I reach around her hips and massage her clit in time with my thrusts. Talia jerks against me, her sex clamping around my shaft. The second she starts coming, I follow her with a choked growl.

She doesn't neglect my brothers, relishing them with her hands and mouth even as she rides out the aftershock of her orgasm. I brace her against me to help her keep her balance as she brings them one after the other to satisfaction.

Then we all sink down on the stone floor. A little

laugh spills out of Talia, the first fully joyful sound I've heard this morning.

I tip my head close to hers to kiss her temple, my heart still thumping hard. I can't think of anything I couldn't do, any length I wouldn't go to, if she needed it. I hope she never doubts that of any of her mates. And if I have my way, she'll have the full loyalty of every other fae in the realms for as long as she's here with us.

May that be much longer than Orion intends.

Talia

The Seelie camp at the base of the hill around the Heart is much more haphazard-looking than its equivalent on the winter side. Rather than orderly rows, the buildings in their various materials stand in irregular clusters. Fae are bustling to and from the several hubs of activity where supplies and food are being distributed. There's a clatter of pans in one direction and the hiss of a knife cutting through fruit in another.

Harper gazes around her with a typical wide-eyed expression. "So many fae from so many packs all here together. And I guess there are just as many out at the front."

Astrid, who's joined us for this visit along with another guard from our pack, nods. "A war is a big undertaking. You should hope you don't have to see it again in your lifetime."

I glance at her. "You've never seen anything this big, have you?"

"Thankfully no, and I wish I could have given this one a miss too." She shoots me a wry smile. "Although at least the ravens managed to work together with us instead of giving us an enemy to deal with on both sides."

We've brought freshly pressed cheese from Elliot's sheep and a huge basket full of loaves of bread that August baked. After handing those over at one of the eating areas, I start to wander through the camp somewhat at random, not totally sure what else I can do but wanting to be here to offer it if the fae around me have any ideas.

They're the ones taking on the most risk in this fight. I've put myself within reach of the Murk army once and only briefly. They've been rotating with their comrades on the front since the first attack.

Many of the fae who are out speaking with each other or grabbing a meal notice me and tip their heads in acknowledgment. Some call out to me by name. "Lady Talia, may the Heart shine on us with you."

"It's good to see you're well, Lady Talia."

"We'll beat the bastards soon, Lady Talia. You can count on that."

There's none of the derision I sensed from the Unseelie last night. I'm not sure how many of the summer fae even know what happened there so recently. And when I haven't let *them* down in any way, maybe it wouldn't matter to them regardless. But even after my thorough worshipping at the hands of my Seelie mates just a few hours ago, the thought of all those deaths travels with me like a boulder in my stomach.

With every fae who stops and offers any kind of greeting or remark, I push a smile to my lips to show I'm keeping my spirits up and ask them, "Is there anything you could use?" or "Do you need help with anything?"

Most don't seem to want to make any requests of me, although it could be they're simply well-supplied as it is. A couple mention that they'd love it if August sent down more of his duskapple pastries. One asks if I can find anyone skilled with a particular plant's true name around, as she'd like to cultivate some for easy camp meals. To make sure I don't forget, I write it all down on a strip of parchment I grabbed from Whitt's office.

We stop at the far edge of the camp so I can rest my warped foot. The sun beams down over us, warm but not oppressively hot. The weather near the Heart is always pretty much perfect. I sit down on the grass, dragging air full of a lilac-sweet scent into my lungs, and study the camp from this vantage point in case I might notice something else that needs doing.

"They've had several days to get into their routines and figure out any problems that have arisen," Astrid says, staying on her feet next to me. "It'll all be minor matters from here on."

"At least minor matters are still something I can help with." I figure as soon as we're done here, I'll go back to the kitchen and work with August to whip up those pastries extra fast.

Harper hunkers down on the grass beside me and tips

her pale face to the sun. Her flaxen hair gleams with the pure natural light. "It's too bad no one needs fancy dresses in a war. I'm getting ready a whole collection for when we can celebrate our win." She pauses. "Not to get ahead of ourselves. I think of it like a good luck charm, encouraging our victory to happen."

"Sounds good to me," I say.

Another familiar figure passes into view briefly before walking on through the camp. Donovan has come down from his castle to check in with his people too. I watch his fiery hair vanish between the buildings and turn to Harper hesitantly. She's looking in the same direction, but I don't see any sign that she's affected by his presence.

"We could go chat him up a little," I suggest. A couple of weeks ago when I was particularly sick, Harper confessed to a crush on the arch-lord.

I expect her to blush, but instead she lets out a light laugh. "No, that's all right. I actually—I've tried to talk to him a couple of times since you and I spoke about it. Because I was thinking about what you said. But... I realized that he doesn't seem to really *see* me. I'm just another random member of Sylas's pack to him, no matter what I say or how I'm dressed. It's better... better to be around someone who notices you for yourself."

Something about her tone makes me raise my eyebrows. "You sound like you're speaking from experience now."

That comment gets me the blush I was anticipating. Harper ducks her head shyly. "There's nothing actually happening. But... I'm not thinking about Arch-Lord

Donovan anymore, so you don't have to worry about that."

Intriguing. I might have pried a little more if Astrid and the other guard weren't standing nearby. Harper deserves her privacy. And if she isn't ready to tell even me about whoever's caught her interest now, that's her right too.

I relax back on my hands for a few minutes longer and then push myself to my feet. "Let's make one more circuit before we head back to Hearth-by-the-Heart. I'd like to find out if there are any—"

My words halt in my throat as my gaze snags on a shape slinking out from between two of the buildings farther down the edge of the camp. It's a wolf, fae-sized and covered in thick white fur with an icy blue sheen. Fur the same color as the hair on the man who took the most glee out of tormenting me in Aerik's cage.

I know Aerik's cadre-chosen Cole when I see him, even in shifted form. My pulse stutters, and I instinctively back up a step. That's all the reaction I would have at the sight of him, except that at the same time, Cole's wolfish head swings in my direction. His lips pull back from his fangs in a silent snarl.

Without any other warning, he charges at me.

It's so much worse than just seeing him with Aerik before. Panic blares through my mind louder than it's ever hit me in the past. In that instant, the sunny summer day around me blackens into a shadowy forest in the dark of evening, with three vicious beasts springing at me and my brother out of the brush. A ghost of the old pain flares in the scars on my shoulder. My skin goes cold, and a scream bursts from my throat.

I come back to myself with the sense of a hand on my back and a firm voice speaking words my mind isn't quite processing. I blink, the world around me coming back into focus. My heart is still racing faster than a runaway train. I've sunk into a crouch, my legs trembling under me, too shaky to fully hold my weight.

It's Harper who's touching my back, rubbing up and down my shoulder blade now, her voice low but frantic. "It's okay, Talia. It's all right. He isn't going to hurt you."

Astrid's voice sinks in next from where she's standing over me, her hands on her hips with one gripping the short sword by its hilt. "I said *back away from her*."

Cole is poised a few feet away from her, now in the form of a man, the sunlight glinting off his icy hair. He sputters an indignant laugh. "All I was doing was running by. *She* interrupted me in *my* work."

I know that's not true. The image of his bared teeth and the way he charged straight at me flashes through my mind, and another shudder wracks my body.

He provoked me on purpose. But why? My thoughts are too scattered for me to piece together any explanation.

Then Cole offers it up all on his own. He turns away from Astrid and me, and I notice the other Seelie who've stopped in their tracks to see what's going on over here. My scream must have drawn a lot of attention. My throat still stings from it.

"This is the human we've elevated so high," Cole

sneers. "She doesn't trust any of *us* at all. She's terrified of our wolves—she thinks we're monsters."

No. He's trying to make me out to be the enemy—as part of Aerik's whole campaign to throw me to the Murk, probably. I suck a breath into my constricted lungs, fighting to get my emotions under control.

He's a monster. And yes, I'm terrified of him. But I don't have to be. I've beaten him and his lord before. I can do it again.

"This is what we're putting up with these days?" Cole goes on with a scoff. "Letting our arch-lords take mates who'll scream at the sight of wolves?"

My pulse hiccups again, but I push myself upright, tensing my legs to hold them straight. It takes me a second to force the words from my throat, but when I do, they're loud enough to carry.

"I'm not afraid of wolves," I say, staring straight at Cole. "I'm afraid of you, because of what you did to me. I've ridden on wolves' backs and fallen asleep with a wolf for a pillow. I have no problem with the Seelie. I only have a problem with *you*."

Cole jerks around. From the stiffening of his expression, he hadn't expected me to be able to talk back, definitely not that coherently. He upped the ante on purpose—planning to send me into a panic so severe I'd be helpless while he made me look bad. When I managed to stand up to Aerik before, I had my mates all around me and there hadn't been anything to overtly trigger my memories of their abuse. He thought if he pushed me harder, he could get the better of me.

But he's underestimated me again. Hopefully for the last time.

He pulls back his lips just a smidge, just enough to show a glint of the fangs he's let protrude again. Trying to send me spiraling again.

Shivers dart under my skin at the sight, but I ignore them and manage to move toward him rather than away. I'm stronger than he thinks. In the ways that matter most, I'm stronger than *him*.

I propel myself forward to stand where the onlookers can see me just as well as him. None of them were at the meeting of the lords in the Bastion. They might have heard whispers about Aerik's treatment of me, but they've never had to really face it.

Maybe it's time I showed the fae I'm living among everything I can. They've seen me break down, but they haven't seen the full cause. I've tried to cover up my old wounds, to even out my limp, but my scars are a part of me. They tell the story of how I came to be here and what I suffered along the way.

Without letting myself think about the consequences, I jerk the neckline of my dress to the side.

"This is what his lord did to me when I was just a kid," I say, yanking far enough to reveal the angry red ridges that mark my shoulder. No one except my mates has really seen them before now, but I've been wrong to hide them. Wrong to pretend that the Seelie can't be villains, that I support every one of them.

I kick off my braced boot and hold out my misshapen foot. At my gesture, Astrid hefts me up by the waist so those farther off can see the malformed lump of bone where Cole broke it all those years ago. "This is what this man did to me when I was already trapped in a cage. If any of you smash up my body, then I'll be afraid of you too. I hope you won't blame me for that."

Several hostile glances are turning toward Cole now. The cadre-chosen's confidence fades. He shoots me a stealthy glare and marches off without another word.

I wish I could feel triumphant about his departure, but all at once I'm exhausted.

As Astrid sets me down on the grass, a few of the fae who were watching hustle over. "Are you all right, Lady Talia?" one asks in a worried voice.

"I didn't realize it was so bad—how could they get away with hurting you like that?" another says.

I don't know how to answer either of those questions. I tug my boot back on, grappling with my words. "What they did—it technically wasn't a crime. Because I'm human. That's why I've spoken up for the other humans here in the fae world. But I'm all right now. I'm just not going to let him accuse me of ridiculous things."

The murmur of agreement reassures me. No one bought into his awful claims.

Astrid squeezes my shoulder. "Maybe we should get you right home." And then, with a mischievous gleam in her eyes, she bends over into her wolf form. She crouches down so I can clamber onto her back.

I guess there's no better way to prove that it's only certain wolves I take issue with. I swing my leg over her back and curl my fingers into her thick fur. The other guard and Harper shift on either side of us, and we set off through the camp to hushed murmurs and hollered well wishes from all sides.

It really isn't any trial to ride Astrid like this. I've faced my fears of the wolves in general so many times over the past months that it was only the sight of that one specific beast launching himself at me that could still trigger a panic attack. Maybe Cole's strategy will backfire on him, and the rest of the Seelie will appreciate my attempts to help even more.

Most of the good things in my life have come out of facing the things I feared rather than running away from them, haven't they? Memories rise up as if jostled out of the back of my mind by the rhythm of Astrid's wolfish lope.

All the times I stood up to Madoc and spoke my mind even when I wasn't sure how he'd treat me afterward. Crossing the border to the winter realm before I knew much of who Corwin was. Crouching in a cage while Aerik and his men stalked over to me, only to turn the tables on them with my hidden magic. Tossing a blood-smeared rag into my Seelie lovers' mouths while they were in the grips of their savage curse.

I linger on those last two events, something stirring amid my thoughts. I've always been underestimated. *That* fact has led to some of my greatest victories too. And I know how much courage I have in me. I once stood my ground in front of Sylas's wolf while he was raging with the curse, ready to tear me apart.

By the time we reach the border castle, I'm trembling

for a totally different reason, one that provokes more excitement than fear. The jitters chase me into the castle, where I find all of my men standing in intense conversation in the living room. They turn at my entrance, but I can't find it in me to hold off this announcement even for greetings.

I halt in the doorway, my heart pounding with determination. "I know how to stop Orion."

21

Corwin

alia's eyes are so wild and defiant they rouse a matching emotion in me. I can't make out any details of the idea that's struck her through our bond, but her resolve radiates into me, as potent as a bonfire.

"Did something happen?" August asks, bristling automatically with his usual protective energy. It's not difficult to see that something must have prompted Talia's sudden furor.

"Yes—it doesn't matter. That's not the point." She marches over to us as briskly as her warped foot allows. "All that matters is it made me think of a way to end the war."

Sylas motions to the nearest armchair. "Why don't you sit down and tell us everything?"

Talia looks a bit reluctant, but she sinks into the chair

he indicated, and the rest of us take seats around her. Madoc's stance is tensed, maybe because any attack against the Murk will be more personal to him than to the rest of us. He stays as silent as we do, though, waiting for Talia to gather her words.

"Do you remember," she says, fixing her gaze on the Seelie men, "how we tricked Aerik and his cadre and got them in a position where you could force their yield?"

"Of course," Whitt says for all of them, in a tone that's both dry and wary. "One of your first brilliant brainstorms."

Talia turns to me and Madoc. I've gotten the gist of the story before through her memories, but she explains for both of our benefits. "Technically I was Aerik's 'property,' and Sylas had stolen me. When Aerik's men found out, they demanded that Sylas give me back or they'd reveal the theft to the arch-lords."

Madoc grimaces. "Even more reason to despise those pricks."

"We arranged to meet them with me in a cage and Sylas and the others taking a vow not to make the first attack," Talia goes on. "But Aerik didn't know that I'd been learning true names. We had bronze chains hidden in the grass attached to the base of the cage, and when he and his men came close, I called on bronze to send the chains to restrain them. The effect didn't last for long, but it was enough to count as the first strike so that Sylas, Whitt, and August could jump in without breaking their vow, and the momentary confusion gave them the upper hand. They overpowered Aerik and his men and forced them to yield with a promise that they'd give up all claim on me."

A fresh waft of pride travels through me, thinking of how frightened she must have been facing those men and how she overcame it to conquer them. "It was very clever of you," I say, offering her a fond smile. But beneath my happier feelings, a twisting sensation is forming in my gut. I'm not sure I like my sense of where this might be leading. "How does that relate to Orion? The Murk can't be controlled through yields since they're not bound to the Heart—at least, he and his followers can't."

"I know. It's not the yield part I'm thinking of." Talia glances at Madoc again. "Orion's never shown any sign that he's aware of my other magical powers, right? You never mentioned that I could wield true names, and none of the other Murk figured it out? He definitely wasn't aware of that factor when he asked me about how I'd found the wrench I was using to try to escape."

Madoc cocks his head. "You cast light during the battle the other day, didn't you? Although I couldn't hear you speak the true name, and you talked about the Heart shining through you, so any Murk who noticed that demonstration probably assumed it was some Seelie trick. As far as I know, Orion has no idea that you can work true names. He thinks of you as his own creature—his 'pet'— and I'd imagine it'd be difficult for him to picture the Heart of the Mists granting you any real power when you're so closely tied to him."

He pauses, and a shadow crosses his face before he

continues. "He couldn't even believe that you could matter all that much to *me*. He expected me to try to cure your curse, and I don't think it ever occurred to him that it might work."

Talia restrains a wince only I pick up on, with a flash of memory that flickers through our bond: the sight of Madoc's limp body as August and Astrid lifted it off her blood-drenched bed. "All right," she said. "Then we have the same advantage over Orion that we did over Aerik—he doesn't know everything I'm capable of. I can use that against him."

"How?" Sylas asks—not skeptical, just encouraging her onward.

She drags in a breath. "We'd have to work out the exact details. But Orion obviously wants to get his hands on me again—because he's upset that I defied him, because he thinks I'm his possession, whatever. So, what if we give me to him, and I have a chance to surprise him and then—and then kill him before he can recover."

Everything in me recoils at the thought of Talia getting close enough to the Murk king to land a killing blow, putting herself within his grasp, and taking on a horrific task that should be any of ours instead of hers. She isn't a killer. Her uneasiness with the idea wafts off of her.

But her qualms don't diminish her determination. She's resolved to carry through with it—and I know she'll try her best, no matter how she feels about it.

The men around me look similarly discomforted. "It takes a lot to kill a fae," August says. "You'd only get one brief chance, and if anything went wrong…"

Talia meets his gaze. "You're the best warrior our pack has. You can teach me the most effective way to aim a quick strike. And I have another advantage over anyone who's fae, like we've already seen. I can use an iron weapon. If I can stab him in the right spot with an iron blade, that would do the trick, wouldn't it?"

Hearing the specifics only twists me up more inside. I smother my reaction as well as I can and try to focus on the practicalities. "To his heart or perhaps deep enough into his throat should do it—but where are you going to get a weapon like that? Humans don't typically make knives or daggers out of pure iron. None of us can wield magic on iron to create one for you. I don't think even the kind of strategy we used to protect your brother would work for a project that requires such careful attention to detail."

"And even if it could, that assumes you'd be able to get close enough to him and distract him well enough to carry it out," Whitt says, frowning.

Talia shrugs, though I can see the tension running through the casual gesture. "The first part is easy enough. We have humans here who'll help however we ask them to. I spoke to a couple of them when we were preparing for our strategy with the tunnels who do metal work. They could create the blade, and then maybe the Murk who've joined us but aren't yet reconnected with the true Heart could use some magic to make it sharper, or at least to hide it so Orion doesn't realize I have it on me."

From Madoc's expression, I don't think he likes this general plan any more than I do. He didn't give his life to save Talia because he wanted to send her off straight into his king's clutches just weeks later. But he nods. "I think they could probably do both. If I can persuade them to contribute. I'm not going to lie to them about what it's for, and a lot of them still have conflicted feelings about Orion."

"We might need even more of their help," Talia says, her mouth slanting at a pensive angle. "Or maybe some of Delta's followers. The hardest part will probably be making sure I can get face to face with Orion rather than him sending lackeys to deal with me… Maybe if I'm already being escorted, or if they provide an additional distraction… Obviously we still need to figure that part out."

"And what is the distraction you're imagining using when you *are* face to face with him?" Sylas asks.

One corner of her lips curls upward with a hint of a smile. "I thought I'd use light. It seems fitting. A strong blast of it, right into his eyes."

All at once, I can picture it: Talia standing before Orion, light flaring from her hands. But I can also all too easily imagine him springing at her and cutting her down before she can strike any kind of blow. My stomach is outright churning now.

"There have to be other ways," I say, fighting to keep my tone even. "You shouldn't have to put yourself in danger ahead of all of us. It's *our* war."

Talia looks at me, her green eyes so solemn my heart nearly stops beating. "No, it's my war as much as any of yours. Orion used me my whole life. He destroyed my family, left me to be enslaved, tortured me, and almost killed me. He stole the child we should have had from us. Maybe none of that is as big as what he's done to the fae, but it's my entire life. I want to take it back."

I don't know how to argue with that. Perhaps I shouldn't attempt to.

"We've mostly been holding them off," Whitt says. "There's no need to rush into a plan so risky."

Talia's gaze snaps to him. "Do you really think we're going to find a definitive move that's less risky? And we're not really holding them off when Orion can murder children hundreds of miles from the front. We have no idea how much farther he'll go or how soon. The longer we leave it, the more likely he'll hurt the fae more, or figure out a way to get at Jamie, or who knows what else. We have to end this as quickly as we can before even more people suffer."

Slowly, the other men incline their heads in acceptance. I can't quite let go of the protest blaring in my head. "We're your mates," I say. "We should be the ones defending you." A desperate urge rises up in me to fly all the way to the front and charge at Orion myself, to do whatever I can to kill him before Talia even has to try, no matter how small my chances.

Perhaps Sylas can read that impulse in me. He's the one who caught me on the verge of racing off to the Murk's Refuge when Talia was dying. He clears his throat and stands up. "As Talia's mates, I think we should discuss the matter amongst ourselves for a moment to determine how we can all best lend our skills." He brushes his hand over Talia's hair. "Why don't you find Astrid and have her see about bringing in the humans who have metal-working skills?"

I manage to hold my tongue until Talia has left the room. Then, holding as solid a wall against our bond as I can, I spit out, "You're going through with this? You think we should let her tackle this monster on her own?"

Madoc's mouth tightens. "She's already faced him on her own before. I don't like it, but I think she's right—her plan could work. His biggest weakness is his arrogance. He assumes he has everything under control, that no one could possibly get the better of him—her more than anyone."

"But she—she shouldn't *have* to." My hands clench at my sides with all the frustration and despair I'm reining in. How can I let my soul-twined mate take on the burden of saving my people on my behalf?

How can I face the possibility of losing her to that fiend all over again?

August has started pacing the room as if he needs to let out similar uneasy energy. He doesn't speak, though.

Sylas folds his arms over his chest. "She shouldn't have to, no. You're not going to get any argument on that subject from us. But she *doesn't* have to. You heard her— she *wants* to. I have tried so many times to protect her, but in the end, she knows her own mind. I swore to myself a long time ago that I wasn't going to let my love for her turn into a cage."

I flinch at that framing of the situation. Whitt speaks up before I can argue further. "You weren't there when she took on Aerik and his men. She was spectacular. I have no doubt at all that she can handle this if we give her the chance, whether we like it or not. She's committed to it. That means our job is figuring out how to mitigate the risks and set her up for success in every way we can."

August stops, letting out a huff of breath. I wait, half expecting him to side with me, but he shakes his head. "There's nothing I'd like more than to kill that mangy vermin for her. But I know where my limits are—and so does she. We have to trust in her strength. All of us. We owe her that much." He meets my eyes, a matching anguish dancing behind his—but one he's managed to overcome.

I look down at my hands. My jaw tightens. I want to yell and rage and tear the room apart, but I won't, because that won't help Talia either.

I have faith in Talia. I love her, so much. It could be that's the problem. I'm not afraid only of what fate she could meet at Orion's hands... but also what fate our bond could meet if she succeeds.

When we realized the depth of Orion's meddling in our relationship, I swore to her I'd be hers no matter what happens. That's still true. But I'm not deluded enough to think that nothing will change if the soul-deep connection between us disintegrates. If my soul then clamors for another.

If Talia is willing to face her worst fears, though,

shouldn't I? I can't hold her back to protect *myself* from the possibility of a complicated future.

I sigh and swipe my hand across my face. Resignation settles into a hard lump in my chest, but I manage to summon a spark of my own resolve alongside it.

If she's going to do this, she needs every one of us behind her, like Whitt said. She needs *me*.

"All right," I say. "How are we going to get her where she needs to be to kill Orion?"

When I cross my domain to the palace of Heart's Cadence some hours later, meaning to consult with my coterie on the plans we're gradually piecing together, the sky is darkening with evening. The purple tones smudging the sky like a bruise match my uneasy mood.

I'm greeted by one of my staff at the front door. "My lord," she says, "Kara of Hazeleven came to call on you. I told her I wasn't sure of your return, but she insisted on staying… She's in the front parlor."

A starker trepidation winds through my gut. But I can't cast off this young woman without giving her a chance to speak. My thoughts have been so much on my relationship with Talia, but Kara has had no compensation for the soul-twined bond she can sense but not fully experience.

I haven't really discussed the situation with her since our first meeting. There hasn't been time what with the war. But perhaps I owe her more consideration than that despite the turmoil around us. And she needs to understand that nothing is separating me from the mate I already have. I've already caught hints from my awareness of Talia that Kara's resentment has led to minor hostilities.

I find her sitting in a chair near the parlor's hearth. She rises up at my entrance, her welcoming smile a bittersweet mix of pain and hope. I wish I could offer more to the second part.

"Good evening," I say. "I apologize—I should have taken the initiative to attend to you sooner." I pause, grappling with my words. "You already know from the messages I've conveyed that I haven't yet tracked down a solution to your predicament."

Kara blinks. "A solution? You mean make the partial bond go away? That's not what I want." She takes a step toward me and then stops there when I remain rigidly still.

"I believe I've made it clear that I have no intention of attempting to sever the soul-twined bond I've already formed, regardless of its source," I say, gently but firmly.

She looks down at her hands and then back at me. "Yes, that has been clear. I came because I've been thinking… Severing it wouldn't necessarily be required, would it? Many lords take more than one partner. And if we spend more time together, perhaps the real bond that was meant to be will emerge on both sides."

The suggestion is more accepting of Talia than Kara's previous approach, but every particle of my body resists it all the same. I don't *want* another woman dividing my attention—and I have no feelings for the woman in front of me at all, other than sympathy. Perhaps that would change if the Heart decides to impose its original bond more firmly, but I have to speak from where my own heart is right now.

"I've found that I prefer to focus my attentions on one mate," I say.

Kara tilts her head to the side. "*She* has four others, doesn't she?"

"Yes, but…" I grope for the right words to convey the impressions I've gleaned of my mate's experiences and emotions, as well as the certainty that's become ever more solid since the possibility of another mate first presented itself to me.

"Talia didn't seek to bring more than one mate into her life," I say finally. "It happened by chance, and to some extent she resisted the idea." It's easy for me to remember that she hardly leapt at the idea of joining herself to me when our bond first exerted itself. "Her heart is so large and generous that she's found herself bound to all of us as circumstances brought us together. I fear my own capacity for affection is somewhat smaller. And I honestly don't know you at all. I would be forcing myself to attempt the relationship, not pursuing it because of feelings that already exist."

"But we were meant—"

I hold up my hand to cut her off, for her sake so she doesn't cling on to hope even a second longer than she has to. "You know I can't feel the bond that might have been between us at all. As long as that remains true, I can't help imagining that it would be far more torturous for you to remain in my presence, seeking a connection that isn't going to form and watching me with the mate I *am* bound to, than for you to set off on a different path. I'll support whatever endeavors you wish to pursue, contribute anything I can that would help you reach a happier future."

Kara's mouth slants at a tense angle. "You don't understand," she says. "Hazeleven is a desolate domain—I have nothing to offer a mate if I have no bond. I don't even have a home right now."

"We're going to get your home back," I assure her. "And—you shouldn't need finery or prestige to find a mate. You offer yourself."

Her eyebrow twitches. "That's easy for you to say," she murmurs, and then shakes herself. "I just—if there is any chance of us—"

I stop her again before she goes any further. "I'm sorry, but as my feelings stand right now, there isn't a chance. I'll do everything I can to improve your situation and help you gain the happiness you deserve, but it won't be at my side. I also ask that you don't raise any further concerns with my mate. This matter is between you and me, and unless forces beyond our control shift what is, that matter is settled."

Kara gazes at me for a long moment. Something comes over her expression—a chilliness that I don't entirely like.

"Well," she says, "I suppose we'll see. We can't know for sure how the future will play out. Maybe the bond will be fulfilled after all."

Then she sweeps out of the room without another

word. She could have simply meant the same consideration I've already had of what may happen when Orion's power is destroyed. But her remark leaves my skin itching with a deeper apprehension than I can fully explain.

22

Talia

I peer over the maps spread on Whitt's desk, doing my best to match the lines and words to my memories of the landscape. "How many sightings have there been of Orion himself? Has he been sticking to any specific part of the front or moving around all the time?"

Whitt taps a spot on the map at the edge of the Seelie realm not far from the border with winter. "We believe he was nearby when we acted out your plan with the salt and iron in the tunnels. He certainly reacted quickly. Other than that, he's been fairly elusive. We've had reports claiming to have spotted him along the front in one place or another, but of course with the Murk's fondness for illusion, it's hard to know how much credence to give those sightings."

"I've spoken with the refugees who've joined us from his army," Madoc says from where he's perched on the arm of the sofa for this late-night meeting. "They say he's been traveling through the ranks regularly, encouraging everyone on... and dealing out punishments for poor performance when he feels it's necessary. With the carriages we've learned to conjure, he could easily make it from the farthest end of the front to the other end in less than an hour."

"Then no matter where I put myself forward, someone should be able to get a hold of him and get him to me fairly quickly." I rub my temple as I wrap my head around the many variables. "We wouldn't necessarily need to give the Murk warriors a heads-up very far ahead of time for the plan to work. That's good. Less time for them to make a counter plan. Right?"

Whitt gives me an approving smile. "I'll totally agree with that reasoning."

I stifle a yawn that tries to stretch my jaw. We spent what was left of yesterday and the whole day today brainstorming possible tactics and gathering the information and resources we need. It's nearly midnight, and my brain feels like it's turned into mush.

I can't hide my exhaustion, especially from my soul-twined mate. Corwin gets up from the armchair where he's been sitting and grasps my shoulder. "You're wearing yourself thin. You'll think better in the morning after you've gotten some rest."

His own weariness comes through in his tone and through our connection—along with a lingering trepidation he can't hide from *me*. But he hasn't argued about this plan again since we started working on it. I know he's grappling with his doubts and making every effort to be supportive despite his worries about my safety.

I slip my hand around his. "I think the same would go for all of you too. You've been working on our strategy as hard or even harder than I have." I pause, my hesitance feeling odd when all five of my mates have been collaborating for days—but they haven't come together in exactly *this* way since Madoc joined us. "I think... my bed is big enough for all of us. I'll feel better having you all around me going into tomorrow."

Tomorrow I might be able to move forward with my plan against Orion. We can't afford to wait if the opportunity presents itself. And that means this could be the last night I ever get with the men I love so much.

Sylas and August were already straightening up from their positions around the room. They halt now, August with the most open glance toward the Murk man, although I can feel all four of my other mates' attention focus on him.

Madoc stiffens a bit, probably sensing he's on the spot. He pushes himself off the chair with an air as if he's making a concentrated effort to pretend he hasn't noticed. "I'd be happy to join you... if I'm welcome."

I don't even have to speak up first. Whitt does, with the playful geniality that's smoothed over so many tense or awkward situations in the past. "I'd say you've well and truly infested our home, and there's no coming back from that. Which is a good thing considering how much our mate enjoys your presence."

Madoc looks like he isn't sure whether to be offended

or pleased by that statement. Sylas chuckles softly and motions us all out of the room. "I'd say we're all coming to appreciate your contributions, if not in *quite* the same ways Talia does. And we've gotten plenty of practice at sharing already."

Madoc's shoulders drop down a bit as we walk down the hall. He comes up beside me, and I grip his fingers with my free hand, still holding on to Corwin at my other side. So much affection for all of my mates swells inside me that I half expect it to spill out of my skin in a giddy glow.

I can't remember if they've ever all been in my bedroom at the same time. It shouldn't feel so momentous after I've already been so intimately entwined with all of them, but it does. Adrenaline starts to thrum through my body, eating away at my earlier fatigue.

Maybe I don't want to sleep *just* yet.

I suspect my mates must be able to pick up on the shift in my mood, but as so often, they let me take the lead in showing what I want. I stop by the edge of the massive bed, picturing myself snuggled there between my five fae lovers, and a strange ache wakes up in my chest that's more bittersweet than I was prepared for.

What if this *is* the last night we have together? What if I don't survive my gambit against Orion? What if his supporters manage to hurt one of my men before I can end the war?

What if it's all for nothing, and I die only for the war to keep raging on?

I close my eyes against that last, despairing thought. I

can't let my mind veer in that direction. There've been so many challenges and enemies before that none of the fae would have believed I could survive, and I've beaten all of them.

I'll keep believing in me for as long as I'm still breathing.

Moving forward, I kick off my boots, climb onto the bed, and sit in the middle of the mattress with my dress pooled across my thighs. My mates circle the bed and sink onto the edges around me. There's something mildly predatory in their approach, but not to the point that it stirs up anything other than desire in me.

Sylas, so often the most confident, eases right next to me first. He kisses the crook of my jaw and teases his fingers along the side of my neck. "What did you have in mind now, my love?"

"I—I don't know," I admit. "I just know I want all of you."

The Seelie arch-lord turns toward Madoc. "Perhaps we should give our newcomer a head start, seeing as he has some catching up to do."

The rat shifter gives the other man a baleful look, but there's no real rancor in it. "I think I'd like to see just how much our mate benefits from having all of us together. But I can definitely make a start of it."

Sliding over, he lifts one of my feet and presses a kiss to the top. His gaze holds mine, the gray irises like molten clouds with the heat of his hunger. He kisses the side of my foot and then my ankle before moving to my other foot, the broken one.

His fingers trace the arch of misaligned bone, an angrier flare sparking in his gaze. He kisses that too, as tenderly as if it were an enhancement rather than a flaw.

As he strokes his hands up my calf, taking his time with this gentle seduction, my other men converge around me. Sylas slides over so he's directly behind me, trailing his fingertips up and down my spine and nipping the back of my neck. August steals a kiss from beside me and caresses my belly. Corwin nuzzles my ear and claims my mouth after August releases it.

Whitt kneels nearby, watching us all with an approving expression. He catches my hand to squeeze it just for a second as if to reassure me that he doesn't feel left out. "I'll take my moment when it comes. There's something to be said for simply taking in your responses. You're radiant when that flush of desire comes over you."

A sharper blush colors my cheeks, and he grins. Then August is kissing me again, Madoc's exploring touch reaches my knee, and there's no room in me for embarrassment.

What's there to be embarrassed about? I'm with my mates as we're intended to be.

Madoc lowers his head to kiss the side of my knee, his hands skimming up my thigh. Sylas helpfully tugs the skirt of my dress higher and then fiddles with the bindings down the back to loosen them. He eases my head around so he can kiss me from behind while August takes advantage of my loosened bodice to cup my breast. Corwin nibbles a path down my shoulder. And all the while I feel Whitt's gaze taking us in, as warm as if he's touching me too.

The flush is spreading through my whole body, from where my breasts tingle with jolts of pleasure to the heady need growing between my legs, dampening my panties. I twist my head around to kiss Corwin more urgently than before. Madoc slicks his tongue from my knee partway up my inner thigh and pauses with a stuttered intake of breath.

He looks up, catching my gaze when I release the Unseelie arch-lord. The emotion in his eyes is so fraught my throat closes up. But then he says, in a voice that's barely more than a whisper, "You're fertile."

Those two words send a stillness over the men gathered around me. Sylas lets out a pleased-sounding rumble and kisses me just behind my ear. Madoc stays braced in front of me, his fingers lightly caressing my inner thigh. They're all waiting for my signal, but he is most of all.

An odd bubbling sensation fills my chest, exhilarating but tinged with grief. I know there isn't much chance I'd get pregnant so quickly after the first time. Even the first time, for it to happen right away, was unexpected. But maybe that's not the point. The point is that I want it to happen again, whenever it does. I want to try as many times as it takes before we have that child our family deserves—and more.

I'm going to believe that we'll have all those chances, no matter what's ahead of us.

In that instant, the decision to simply hold on to faith

feels so momentous that I have trouble speaking. "Good," I say. "We have a chance to try again. Maybe the Heart will shine on us now, but if not, there's lots more time for it to come."

Corwin's love courses into me through our bond like a wash of sunlight. Madoc still looks oddly uncertain.

"Are you sure—?" he starts, and seems to grapple with his words. "We aren't officially mated yet…"

I don't know if that's what his hesitation is really about or if it's because of what he is, but he should know that I don't see him as any less than my other men. I told him so before, but after everything he's experienced, it isn't surprising it'd take a while sinking in.

I push myself forward so I can touch his cheek. "We're mated in every way that needs to count as far as I'm concerned. I'm your mate as much as I am anyone else's in this room. Don't hold back on me."

Heat flares in his eyes again, and a small but sly smile curves his lips. "Well, I don't see any reason to rush to the finish line. You still deserve to get every bit of enjoyment out of tonight that we can give you."

He drops his head to my thigh again, tasting my skin in a steady path toward my core. My sex aches with anticipation. Corwin finishes the job Sylas started by tugging my dress off me completely and continues to nibble my shoulder as he fondles one of my breasts. The Seelie arch-lord reclaims my mouth, August teases my other breast with his teeth, and I'm adrift on a whirlwind of bliss.

As Madoc reaches my sex, that storm becomes a

tsunami. He presses his mouth to me, his hot breath spilling through the fabric of my panties to delicious effect, and then wrenches them down to lick my sensitive nub directly. I whimper, unable to stop myself from squirming.

Madoc worships me with his lips and tongue, drawing more and more pleasure into my sex with every skillful movement. Quivers race from my core to the tips of my toes and the top of my scalp. I moan again, into Corwin's mouth now, my hips arching up of their own accord. Madoc grips them and urges me to buck into his mouth as he drives me closer and closer to that edge of ecstasy—and then sends me careening right over.

I come, gasping and quivering, and then he's surging over me with a groan of need that can't be denied. As he fumbles with his pants, I throw my arms around his shoulders. He plunges his shaft into me, filling me so perfectly.

I'm so sensitized it only takes a few strokes before I come again, my sex clamping around him. Madoc's chest hitches. "You always feel so fucking good," he mutters, and kisses me hard, thrusting into me almost frantically. I clutch him and rock against him, supported on all sides by my other mates, propelled toward even greater heights by their mouths and hands.

Another groan escapes Madoc as he comes. He kisses me again, long and lingering, and then he withdraws, glancing around him.

August is there in an instant, with no hint of any resentment at the new man in my life or the role he got to take first tonight. He kisses me with a flick of his tongue between my lips and kicks off his trousers. I grasp his rigid length, reveling in the twitch of it against my palm, the strength that emanates from it. "Please," I murmur.

August doesn't make me outright beg. With a joyful sigh, he slides into me, nipping my lip as he sinks all the way in. Another wave of desire swells inside me. I hook my feet around his waist and urge him onward.

"Always so sweet," he murmurs in a rough voice, picking up speed. "My Sweetness."

I whimper and cling on as pleasure blazes through me again. My fingers tangle in the short tufts of his hair. August grunts at the tug on his scalp, his thrusts turning wilder, and then he's spilling himself inside me with a low, drawn-out growl.

My reaching hands find Corwin next. My soul-twined mate pulls me around and onto his lap where he's already stripped off his slacks. I find him with eager fingers and line him up so he can push up into me.

My muscles feel as if they've turned to jelly, but somehow I find the energy to ride him, rewarded by the surges of bliss that race through me with every plunge of his shaft. Corwin dapples kisses across my face and neck, his inner monologue a constant stream of praise and devotion as he careens toward his release. *My mate. My love. My soul. You are all I could ever have asked for.*

His delight spirals into me in that familiar giddying cycle. As he comes with a spurt of heat inside me, I come yet again, shuddering in his arms.

Corwin draws back, but not too far. As he eases me

into a kneeling position before him, kissing my neck and stroking my breasts, I realize what he's getting me in position for. Or rather who. Sylas nuzzles the other side of my neck, his rich earthy scent filling my nose, and fills me from behind.

I sway between the two arch-lords, soaring higher with every buck of Sylas's hips and every swipe of Corwin's thumbs over my breasts. Madoc takes the initiative to slip his hand between them and finger my nub, and something in me explodes. My eyes roll back, every nerve quaking with fulfilled desire, my vision fracturing with a burst of stars. Sylas follows me with a roar.

When the Seelie arch-lord releases me with a gentle peck to my shoulder, my sly strategist is waiting. Whitt takes in my sated body and bliss-hazed eyes, and grins. "You are well-loved, aren't you, my mighty one?"

He lays me back down on the bedspread and takes his time kissing me and caressing me between peeling off his clothes. I run my hands over his muscular, tattooed chest, thinking of all the power those true-name marks speak of. All the trust this man has in me that he's supporting *my* strategy, letting me call the ultimate shots.

I am well-loved—so well it takes my breath away.

By the time Whitt's practiced fingers drift over my sex, I'm already quaking with renewed desire. He strokes me carefully, running his hand over my nub and slit and then delving his fingers inside, until I'm writhing and moaning beneath him. Then he sheaths himself in me with one swift movement that brings a gasp to my lips.

I'm tossed up on wave after wave, floating on a heady

current that races toward that inevitable peak. Whitt brings out his claws just long enough to tease them down my side, his fangs nicking my shoulder, and I shatter apart beneath him with a cry.

"That's right," he says. "Just like that." The words come out ragged, and a few moments later, he's bowing over me with the impact of his own release.

There's nothing left in me but joy and satisfaction. I drift in that bliss, holding on to it tightly, ignoring all thought of how long it might last—or not. My mates assemble themselves around me, sprawling out across the huge bed with an arm tucked around me here and there, and my eyelids slide shut.

If this is our last night, then I couldn't have asked for a better one.

23

Talia

The three humans who've ended up taking over the metal workshop in Heart's Cadence bring the best of their efforts out for me to examine by the light of the mid-morning sun. They lay the weapons on the long table next to the forge building and then step back as I walk right up to it.

Zelpha and Domhnall, today's babysitters from Corwin's coterie, don't come any closer. Based on Zelpha's grimace as we approached the workshop, just the faint whiffs of iron that've caught in the breeze made her uncomfortable. There's no way any of the fae of the seasons could have done this work themselves.

Madoc crosses about half of the distance between them and me before halting there. With his new connection to the Heart of the Mists, I know the noxious substance bothers him too.

Altogether, there are ten weapons lying on the table. The man in the middle, a grizzled figure with a trim beard who took over as leader after we determined he was the most experienced of the bunch, nods to them. "We felt it'd be best to offer a range of sizes and shapes so you can find what you'll be able to handle well. These were our best creations. We haven't worked with iron like this before… If you need us to go back to the drawing board, we can."

I shake my head. "I'm sure one of these will be fine." Madoc has convinced a few of the Murk newcomers to perfect the weapon once I've chosen it. The blades before me already look deadly.

I pick up one and then the next, testing them in my hand. First I simply get a feel for the grip, each of them wrapped with a thin leather binding, and practice drawing them from my pocket. Then I take a few trial jabs with the dagger.

August led me through several training exercises yesterday to hone the moves I'll need. We quickly decided that I'm best off going for Orion's throat. As satisfying as stabbing him in his heart might be, it's guarded by ribs I'd have to pierce at just the right spot and angle to avoid them deflecting my blow. The throat has cartilage to get through, but it isn't as tough as bone, and there's a broad expanse to work with. August showed me exactly where I should strike if I get the chance, a little to the side where the flesh is softer.

I run through those movements with nausea pooling in my stomach. As much as I hate Orion and what he did to me and so many of the fae—what he's still doing to us now—I don't get any joy from imagining his blood splattering all over me like Madoc's did not long ago. Killing has never been a talent I wanted to add to my repertoire.

But if this is the only way to protect myself and all those other people, then I'm not going to let my personal preferences get in the way.

I narrow my options down to my favorite three and experiment with each of them again. I like the ones that are on the longer and thinner side—they move more swiftly in my hand and fly free of my clothes more easily. But the length makes them more difficult to carry and conceal, and I need some heft to the blade if I'm going to be sure of it completely severing Orion's life from his body.

Finally, I settle on the middle one, not the longest or the lightest. As I swing it through the air once more, the sunlight glinting off its surface, a sense of rightness fills my chest.

Yes. This is the one.

"Thank you," I say to the metalworkers. "This is exactly what I needed. I guess you should hold on to the others just in case it turns out this won't quite do the job —I'm not really the best judge of that—but I think I'm ready."

All three of them bob their heads. "Thank you, and God speed," the woman on the left murmurs. They have a vague idea that I'm going to use this weapon to win their freedom, which is true in a roundabout way.

I pull a silk pouch reinforced with shielding magic out

of my pocket and slip the dagger into it. Only then do I walk over to Madoc to hand it over. His mouth twitches uneasily as he tucks the pouch into a carry-sack slung over his shoulder.

"They should make the blade as sharp as possible, with a sheath it'll slide free from quickly but won't cut through, and dull whatever impressions the metal gives off so Orion and his people won't realize I have it on me beforehand," I remind him.

My Murk mate touches the side of my face. "I know. They've already researched the spells. And I'll be right there the whole time to make sure they stick to the plan." He pauses. "Then you'll train a little more with August now that you have the specific weapon, while we get the rest of the pieces in place… and that's all there is to it?"

"We can only hope," I say with a halting chuckle. My stomach clenches tighter.

Madoc brushes his thumb over my cheek and hurries off to cross the border so his Murk companions can get started right away. I linger behind for a while, helping the humans tidy up despite their faint protests. August won't need me until the dagger is ready.

"You can go to the palace and get washed up," I say, pointing to the tall diamond building a short distance across the snow-swept plateau. "Then Arch-Lord Corwin's chef will have a hot meal waiting for you."

The metalworkers offer more thank yous and set off for the palace. I turn toward the border castle. As soon as I leave the workshop behind, Zelpha and Domhnall fall into step on either side of me.

"Are you sure it's a good idea to trust the rats with the task of enhancing the blade?" Domhnall asks, frowning. "I don't like so much relying on them staying true to their word."

Zelpha swats him behind my back. "You've been off wrangling the lords in the far-flung domains for too many of the past few months, Dom. Madoc's a good one, and he'll watch over the others more closely than *you* would. There's no way he'd risk Talia getting hurt if he can help it."

Domhnall looks abashed, and I can tell he's heard the story of how Madoc cured my curse. "I'm sorry," he says to me. "I just—I'm so used to thinking of all of the Murk as vermin."

I give him a tight smile. "I know. It's been an adjustment for everyone. But you can definitely trust Madoc. He's more honorable than an awful lot of summer and winter fae I've met."

Zelpha clucks her tongue. "Sad but true. What are you going to do while you're waiting on them enchanting the dagger?"

I blow out a breath. "I guess I'll see what progress Whitt has made on figuring out the final details of how we'll draw Orion out."

When I spoke to him earlier this morning, he was making some kind of calculation about the most ideal spot for me to venture across the front. We're still waiting to see if any of the Murk will agree to go in a little ahead of my arrival and make sure Orion knows to expect me. I'm going to say I'm giving up to save any more deaths among the fae children, but that I want to hear Orion tell me he'll back off on them to my face.

I don't actually expect him to do that. I figure he'll come specifically so he can rub it in my face that he'll attack the fae of the seasons however he wants. But that'll still bring him to me, which is all I need.

If we can't find a rat shifter who's willing to pass on the message, though, we'll have to come up with some other way of getting the king's attention. One he won't suspect is a trick. Too much depends on this gambit for us to get careless with any part.

We're just coming up on the winter side of the joint castle when a shout rings out from farther down the border. My head jerks up to see a slim form, face obscured by a heavy hood, waving to us maybe a quarter mile along the hazy wall. There's a panicked jerkiness to the movement that sets my nerves immediately on the alert.

Zelpha tenses, probably torn between sticking with me and going to investigate. But then the figure calls out, "Lady Talia, please hurry!" and it becomes clear that I'm the one who's most needed there.

We hustle over, my bad foot starting to ache against the frozen ground. As we get closer, I make out the woman's features within the hood. It's Kara. I'd stop in my tracks, the memories of our most recent encounters making me wary, but at the same moment she gestures toward the border.

"A couple just came with their child. We assumed you were on the summer side. The little girl's been taken by the curse—I think she's almost gone."

Her frantic tone and the words themselves send a jolt of chilling adrenaline through my veins. Every second might make a difference in whether I can save this child. I dash in my uneven way into the haze where she's indicating.

If I wasn't in such a hurry, if the past deaths hadn't weighed on my conscience so much, I might have wondered why the couple wouldn't have come to the border castle on the winter side, where the attendants could have told them exactly where I was. Or why Kara happened to be wandering around in Corwin's domain to coincidentally encounter them. But in the moment, horror drives me onward with no thought in my head except reaching the cursed girl.

After just a few steps, a yelp and a grunt sound behind me. I've already dashed across the dwindling ice onto the grass of the summer side of the border. I spin around, squinting into the haze for my companions who've unexpectedly vanished—and rigidly muscled arms slam around me from behind.

One hand yanks a swath of dark fabric over my face, shutting out all light. In the same motion, it clamps over my mouth to muffle my instinctive cry of protest. The other arm locks my arms against my sides, pressing into my ribs so hard my next breath comes with an ache.

"Quickly," someone hisses, and I'm heaved off the ground. I squirm and kick in every direction, but the arms around me only squeeze tighter. Someone else snatches my flailing legs and wraps a stiff cord around them.

There's a murmur, and a fog starts to sweep over my

mind. I fight against it, mumbling the true name for light against the fabric nearly smothering me. It slips out faintly, but it's just enough to drive back the worst of the mental haze. I cling to consciousness by a thread.

Corwin! I call out through our bond with the tenuous focus I have left. *Corwin, help!*

The figures who've grabbed me dump me onto a hard surface and tie another cord around my hands behind my back. They don't seem to have noticed that I'm not totally unconscious, but I can't command my body well enough to take any advantage of that oversight. My limbs refuse to respond. It's all I can do to hold my mind from spiraling into darkness.

What's happened, Talia? Corwin's voice reaches me from inside. *Where are you?*

The surface beneath me lurches into motion. I recognize vaguely that I must be in some kind of vehicle— a carriage from the feel of it. Wind whips over me even sprawled on the floor, tugging at the fabric pulled over my head. My captors are getting out of here as fast as they can, which isn't surprising.

I was— It's a struggle to form my thoughts into anything coherent. *The border... with Zelpha...*

Then the men poised around me start to speak, and I let my inner voice go silent, instead opening myself up so that hopefully Corwin will make out their words through my ears. They might reveal more than I'm able to convey.

"Are you sure that vermin 'king' wants her enough to barter much of anything?" one asks, and a deeper chill sinks into me. I know that voice. It's Cole.

And the one that answers is his lord. "Half of what he's done to us seems to be because of this blasted dung-body. We offer her in trade and win some concession that'll show our arch-lords and the others that they all should have listened to me to begin with."

A hysterical laugh bubbles in my chest. Aerik and his cadre are going to hand me over to Orion just like I was going to hand myself over—except I don't have my weapon, and who knows if they'll even let me be conscious for the transaction. They could have had exactly what they want if they'd just waited until the end of the day.

Except that's not totally true, is it? They didn't just want to bargain with Orion and score a win against the Murk. They also wanted the glory of doing it for themselves. And I have no doubt that Aerik would love to never again have to see me standing alongside one of his arch-lords, stirring the people's sympathies for me.

Did you hear? I think at Corwin. *It's—Aerik—they're—*

Before I can get any further than that, the carriage jostles, and my body flinches instinctively. One of my captors lets out a curse. A hand smacks onto my head alongside a muttered word, and I lose my grasp on the world around me completely.

24

August

"He *what?*" I burst out with an edge of a roar when Corwin finishes his hurried explanation of his last contact with Talia. Rage sears through me, and my vision flares red. "I'll tear that mangy bastard limb from limb, and his cadre too."

The Unseelie arch-lord is looking even paler than usual, adjusting his weight on his feet as if he's seconds away from launching himself after her. I guess I should be glad he took the time to tell us at all.

"I tried to give chase, and I sent the members of my coterie nearby and a few other guards as well," he says in a strained voice. "But Aerik obviously planned this carefully. We couldn't pick up any clear trail or spot him from above. They're concealing themselves too well. And unfortunately, I don't have very many people to call on for the search with so many focused on the war."

"We know they're headed toward the front," Sylas says. He's gotten up from behind the desk in his study, his dark eye glowing fiercely. "We have to catch them there before they have the chance to set up their 'trade'."

"What if they hurt Talia before they get there?" I demand. My claws come out where I'm gripping the top of the nearest chair, piercing the fabric, but I can't draw them back in. "They've done it before—to make her easier to restrain. They might even think Orion will be happier if they show they've tormented her first."

Whitt lets out a low growl. "We won't let it come to that."

"How could they even have taken her at all?" I ask. "They vowed to leave her alone with their yield."

Sylas grimaces. "There must have been some loophole they worked around with the wording. I believe I said they couldn't attempt to put her under their control. It could be that taking her for the purpose of letting Orion control her made enough of a difference that the vow didn't stop them. Or perhaps someone else helped by taking the initial steps to subdue her." He gestures to Corwin. "You said that Unseelie woman, the one who claims she should have been your soul-twined mate, was involved?"

Corwin nods like he's got a heavy weight on his shoulders. "I suspect she believed that if she removed Talia from consideration, her soul-twined bond with me would solidify after all. She set up the trap and prevented my coterie from intervening. Zelpha would have been right there with Talia if Kara hadn't tangled her in a spell. They have her in custody now. No one saw, and she didn't say—we're not sure if anyone else was helping Aerik."

"He could have had a couple of his pack-kin with him if necessary to pull it off." Whitt lets out a rough breath and turns to Corwin. "No offense to your sharp raven eyes, but I think wolfish noses will tackle this task more easily, especially when the trail should be fresh. Exactly how long ago did this happen?"

Corwin winces. "About half an hour ago now. I went after her first—there wasn't any way to quickly tell the rest of you—"

"That's fine," Sylas says. "That still gives us plenty to work with. The trail won't go cold immediately. We'll set out at once—with Astrid and the best trackers we can summon from the packs around the Heart—if we can get a message to our forces on the front to keep watch in case they reach it ahead of us—"

"I doubt Aerik will race right in without any preamble," Whitt says. "He's a prick, but he's not stupid. He'll have to make arrangements with the Murk for a hand-off and figure out a way to do that without tipping the rest of us off. I wouldn't be surprised if he finds a place to camp out until after nightfall when he'll have darkness for additional cover."

It's not even noon yet. If my brother is right, that should give us more than enough time to track the brutes down. I swivel toward the door, every muscle itching to get started on the rescue. "I'll find Astrid and send out the word for trackers. We should get going as soon as—"

I open the study door to find a sentry standing on the

other side with her hand raised to knock, her face flushed with exertion and her jaw tensed. I step back, startled. Does she already have news about Talia?

But her hasty report has nothing to do with our mate at all.

"My lord, the Murk have pressed forward in another attack along the front," she says, her gaze seeking out Sylas beyond me. "They're sending some sort of projectiles at our warriors that are weakening their powers. When I left, we'd already lost another two domains. I don't know if the fae already on the front line will be able to hold them off at all."

Sylas growls a curse under his breath. "We'll have to send everyone from the camps—every fae who can contribute any magical power at all. If they press forward all the way to the Heart…"

He doesn't finish that sentence, but he doesn't need to for dread to wind around my gut. If the Murk topple our forces, it won't matter what happens to Talia. We'll all be done for.

The sentry dashes off to alert the other arch-lords. Sylas strides out of the room with Corwin close at his heels. The Unseelie arch-lord looks just as sick as I feel. "If they're advancing on the summer side, they'll be doing the same in my realm as well. I'll have to get back."

But he doesn't want to. None of us wants to be shepherding our people into a desperate battle with the Murk while our mate is in the hands of fae who are just as villainous. My lips pull back from the fangs that've sprung free from my gums. One clear thought blazes through all the rest.

"I'll go after Talia," I say. "I'm the best tracker out of us, and I'll be able to take on all three of those bastards in a fight when I find them, as long as I catch them by surprise. If the Murk have taken up some unexpected new tactic, you won't need one more fighter on the front that much. Our people will need leadership and strategy."

Sylas grits his teeth, but understanding simmers in his eyes. "I don't like you going alone."

"I'll travel faster that way. Chances are they'll be close to the front as it is by the time I catch up with them, and I can call on a little assistance if anyone's able to offer it then." I hold his gaze, my own imploring. "Let me do this. The faster I go after her now—"

Sylas waves his hand, releasing me from any other obligations I had to him. I dash down the hall, already springing into wolf form as I go. "Be careful as well as fast," my brother calls after me. "Aerik has to know someone will come after him."

I charge out of the castle to find the fields outside are already a swarm of activity. Warriors are shouting to each other and passing weapons to pack-kin who look much more uncertain. Every fae on hand is being ushered to the front. Messengers are rushing this way and that through the chaos.

I dodge through the bustle and plunge into the thick underbrush of one of the stretches of forest. Corwin said Aerik stole Talia from a spot just north of here, near where the hill starts to slope downward. I'll sniff him out, whether with my nose or my magic.

He won't get away with this. And when I'm through with him, he's never going to terrorize my mate again.

As I emerge again farther along the border, I mark the spot where the carriage took off easily from the disturbed grass. They raced away too hastily to totally cover their tracks here, probably figuring that there were too many witnesses to the scene of the crime to bother with it. But after they left this spot, they vanished.

To Corwin and his coterie's senses, anyway. I circle the area, expanding my search a little farther with each iteration, taking deep whiffs of scent into my wolfish nose. It takes five circuits, but then I pick up on the clue that will lead me to them.

All of the smells I'm taking in are what you'd expect for this strip of land, no trace of recent fae or human presence. But along one path away from the launch spot, those scents take on a slightly more pungent edge. It's an incredibly subtle difference, and with Corwin and the other Unseelie being unfamiliar with the odors of the summer realm, I'm not surprised they'd have failed to pick up on it.

But I know it for what it is. Aerik used magic to exaggerate the other scents just enough to swallow up his own. The effect will dissipate over time—it's already faded so much I'm lucky I caught it at all. I have to follow it quickly.

I set off at a lope, veering left and right at periodic intervals to make sure I'm still on the right track. As

Aerik's course takes clearer shape in my mind, I speed up to a full-out run.

I should have gotten a small carriage of my own before I left Hearth-by-the-Heart. I can't conjure one myself. Is it worth racing back to the castle to see if I can take one now? Will I lose more time doing that or staying on foot?

Before I can finish debating, a shape flits into view at the corner of my vision. I jerk my head around to see a ragtag vehicle made of what looks like scraps of wood and woven leaves, only about twice as big as I am. Madoc is braced by the bow. When he sees me looking his way, he raises his hand.

As he draws up next to me, I straighten up in the form of a man, my pulse thrumming with the need to keep on the move. "What are you doing here?"

The Murk man's expression reminds me of the morning I found him standing over Talia's bed with a knife in his hand, ready to sacrifice himself to save her. "I heard what happened. I have the feeling I'll be more useful helping you than doing battle on the front. Stealth and sneaky escapes are much more my thing than combat."

Some part of me bristles a little, as if it resents his intrusion on my mission, which is ridiculous because it was a risk making the journey alone—and he has gone as far as supplying a vehicle so I don't even need to worry about speed. "I'll accept your offer," I say. "So far the trail leads that way." I motion to the southwest. "Can you handle the steering and change course quickly as need be? I need to focus all my energy on scenting them."

Madoc nods and motions for me to get in. I shift back into wolf form as I leap.

The carriage is narrow enough that I can swing my body from one side to the other and catch the edges of Aerik's concealing spell without needing to divert from our course farther. Madoc sets us off at a pace about twice as fast as I could have run, urging the carriage swifter still at my barks of encouragement. When the trail of exaggerated scent veers farther west, I thump my paw against the hull, and the Murk man adjusts our angle. Sometime later, I smack the other side to get him aiming more south again.

During the straight stretches, Madoc murmurs a few spell words around us, chaining bits of magic together with a tingle that washes through the atmosphere. "I'm disguising us too," he tells me. "Better if they don't see us coming, right?"

I can't argue with that point. I should have thought of it myself.

The extra vividness of the landscape's smells has thickened, still subtle but obvious enough now that I don't need to strain as hard to keep track of it. We must be getting closer, catching up with them. I wonder if Aerik even realizes that the Murk have launched a renewed attack. How will that fit into his plans?

If he's just picking a spot a good distance from the front to hide out until nightfall, he may not have any idea at all what a mess he's set himself up to wade into. Of course, if I have my way, he's never going to get the chance to go anywhere near Orion and his army.

The sun is starting to sink toward the horizon when

the carriage slows. I glance at Madoc with a huff of consternation, but he points into the distance where there's a clump of forest with gold-tinged leaves. "I think they've taken shelter there. There's a quality to the light around that spot... Some kind of illusionary magic's been cast there."

I guess as an expert on illusions, he should know.

He draws us up within about fifty feet of the patch of woods, and we both leap out. I stay in wolf form. Madoc casts another spell around the two of us, and we set off toward the trees.

"They won't be able to hear us or see us," he says under his breath. "But if we bump into them, they'll feel us. So don't go barging in there until you're sure you're ready."

I snort to say that should be obvious.

We slink between the trees, which grow sparsely at first and then closer together as we get deeper into the woodlands. I almost miss the glade until Madoc points out the shimmer in the air nearby. Aerik's people have had to get less subtle to expend enough magic to hide their presence entirely. I can't see, hear, or smell the fae themselves yet, but this close, there's an obvious visual clue.

When we reach the edge of the glade where the spell was cast, the figures swim into focus where moments ago it appeared to be empty. My stance goes rigid.

If Aerik had one of his pack-kin helping with the abduction, they left that person behind. Or maybe they sent that one off to try to barter with the Murk. It's just him and his two cadre-chosen sitting on a semi-circle of logs, eating slabs of smoked meat they brought along for the journey. Their narrow carriage, which they must have navigated carefully through the trees, is parked off to one side of the glade.

I straighten up as a man and ease closer, setting my feet softly even though Madoc's spell should stop the other fae from hearing me. With just a few steps, I make out Talia's slender form curled on the floor of the carriage between two of the benches. There's a loose sack over her head, hiding her face and her vivid hair, but she's wearing her usual boots, and I'd know the curves of her body anywhere, just as I know her other features.

My lips pull back in a silent snarl. At least they don't appear to have hurt her—yet—other than binding her wrists and ankles. From the slow rise and fall of her chest, she's unconscious.

My attention slides back to the men who wrenched her away from us and meant to barter with her like she's worthy of no more consideration than the meat they're digging into. My claws spring from my fingertips. But something in me hesitates just for a second.

What will Talia think if we wake her up to a clearing splattered with blood, to that same blood splattered all over me from my rage? How will she look at me?

I close my eyes, gathering myself. Talia has reassured me again and again that she doesn't see a monster in me. That she appreciates the ferocity with which I'm willing to protect her. There's no way I can keep her safe when she goes through with her plan to confront Orion, but right here, right now, I can defend her in the most primal way there is.

She deserves that.

When I open my eyes again, Madoc has come up beside me. My muscles have bunched, ready to spring. I'm not going to bother with my sword for the initial assault. I can't wield it as effectively as I can my fangs and claws anyway.

"I'm not a particularly skilled fighter," Madoc says, "but I can help even the playing field. If you want, I can use an illusion to distract them, scatter them so it'll be easier for you to tear through them all."

He says it without any judgment of the tactics he assumes I'll take or the slightest hint that he'd argue with them. I find myself smiling at him—a real smile, with a sense of companionship I hadn't quite felt toward the newest member of our family before.

"Be my guest."

Madoc smiles back, grimly but determinedly, and steps to the side again. He intones several words under his breath, his gaze trained on a point at the other side of the glade.

There's a rustling in the underbrush. All three of the men's heads jerk up. Twigs crackle and then a stomping sound rushes off as if away from the glade.

"What in the lands?" Cole mutters, leaping up.

Aerik waves at him. "Go see what that's about, but stay hidden unless you need to… deal with it."

The pale-haired man strides off between the trees. The second he's vanished from view, Madoc murmurs again—

and an image that looks just like Sylas appears half-cloaked in the shadows at another end of the clearing.

Aerik sees it first and startles, springing up. As he strides forward, his other cadre-chosen stiffens on his log. And I see my perfect opening.

I burst through the trees and launch myself at the man on the log. He barely has time to get out the start of a yelp before it turns into a gurgle as my claws slash through his throat. I slam his skull under my heel for good measure and spin toward Aerik, my pulse thumping, my blood humming with anticipation.

Aerik whirls, but it's Cole I have to deal with next. He bolts into the glade in wolf form, gnashing his teeth. I fling myself forward and shift at the same time. My paws slam into him, digging in as I slam him to the ground.

His claws rake across my side, but I ignore the stinging sensation and snap at his throat. He manages to wriggle just out of reach. I pummel him into the ground with all my weight, hard enough to crack ribs.

A frantic whine creeps from Cole's wolfish mouth that only spurs me onward. He *should* be afraid. I hope he feels every bit as terrified as he's made Talia so many times.

He tries to squirm away, and I shift in an instant, snatching the sword from my belt and driving it into his chest, straight through his heart.

I look up to see Aerik standing over me, his own sword in his hand. He lunges at me, and I dodge to the side, rolling across the blood-damp grass. Then more illusionary images flicker into being around him.

They're all Talia—a Talia at every side of him. They

glare at him with the fierceness my mate can bring to bear so well and open their mouths to say in a chorus, "You shouldn't have done this. You're the vermin here."

Aerik can obviously tell they're not real, but they shake him for just long enough for me to recover my balance and hurtle toward him. I ram my elbow into his wrist as I crash into his body, snapping the delicate bones there and sending his sword flying. He slices clawed fingers at my neck, but I twist away and sink my fangs into his shoulder.

Words start to rasp over his lips, but I cut them off with a barked spell of my own that deflects his magic. My feet kick his legs out from under him. As he falls, I rear back to make my final blow.

"Hold!" he sputters, his eyes wide. "I yield. I yield. You can't—"

I snarl at him. "You already broke the terms of our last yield, however you weaseled around them."

"I stuck to the letter of the—"

"I think the Heart will side with me and justice," I roar, and clamp my fangs around his throat to tear it right out.

Blood sprays across me and the glade. Aerik's body sags beneath me. I push away from him, disgusted with the taste of him in my mouth but with a rush sweeping over me that's more relief than triumph. I stare down at his limp form and swipe the back of my hand across my mouth.

It's over. It was a long time coming, and he's finally finished. He'll never lay one more finger on my mate.

25

Talia

My mind swims back into consciousness. I blink, my vision blurring and then steadying to reveal two faces hovering over mine with matching looks of concern.

"Sweetness?" August says, and my pulse hiccups. All at once, I register the hard slats of the carriage floor beneath me, the ache around my forearms and ankles where a rope bound them not long ago, the faint throbbing in the back of my head.

I jerk upright, and Madoc catches my shoulder to steady me. "Aerik," I gasp. "He and Cole and—and I don't know who else."

"We dealt with them," August says with a savage smile, and only then do I notice the flecks of blood at the corners of his lips. There's more splashed across his shirt. My gaze darts over him, but he doesn't appear to be at all injured himself.

I can't stop myself from throwing my arms around him, hugging him tight. August lets out a pleased rumble that sounds a bit choked as well and nuzzles the side of my face. "You're all right now. And he's gone for good." He lifts his head to glance over at Madoc. "Your new mate showed some creative battle skills to help make that happen too."

I pull back and glance between them. There's a new warmth in the grin August aims at Madoc and an ease to the way the Murk man tips his head in return that wasn't there before. It looks like my mates accomplished more than just destroying Aerik and his cadre.

Talia? Corwin speaks through our bond, his voice both eager and oddly harried. He's supressing most impressions of the world around him. *August reached you? You're well?*

As well as I can be when just rescued from a kidnapping, I think back. *Where are you? What's happening there?*

Don't worry about that, my soul. Let August help you recover, and we'll take care of the rest.

The rest of what? I'd ask, but he's muted our connection completely. Trepidation coils around my gut.

August helps me to my feet and lifts me over the side of Aerik's carriage. I stare into the glade we're at the edge of, taking in the three bodies sprawled there. Aerik's neck is nothing but mangled, bloody flesh, the grass around him soaked red. The burly man's throat has been slashed too and his skull cracked open. Cole lies nearby, his eyes staring sightlessly at the sky, a little blood still oozing from a stab wound on his chest.

My stomach turns at the gore and the meaty smell that's rising into the air, but I don't feel any actual horror at the scene. This is exactly how these men would have happily treated me and my mates if they could have gotten away with it. August ensured they'll never get that chance.

I turn my back on them, a heaviness expanding in my chest before my spirits have much time to lift. Corwin's words and the vague sense of disarray I got from him are still niggling at me. I turn back to my men. "Is everyone *else* all right? They only sent the two of you to look for me?" Not that I'm complaining when they obviously got the job done, but it does seem strange, especially when my mates had to suspect they'd be up against at least three opponents.

August opens his mouth and closes it again. Before he can figure out how to answer, Madoc steps in, his voice a little hoarser than usual but still even. "Orion pushed forward another attack. We didn't get many of the details, but it sounded bad. They needed everyone who could be spared on the front to try to stop his advance. I know Sylas, Whitt, and Corwin would have been racing to your rescue too if they hadn't been determined to ensure you have a home to go back to."

Any relief I'd felt before flees my body. I suck in a shaky breath. "I have to do it, then. The plan. I have to—I need the dagger—did the Murk have a chance to finish it? And we need to get to Orion... I can't let him keep going like this!"

"Hey." August strokes his fingers over my hair. "One thing at a time. You only just came out of Aerik's spell. We *don't* have the dagger you need, and—"

Madoc coughs. "Actually…" Gingerly, he pulls the pouch I gave him out of the deep pocket of his trousers. He hands it to me, looking glad to have it farther from his body. "My people have learned to work quickly. They were just finishing up when I heard what'd happened to you. I thought… better to bring it to wherever you are than leave it behind."

August lets out a noise of disbelief. "I couldn't even tell you were carrying it. Are you sure that's iron?"

Madoc smiles thinly. "Very sure. The essence seeps through a little when it's very close to you. But I'm glad to hear the disguising spells did the trick. Talia should be able to walk right up to Orion without him realizing what she's carrying until she's jabbing it into his throat."

I slip my hand into the pouch and pull out the dagger. When I ease it from its thin but hardy sheath, the blade gleams even brighter than before in the late afternoon sunlight. I slash it through the air, and it seems to sing. Even without trying to cut anything, I can tell how sharp it is.

"We didn't get the chance to practice," I say to August. "Not with the actual weapon I'm going to be using."

August glances off through the woods. "We've got a bit of a trek from here to the front, and we'll want to give that a wide berth until we see what the current situation is. Madoc can steer the carriage, and you and I can try out the motions while we're traveling. His vehicle is steady enough." He turns back to me. "But that isn't the important part. We already trained quite a bit. How are we going to get you in a position to take on Orion while his army is in the middle of battering us?"

I frown. "They can't keep going full tilt forever, right? They'll have to slow down to rest at some point. There'll be a lull."

August nods slowly.

Madoc makes a dismissive motion toward the corpses behind me. "As much as I hate to give those fuckheads any credit, we could take a page from Aerik's strategy book. It seemed like he was waiting until nightfall before he'd attempt his 'trade.' You might be better off approaching Orion with the cover of darkness too."

"Yes." I don't know if that will be enough, though. And what if the Murk topple the Seelie and Unseelie forces before they ever need to rest?

"I need to know what's going on," I say. "You said the others all went to the front?"

"As far as I know," August says. "That's what we discussed when I set off to look for you."

"They were just heading out when I left the hill around the Heart," Madoc puts in.

"Let me try to talk to Corwin and then Whitt," I say. "I'm going to find a quiet spot so I can totally concentrate." Distractions shouldn't matter much when it comes to my soul-twined mate, but reaching out to Whitt with his true name has always been harder. At least I'm nowhere near as far away as when I tried to speak to him from the Refuge.

August and Madoc let me pick my way a short distance from them into the trees. I find a mossy stone at the base of a broad oak and sink onto it, leaning my back against the trunk. Closing my eyes, I focus on the energy of the bond inside me.

Corwin? Please, I realize you're dealing with a lot, but I have to know what's happening. August told me the Murk were starting to overwhelm the rest of you. Have you managed to stop them?

Corwin's voice reaches me a moment later, more frayed than before. *Not quite. We've slowed them down, but we haven't found a strategy that completely offsets their new one.*

What's that? What are they doing?

They've brought out these devices that launch projectiles, and they've been shooting spikes of iron at us. They can't launch very many at once because having the metal around affects them too, but the things can pierce right through any defensive wall we throw up and they weaken us faster than they do the Murk. We've had to keep pulling back as they pollute the territory.

I think back to my own strategy using iron. *That means they're advancing over land that's already got iron scattered across it, and you're pulling back onto clean terrain. It should be wearing down on them the longer they're surrounded by it.*

I agree—and that may be part of the reason their advance has slowed. I don't know if it'll be enough for them to stop for good, though.

I might not need them stopped. I just need there to be

enough breaks in the fighting for me to have a chance to get Orion's attention. I bite my lip. *Have you seen Orion? Is he on your side of the border?*

What are you thinking, my soul? You can't go after him in the middle of this.

I'm not asking you for permission. If I see an opening, I'm going to take it. I'll be a lot safer doing that if I have a better idea what I'm up against.

I get the impression of a mental sigh, and distant yells that Corwin's trying to keep from traveling through our bond. *I understand. That determination is part of why I love you, and I won't stifle it. I haven't seen any sign or heard any report of Orion's presence along the front. That doesn't mean he isn't here, but he hasn't shown himself at all if he is.*

Thank you. Stay safe—as safe as you can be. I send him an image of me kissing him and let him refocus on the war waging around him.

I shift my attention to Whitt next, picturing his sparkling ocean-blue eyes and sly grin. "*Wye-con-ell,*" I whisper. "Hear me and let me hear you."

Reaching out to the spymaster this time doesn't provoke the same instant headache that came when I tried from the human world. I hear his voice as if through a long tunnel, faintly echoed. *Talia? What's going on? August was coming for you—has he—?*

Yes, I say before he has to go on. *I'm safe now. But from what I'm hearing, the rest of you aren't. Corwin says the Murk are firing iron spikes at the Unseelie. I assume it's the same on the Seelie side?*

Yes, Whitt says. *We've had a little luck deflecting them. A squad of Madoc's Murk followers decided to come with us, and their magic isn't as weak to the iron. But Orion's still gained a lot of ground. We're in a stand-off now.*

Have you seen Orion himself? I ask quickly. Now an ache is starting to creep up the back of my head, and I can tell it'll soon get harder to say or hear anything completely coherent. The true-name connection isn't meant for extended conversations.

I get a sense of Whitt shaking his head. *Not directly. But he hollered out a few taunts with that megaphone spell of his earlier.* He pauses. *What are you thinking, mite?*

Orion's probably on the Seelie side, then. I know where I need to go. *I still have my plan to go through with,* I tell him. *Try to hold your ground until I can make it there. It'll be a lot easier if there's not a battle in full swing.*

I'll see what I can do. There isn't—

My connection to him falters. The ache in my head has only deepened to a dull throbbing, but Aerik's spell has left my mind a little groggy as well.

I know enough, don't I? I get to my feet and head back to August and Madoc. Now I have a destination, and I have my weapon.

I just don't know how I'm going to convince Orion to meet me halfway—the part that we were stuck on all along.

"Did you find out everything you were hoping to?" August asks me when I rejoin them. "Are the others okay?"

"Whitt and Corwin are," I say. "And I'm sure Sylas must be, or I'd have been able to tell something was wrong. I just…"

As I rub my forehead, my gaze drifts across the ruined bodies in the clearing again. My body goes abruptly still. The idea flickers to life like a flame inside my skull.

"What?" Madoc asks, watching me.

"I think I know how I can make it to Orion," I say slowly. "Aerik might have had the right idea in a very wrong sort of way. Let's go, now. I need to try to speak to Whitt again. If they can have everything ready by the time we get there, we might be able to end this war tonight."

Sylas

I prowl along the crowd of warriors, casting my gaze between those poised to fight at the first sign of another Murk offensive and those scattered behind that line of protection with healers kneeling by their sides. Exhaustion shows on too many of the faces around me. We've been fighting off the Murk onslaught for hours, and we're all wearing thin.

My only comforts are the signs that our rat enemies have also tired and the knowledge that my mate survived her kidnapping uninjured. But even that second fact comes with other worries. Talia is coming back to us, but only to throw herself before the Murk in an even more dangerous scenario than she was facing before.

Whitt finds me as I reach the end of the front near the border haze. He looks weary too, but there's enough optimism in his expression to bring a little hope into my chest.

"I think I might have what we need," he says. "But they want to speak to you first. I think they want some kind of arch-lord guarantee."

I let out a huff, but I'm not going to blame the Murk refugees who've recently come among us for negotiating. Their position here is more precarious than anyone's. "All right. Talia said she needs just two to accompany her?"

Whitt falls into step with me as we head to the area where the rat shifters who volunteered to join us in battle have been sticking together in one small squad. To my pleased surprise, Delta and a contingent of her warriors arrived as well, but they've been keeping their distance from Orion's former followers.

"Yes, just two, as far as I gathered," my strategist says. "The second time she reached out to me, she was struggling more to get her message across. But that number would make sense. Two gives her a decent amount of protection without making Orion feel overly threatened."

"They won't be much protection if he strikes her down too quickly," I can't help muttering.

Whitt sighs. "No. But Talia's been around him; she's seen how he thinks and behaves. And she's got Madoc with her to advise her. I think we have to go by their judgments over our own."

"I know." I restrain a growl of frustration. "If we could kill him ourselves right now…"

"Obviously I'd opt for that plan too if it were available.

But he hasn't shown himself to us at all. As much esteem as I have for both the two of us and the rest of our forces, I have to admit we can't offer much that would tempt him."

But the Murk king has had it out for our mate from the moment she fled his colony. The reasoning for her plan is sound. I'll support her in it as much as I can. There's simply nothing that can make me *like* it.

If another opportunity to end Orion's life presented itself right now, I'd take it in an instant.

We have a few dozen Murk who've arrived at the temporary settlement near the Heart, but only eight of them had the courage to accompany us in fighting back directly against their former allies. One of them fell under the first barrage of attacks after we entered the fray. At the moment, the other seven are sitting in a tight cluster, gulping down the rolls other fae have been passing out so the warriors can keep their strength up. From the wary glances they keep shooting over their shoulders, I suspect they haven't gotten the warmest reception from the rest of the fae here.

"Has anyone harassed you?" I ask as I come to a stop before them. If there's been any outright hostility, I need to stamp that out immediately. Not only does it undermine our best chance of finding a peaceful resolution with the Murk even after Orion is gone, but it could threaten Talia's plan to ensure that first part happens at all.

The Murk man who's been the most talkative of the bunch, Flynn, peers at the groups of fae gathered across the plain around us and wrinkles his nose. "Nothing like that. But we'd rather not stick our necks out too far trying to make friends while our lives are already literally on the line, if that's all right with you."

"Of course," I say evenly. "I only asked so that I could set *my* people straight as need be." I motion to Whitt. "I gather that my strategist has informed you of Lady Talia's request? I understand it would be an even more dangerous undertaking than simply standing with us in battle. We wouldn't ask it of any of you if we didn't feel it was our best chance at ending this war."

One of the two women in the bunch narrows her eyes at me. "By killing Orion."

I give her a grim smile. "You must realize that there's no way we can find any kind of peace while he's still determined to take the Mists completely for himself. Can any of you honestly see him agreeing to compromise and live in cooperation with the rest of us?"

The gloom that settles over all their faces is enough of an answer.

"He isn't going to be happy with us," one of the other men says. "Chances are no matter what we say or do, he's going to want to set an example. We'll be walking in there just to be slaughtered if your mate can't put her plan into action the way she's hoping."

I tip my head. "I acknowledge that. As I said, it'll be dangerous. But Lady Talia has accomplished quite a lot of difficult tasks in the past. None of us is safe if we can't defeat Orion—and soon. I honestly believe it's by far the route most likely to see all of us, including the Murk who are willing to work with us, survive."

"Why does it have to be us going with her?" the woman mutters.

"He'll be much more inclined to believe that a couple of *his* people would have regrets and try to make amends than that any of the fae of the seasons would go over to his side," Whitt says. "That'll mean he's less suspicious, more willing to let down his guard, which means more chance for Talia to make her move."

Flynn rubs his mouth. "What does Madoc say about all this? He went after her, didn't he?"

I nod. "Yes, and he's with her now. He'll have consulted with her on this plan. You should have an opportunity to speak to him directly before you actually set off. We'd need you to head west of the front to meet with them and approach the Murk forces from there."

"It won't be easy to back down once we've gone that far," the other woman puts in.

"That's true," I say. "And I gathered you have some conditions you'd like to put on your help. I'm willing to take a vow related to any requests you have—within reason, of course."

One of the men snorts, but Flynn sits up straighter, holding my gaze. "You've got to use plain language, no flowery garbage that's easier to maneuver around. We know the fae of the seasons can be just as tricky as you say the Murk are."

"I have no problem with making the vows as simple as possible."

"All right. We want a guarantee that no matter which of us takes this on, all of us who came out here and have been fighting with you against our own people will be safe in the Mists for the rest of our lives. No banishing us, no attacking us—we'll have a good home and not be hassled about it."

That seems fair. "I can offer you that," I say. "But I'll need to include a caveat that it will only be enforced as long as you don't commit any major crimes. And I can only speak for myself and what I'll insist on. I may be able to get my fellow arch-lords to swear as well, but we can't vow for any future arch-lords, the Unseelie rulers, or anything beyond our scope."

The Murk appear to think this over. Flynn makes a gesture of acceptance. "That's the main thing. I also want —we should have approval to associate with the fae of the seasons however we want, if the other fae want it too. I mean, as friends, or mates, or whatever else comes up."

I restrain myself from raising my eyebrows at that request, wondering if he already has someone in mind. I wouldn't have argued against it even without a vow. "That's not a problem either. Is there anything else?"

The Murk murmur amongst themselves for a few minutes, and then Flynn turns back to me. "That would be enough. We need to approve of the wording before you take the vow. And then we'll decide who goes. We'd like all of the arch-lords to take the vow if possible."

Somehow I suspect he'll be one of those going no matter what. I recognize the determined fire in his eyes.

"I'll speak to them now," I say. "Thank you. We do appreciate the risks you'll be taking."

I expect to have to roam for a while before I can locate

both of my colleagues, but I've only just left the Murk when Celia and Donovan stride into view just a short distance away amid the crowded camp. They head straight toward me. Whitt considers them and mutters from the side of his mouth, "This looks like trouble."

I have to agree with him. Both of my fellow arch-lords look solemn and strained.

"What's the matter?" I ask when they reach me. They wouldn't be coming to me together if it wasn't official business.

Donovan glances toward the Murk army on the other side of our latest attempt at a magical wall. "We're seeing new activity among the Murk. We suspect they're gearing up for another large-scale attack, maybe something different than they tried before."

"Maybe something even worse," Celia adds, a stormy expression crossing her dark face. "I say we launch an assault of our own as quickly as possible with all the power we can muster. Catch them before they have the chance to get another edge on us."

My heart sinks. "We've already been fighting them for days without managing to push them very far when we're not implementing a special strategy. What's going to turn the tide this time rather than simply exhausting us even more so we can't even hold our ground after?"

"We have a much larger force assembled today than we've had before," Donovan says, though there's a trace of doubt in his tone. "The Murk have been lingering amid the iron projectiles they fired into that territory—we can hope they've been weakened."

"As we will be if we charge back into that territory," I remind him.

Celia's eyes flash. "We can't simply sit around and wait for them to savage us again."

"We won't," I say with all the confidence I can summon. "Talia is on her way here. The Murk have all but agreed to support her plan. Within the hour, we could see Orion fall, and the majority of his supporters will falter without him leading the charge."

"So you claim. But where is your mate? She may not make it to us at all. And what guarantee do we have that the Murk will follow through? Just days ago, they were on the other side of this war. If we don't act now, we may lose any advantage we could have had."

"If we *do* act now, we'll definitely lose the even greater advantage Talia means to give us." I look at Whitt. "Have we had any other news from her party recently?" I've avoided telling my colleagues exactly how we've communicated with them, letting them make their own assumptions about messenger spells.

Whitt shakes his head, his mouth slanting at a crooked angle. "I don't think it should take very much longer, though."

Celia exhales roughly. "We can't rely on assumptions."

My chest constricts, the responsibilities of my role pressing in on me as never before. I have to make the right choice for my people. Donovan is wavering—I can see I've started to persuade him. But what if I push for this outcome and the Murk tear through our ranks before Talia even arrives?

What if I send so many Seelie to charge at the Murk only to watch most of them fall under the rats' blades and claws?

I think of Talia, standing up to Aerik in the Bastion with all the brilliant strength I've watched growing in her for months. I think of my younger brother, who's fought with unrelenting devotion, and of the rat shifter who was willing to sacrifice his own life for a chance at peace for the rest of his kind.

Resolve winds through me. All three of *them* are my people, and I trust in them. I fully believe that they can see us through this war if we only offer them the chance. If I've learned anything about being a true arch-lord, it's that you need to be able to recognize when those around you are capable of more than you yourself can accomplish—and give them free rein to do so.

"Leave it for half an hour," I say, taking a gamble so I can persuade Celia as well. "If we haven't set Talia's plan in motion by then, we can make our brute force attempt. I swear it. But only if you'll also swear to the conditions of the Murk who'll be risking their lives for that plan. They aren't asking for anything that the rest of us fae don't already have."

Donovan nods slowly. Celia's lips purse, but when she looks toward the opposing army, a flicker of doubt crosses her face. She *wants* to believe we could barge right through their forces, but she must know how precarious her plan is too.

"All right," she says, turning back to me. "I'll hear the

Murk out and prepare the pieces of this gambit. But you only have that half an hour."

As we set off toward the Murk squad, Whitt abruptly stiffens. He covers it quickly, but I fall back beside him as his pace slows. After a moment, his gaze clears again. He aims it at me with a crooked smile, lowering his voice.

"She's here. All we have to do is send her rat accomplices to her."

Somehow my spirits lift and plummet at the same time. All we have to do is set the final part of her plan in motion—and hope she comes out of it alive.

27

Talia

The terrain where the war has currently halted is mostly flat with not much available shelter. Madoc has kept a concealing illusion around us during the whole trip, but we stop the carriage behind a small stand of trees for extra camouflage.

As soon as I've hopped out, I touch the pocket on my dress where the iron dagger is equally well hidden. August adjusted the stitching of the pocket so we can be sure the weapon won't shift too much no matter how my body moves. I've practiced snatching the hilt and brandishing the blade in one swift movement so many times I almost do it automatically the moment I bring my hand near it.

August also carried out more drills on the exact best place to strike for a quick kill. My stomach doesn't outright churn anymore at going through the motions, but it stays knotted as I take in the landscape around us.

What if I falter when I actually have to do it, when Orion's right there in front of me and I need to dig the blade into his literal flesh? It's one thing to imagine it and another altogether to go through with it.

But I have to, because the thought of what will happen if I fail horrifies me even more.

The two men scan the terrain. "Whitt said someone was coming?" August checks.

I nod. "He told me that they were just finishing arrangements. The Murk who agreed to help should be heading this way soon. But I could only give him the general area we're in. We should make some kind of signal so they can find us."

"A signal that Orion's people won't notice," Madoc puts in.

August hums to himself and considers the trees. "They should be coming from the east. I'll make it something that won't show to the south."

Focusing on the branches above us, he speaks the true name I'm planning on using myself in just a little while for an even more crucial task. "*Sole-un-straw.*" Light sparkles into being amid the trees, nestled where it should shine clearly to anyone coming at us from the direction of the Seelie camp but where the foliage will hide it from every other direction.

"Nicely done," Madoc says with genuine approval, and August grins as if the praise matters a lot to him. Even with the danger so close on the horizon now, I have to appreciate their newfound comradery.

While we wait next to the carriage, I practice the fatal

strike several more times: standing, crouching, on my knees, even lying down imagining Orion bending over me with his horrible smirk. When my fingers start to ache, I slip the dagger back into its sheath in my pocket. There's a point where more practice will make it harder for me to perform when it counts rather than easier.

August sniffs out some berries on a nearby bush and offers them to me to restore my energy. I'd insist that he and Madoc eat too if I wasn't a little lightheaded. Too much rests on what I do next for me to take any chances with my physical wellbeing.

I'm just gulping down the last of the berries when Madoc lets out a hopeful sound. He straightens up from where he's been leaning against a narrow pine. I squint at the plain ahead of us with its fluffy, pinkish grass. It takes another minute before my human sight picks up on the two small rippling lines weaving through that grass.

The rats reach us within moments. They pause while Madoc extends his concealing spell around them too and then shift into human form. Somehow I'm not surprised to see that one of them is Flynn. His previous bravado obviously wasn't for show.

He stands with his chin high, his eyes bright but his stance a bit rigid with tension. He might have been snarky before, but I can tell he's taking this mission seriously. The woman next to him folds her arms across her chest, but the clenching of her jaw looks determined rather than frightened.

"Thank you for coming," I say to them.

"Yes, you have no idea how much we appreciate you

coming through." Madoc tips his head to both of them. "I wish I could join you or take this on completely on my own, but… you already know how Orion feels about *me* right now. Do you understand the basics of what's needed?"

"I think so," Flynn says. "We put a call out for Orion and get him to come, saying we've captured Talia to hand her over to him as a gift with the request that he welcome us back."

"That's the gist of it." Madoc walks around them, checking them over—I guess for anything about them that might tip Orion off to the trick. He finishes his circuit and comes to a stop, apparently satisfied. "We want him away from as many of the other Murk as possible. That'll be safer for you and make Talia's job easier. Walk from here until you're just in view of the front, and a sentry or two should come over to find out what you want. Explain that you're offering up Talia, but that you're not going any farther or handing her over until you can speak to Orion himself. Hold your ground until he comes."

"And if he doesn't come?" the woman asks.

"If you see a larger force heading your way, retreat as quickly as you can," August says. "We don't want this to become a suicide mission."

Flynn's gaze darts over me. "Should we restrain her?" he asks doubtfully. "She's supposed to be our prisoner—but she'll need her hands free to have a go at Orion."

"You'll say that you managed to get her drugged up with cavaral syrup to make her compliant," Madoc says. "Talia can put on a show of supposedly being intoxicated."

"I've had that stuff before," I put in with a wry smile, remembering the time that feels so long ago now when Whitt shared his supply with me at my demand.

"And you should keep a blade on her," August says. "You can borrow my sword if you don't have your own. The implication should be that if the other Murk try to take her from you without Orion coming, you'd rather kill her than give up your bargaining chip. He'll want her alive."

"He will." Flynn exhales sharply and holds out his hand for the sword. "We'd better get going right away. The wolves have spotted some unusual activity on the Murk side. They might be gearing up for a fresh attack, and there's no telling when they'll launch it."

The thought of setting off right now makes my pulse skip even though I've been preparing for this moment for days. Somehow I expected to be able to settle into the mission a little more gradually once it actually started.

I pat my dagger again and drag the warm summer air into my lungs. My heart thumps onward, faster now. I can do this. I *will* do this. I'm not going to let Orion ruin any more of my life than he already has.

"All right," I say. "Let's go."

"Just one second." August tugs me to him and kisses me hard before wrapping me in the tightest of hugs. I lean into his embrace, willing back the nervous tears that want to spring into my eyes. When he lets me go, Madoc grasps my hand and raises his other hand to my cheek.

"You're stronger than he is," he tells me. "By a mile."

I manage an anxious smile in response. Then I turn to our two Murk accomplices and set off toward the front.

Flynn keeps August's sword out but not too close to me. The woman stays at my other side. After the first few steps, I start to put on my performance of being high on faerie drugs.

My limp makes it easy for me to bring a waver into my gait. I gaze around me as if finding every blade of grass and puff of cloud fascinating. I even swerve off course here and there, letting the Murk guide me back.

The woman snickers and glances at Flynn. "She's good."

"She'll have to be," Flynn says, but he swings the sword with a flourish that's all confidence.

I can't afford to pay too much attention to what's directly ahead of me while I'm supposedly in such a daze, but I do periodically snatch glimpses of the Murk forces in the distance. I see when a few men posted near the edge of the battlefield peel off from the others and trot toward us. Flynn stops me with a hand on my arm and holds the sword ready.

"Hold it there," he snaps when the approaching Murk are several feet away. "We're not here to deal with you. We want to speak to Orion."

One of the sentries sniffs. "I don't think you're anyone to be making demands like that." But his gaze lingers on me. I mumble to myself and cock my head at the sky.

"We've got his human 'pet,'" the woman next to me says. "We stole her from the Seelie while they were distracted with the fighting, and we're bringing her back to her rightful owner. I think that's proof enough that our reasons for leaving were always in support of Orion."

"But we want to hear from his own lips that he recognizes our contribution before we hand her over," Flynn adds. "Why don't you go tell him, and we'll see what he thinks about it? We'll stay right here. For now, she's ours." He motions the sword toward me in a vaguely threatening gesture.

The sentries shift on their feet uneasily. The woman next to me scoffs. "You wouldn't want to make the decision yourself and then find out Orion isn't happy with it, would you?"

She's pushed the right button. The three of them tense, and they scuttle back to the larger mass of Murk warriors. One of them breaks into a sprint, heading for a carriage I can make out past the edge of the crowd.

"And now we wait," Flynn says under his breath with audible trepidation.

I breathe as steadily as I can, willing the rhythm of my lungs to even out the pounding of my pulse. To make the waiting easier, I crouch down and pretend to examine the grass by running my fingers through it, giggling to myself. It's easier to keep up the façade and not give in to the emotional strain when I have something to focus on—and when I don't need to hold myself upright.

The woman's faint cough alerts me that something has changed. The sun has sunk so low by now that our shadows stretch like skinny giants across the plain. I act as if I haven't noticed anything significant, but after a few moments, I let my head swing around in a lazy arc and spot a familiar figure with a head of spiky white hair striding away from his army.

Orion brings a few warriors with him, and he stops a mere ten feet ahead of the rest of his army, where he makes a beckoning gesture. "Let's see her then," he calls. "Let's discover if you've earned your way back into my good graces."

There's an edge to his tone that sets all my nerves on the alert. He doesn't sound happy. He probably assumes that these two fled for real and only recently came to regret that choice.

I can't let him hurt them. I've got to keep them safe too.

But I can't ready myself, can't risk reaching for the dagger or doing anything other than walk with swaying steps as my supposed kidnappers usher me over to where the Murk king is waiting. He sneers as he takes me in, his expression all vicious derision.

"Didn't take much to addle her mind, did it?" he says. "So easy to mold to our will."

Anger swells inside me. I want to raise my fists and shout at him that he doesn't own me, that he never did and he never will, that he's the sorriest excuse for a king I could possibly imagine. To rain judgment down on him like I did with Aerik and Cole.

But that approach isn't going to work here. I'll only get us all killed.

One more time, I'll play the victim—the helpless, frail human. One more time, I'll let the fae around me believe they control my fate. It'll be worth it in the end.

I have to remember that my deception is its own kind of power. I can create this illusion without a single spark of magic, and even Orion buys into it wholeheartedly.

That last thought solidifies the resolve in my chest. I let my glazed eyes continue to drift this way and that as my body weaves from side to side, but within, my attention narrows down to the stance of the man in front of me and the distance from the blade in my pocket to his throat.

My escorts stop again before they've quite reached Orion and his guards. I'd imagine they can pick up on his hostile vibes even better than I can. "You can see what we've brought you," Flynn says. "We've served you the best way we knew how, my king. Will you welcome us back?"

"I think I'd like to examine the merchandise first," Orion says. "Throw away your sword."

Flynn hesitates, but he only needed the weapon for show when he was dealing with the initial sentries. We both know he isn't going to survive a real fight so close to the Murk army, no matter how well-armed he is. He flings the sword off across the grass.

"Back away from her," the king orders next. The two Murk comply, taking one step and another in opposite directions from each other until they're well beyond my reach.

Orion gestures for his guards to walk over to Flynn and the woman. He stalks toward me on his own. Totally assured, never suspecting that I might be more of a threat than they are.

But I am. I can do this. I can sever the life from that

smirking face forever. I can silence the voice that's ordered so much pain, still the hands that have dealt so much themselves.

He comes to a halt directly in front of me, close enough that his breath tickles my forehead. I cock my head to the side and peer up at him, still swaying. "Hello?" I say in a dreamy voice, forcing it from my constricted throat.

Orion cackles, a chilling sound that rings across the plain. "You poor, pathetic thing. You should have stayed with me while I was good to you. Now you'll only—"

He starts to move, and adrenaline jolts through my veins. I may not get another chance.

While one hand jerks to my pocket, I whip the other up in front of Orion's face, summoning the joyful memory of drifting off to sleep last night in my mates' combined embrace. The true name tumbles from my lips. "*Sole-un-straw.*"

Light flares from my hand so brightly it glares through my eyelids, which I closed in anticipation. Orion sputters, falling back a step, but I'm already moving with him. My eyes pop open. I lunge at him with a swing of my arm, my fingers clutched around the hilt of the iron dagger.

My strike flies with August's careful training guiding it, with all my fury and horror fueling my strength. The blade plunges into the side of Orion's neck in just the right spot, slamming all the way to the hilt so the point protrudes from the other side.

Blood sprays over my hand and across my arm. Orion gags and gurgles. Even as his legs crumple, he gropes at me, his claws springing from his fingertips. They rake across my forearm before I've quite shoved myself away.

Thin lights of pain sting across my wrist. Every nerve in my body screams at me to get away from him, but I have to make sure I'd done this right. I smack my hand into the hilt of the dagger, driving it even deeper before scrambling backward.

The Murk king crumples further. As blood sputters across his lips, his knees give. He topples over, his head smacking the ground with a dull sound that seems to echo in the sudden silence around us.

The dagger still lodged in his neck gleams in the fading sunlight. His body twitches and then sags.

One of the guards lets out a startled shout. He swivels back toward Flynn, who's backing away with his hands raised.

"It's done now," Flynn says. "It's over."

"It's over!" I repeat, hollering even louder, pitching my voice as far as I can along the front. "Orion is dead. *I* killed him." The words bring a weird mix of exhilaration and dread into my gut. I raise my hands, one of them streaked red with the Murk king's blood. "He died, and so did his war. You can fall like he did, run back to the sewers and subway tunnels, or find a way to make peace with the rest of the fae. They're waiting to welcome you home. The Heart of the Mists is waiting."

Cries ring out along the front. Spells and projectiles hurtle across the gap between the armies, and several Murk warriors charge forward in a last, desperate attempt.

A bunch of them at the end of the crowd stalk closer to us, their weapons raised, their lips forming spell words.

My pulse stutters. I retreat as quickly as I can, Flynn and the Murk woman falling in on either side of me—and then a blaze of light sweeps over us all, halting our Murk opponents in their tracks with startled expressions.

It's coming from the Heart of the Mists. The familiar thrum seeps into my skin, recognizable even from so many miles away. The glow like sunlight lights up the ground, and more concentrated beams narrow in on Flynn and his companion on either side of me.

Flynn gasps, his hand smacking into his chest. The woman lets out a choked sound and then a breathless laugh. They glance at each other with matching expressions of awe.

"The Heart," Flynn murmurs. "I can feel it. I never—I never knew it could be like this." He turns to the watching Murk. "You could have this too! Stop the fighting, start negotiating. The Heart of the Mists knows we belong here too."

Our opponents waver on their feet with uncertain expressions. More beams are landing amid the Seelie army where the other Murk who've joined us must be, a few even touching on spots among the Murk forces. I don't know how the Heart is choosing who it welcomes now, but the next cries that ring out are joyful.

A couple of the warriors facing us gnash their teeth and charge forward again. But at the same moment, a Seelie carriage races into view. It plows right into the figures on the attack, knocking them to the ground. My Seelie mates and Madoc lean over the side.

August and Whitt extend their arms to help the three of us in. Sylas directs the carriage to whip around and speed back toward the Seelie side of the front. Then he's with me too, four of my mates around me, passing me from embrace to embrace with soft words of awe and comfort.

"You were amazing," Madoc says. "To face him like that… He had no idea."

My heart still hasn't stopped racing. I meet his gaze. "That was his problem all along."

As the carriage slows behind the Seelie's defensive wall, I glance around to take stock. It looks like maybe a quarter of the Murk force is still hurling attacks at us, although they're so outnumbered now that they hardly feel like a threat. Most of the others have darted off toward the fringes—most likely to the portals that'll lead them to the human world. I'm not sure if they'll hide away for good or if some of them will find the courage to come back to the Mists once they've had time for the new reality to sink in.

There are others crossing the battleground along the edges, their hands raised in surrender. The Murk on our side are hurrying over to beckon them onward.

The Heart's thrum has faded. Orion's body still lies limp where I stabbed him. The sense rises up in me that this isn't totally over after all. The most immediate part of the war is finished, but Orion's legacy doesn't totally die with him.

"The curse," I say. "There's a full moon in a few days.

More Unseelie will be hit by the freezing sickness. It isn't going to stop just because Orion died, is it?"

My mates exchange a somber glance. "No," Whitt says. "Most likely it won't. For that, we'd either need to know the counter-curse… or we'd need to destroy the source of the magic that fueled it." He turns to Madoc.

The Murk man grimaces. He might not draw on the power of the Murk Heart anymore, but an awful lot of his people do. He protested before against extinguishing it.

But now he sighs and squares his shoulders. "It has to be done. The Heart of the Mists has shown it'll accept us. You can't lord your magic over us."

"We can't, and we won't," Sylas says firmly. "All of the Murk have a place here if they choose to take it."

"Then we have one last problem to deal with." Madoc's gaze slides toward the fringelands out of view beyond the horizon. "To the Refuge we go. I can lead the way."

28

Madoc

If you'd told me a few months ago that I'd end up bringing a bunch of fae of the seasons to the Refuge so they could dismantle the power source Orion so painstakingly grew for our people, I'd have laughed so hard my ribs ached. But here I am, picking apart the spell that guards one of the main entrances in the furnace room of an old mall.

Sylas, Corwin, and a contingent of Seelie and Unseelie fae stand in the dark room around me, waiting for me to finish. I brought a handful of the original Murk refugees too in case their connection to the Murk Heart is needed for whatever we decide to do. Talia insisted on coming as well, even though I can see the tension creeping into her the closer we get to the place where she was essentially held captive for several torturous days.

I understand her wanting to see this through to the

end, though. That's why *I'm* here, even though I could have asked any of our other Murk allies to show the way.

If the source of magic that's fueled so many of my people for so long is going to be destroyed, I want to be able to have some say in when and how.

It's clear that Orion brought pretty much all of the Murk who were on his side into the Mists to fight his war. He'd have needed to in order to have any hope of winning. When I intone the last words to release the protective and illusionary spells and the door grinds open, a sole guard peers out at us, the knife in his hand jerking up. I recognize him from doing my rounds here before I left.

"Orion is dead, Hender," I say, in a sympathetic tone I don't have to put on. "But you can still go home to the Mists. We'll even take you there when we're done here if you want. We've just got a little more business to take care of. Will you let us through without a fight? I don't want to see you get hurt."

Hender's jaw works. He'd have trouble taking on me even on my own—I might not be an avid fighter, but when push comes to shove, I give it my all. I wouldn't have made it to my position as Orion's knight otherwise.

And I'm not on my own. The other man's gaze skims over the arch-lords and gathered warriors behind me. I can only imagine the calculations he's making. He has to note the other Murk standing freely in their midst, though.

"Orion's dead?" he repeats, sounding a little hopeless.

I dare to reach into the range of his knife and squeeze his shoulder. "No more unnecessary killings. No more lashing out at anyone who questioned him even a little.

No more insisting that every problem be solved through violence and bloodshed. I promise you, it's going to be for the best, if you can let yourself accept it."

He lets out a shaky breath, his eyes searching mine. Then he lowers his knife. "He told me I should stay behind because he didn't think I had enough guts to handle an actual battle. Because I was upset when one of his other knights beat up on my cousin. He didn't even give me a chance."

"It wasn't the kind of chance that'd have brought anything good anyway," I say. "The Heart of the Mists will welcome you back. It's already reached out to me and some of the Murk who came over to us earlier. We're setting up colonies throughout the Mists. The fae of the seasons are *helping* us. It's going to be okay."

His expression still twitches nervously as the other fae draw closer, but he heads on down the tunnel, letting us follow him. At Sylas's motion, the warriors with us keep their weapons sheathed.

"Do you think many of the Murk who fled the battle will come back here?" Talia asks quietly.

I shake my head. "Not right away, at least. This was always Orion's domain first and foremost. They'd have a hard time seeing it as safe after his death. I'm sure they'll be back after they have a chance to realize that his loss isn't the end of the world, though, at least to scrounge up belongings they left behind."

Which makes me think of one particular item I'd like to scrounge up myself. Something that never should have been taken from its owner in the first place.

We tramp along the dark and winding passage for close to half an hour before we finally reach the doorway that leads into the subway tunnels. Hender has fallen into conversation with a couple of the Murk who joined us, and by that time, he's relaxed enough that he opens the entrance for us.

On the other side of the door, the station we come out into is lit with the usual stark yellow glow. Orion didn't cut off the electrical power he got running for this place when he left. But the platforms are eerily vacant, only a couple of my people standing up to gape at us at the far end, the rest of the homes apparently abandoned. The place is unsettlingly quiet with none of the forges or other workshop machinery in operation.

"We're here peacefully," I call out to the women watching us. "You can pass on word to anyone else who stayed behind that the war is over, and we can all move into the Mists now. If you're willing to share our real home with the fae of the seasons, who we've convinced to make plenty of room for us, you're welcome to make your way there with us when we return."

The women murmur to each other and vanish into the nearby tunnel, their tails swishing behind them. I can't tell whether they believe me or not, but I guess we'll find out before too long.

I lead my procession down the tunnel at the other end of the station. The air there is taking on a dank quality it didn't use to have. There haven't been enough Murk around to keep up with Orion's previous cleaning schedule. My pride rankles at what the fae of the seasons must think, imagining we lived like this, but none of them comments on it. I'm sure the warriors have a few thoughts, but the presence of their arch-lords keeps their tongues still.

They can think whatever they want as long as they keep it to themselves. I know what my people were capable of, how much we made of the lot we had. And who was responsible for keeping us in this low situation.

We pass through another station and on into the tunnel Orion's throne room branches off from. At the sight of the quavering orange light spilling across the tracks up ahead and the feel of the erratic thrum of energy that tickles over my skin, I have to restrain a shudder. Now that the magic of the Heart of the Mists courses through my body, I can't tune out how dissonant Orion's Heart is by comparison. No wonder Talia always tensed up in its presence.

She's holding herself steady approaching it now, limping along without a second's hesitation. As much as it might have unnerved her, she never let it get in the way of what she was trying to do.

When we turn the corner into the throne room, several of the fae around me suck in their breaths. "Heart help me," Whitt mutters, staring at the spastically pulsing mass of light at the far end of the dais. "Even after Talia's stories, I didn't imagine it'd be so... so *much*."

Queasiness pools in my stomach, both because of the false Heart before me and because of the thought of what we're going to do with it. First, I walk to a narrow passage in the wall partway down the room. "I'll be right back, and then we'll talk about what to do about it."

I slip down the passage as quickly as I can, Orion's scent thickening around me and raising the hairs on the back of my neck. The tunnel opens up to the room where he usually slept, next to the hoard of his favorite treasures. I paw through them, finding the item I wanted quickly since it was a recent acquisition, and hurry back to rejoin the others.

As I reach them, I hold out the delicate crown in my hands to Talia. "This should never have been taken from you, Lady Talia."

My mate arches her eyebrows slightly at the formal title, but there's no missing the poignant mix of emotions that crosses her face. She takes the crown from me gingerly, her fingers curling around it. No doubt she's remembering the moment it was gifted to her, just as I am —when she took her three Seelie mates with her soul-twined mate's blessing.

That was the night I stole her from her mates and brought her here. How bizarre that committing the crime was the best thing I could have done for my people, but not at all in the way I thought it would be.

Maybe before much longer, she'll bless me with a ceremony like that too, to make our union official. There hasn't exactly been time yet. I can wait. At this point, I trust her and the men she's bound herself to enough to know I'm already part of the family.

"Thank you," she says in a soft voice, and shoots me a

smile that could stitch my heart back together even if it'd shattered to pieces.

But it's not my heart we need to worry about now. I turn toward the one Orion created in all its monstrous glory. "What do we do with *this*?"

Sylas lets out a huff, still taking in the mass of energy. "I was hoping you'd have some ideas on that subject."

I speak several words of magic, testing the currents around the Heart. It doesn't feel solid, but in a way that makes the idea of dismantling it more difficult. There's nothing to really get a hold of to tear it apart, nothing to smash or blast to bits.

I motion the other Murk with me who are still connected to its power closer. "Can you get a sense of any weaknesses or a spot where we could even start to prod at it and unravel it, or anything like that?"

They can't hide the reluctance that briefly crosses their faces. "Before long you'll have the other Heart's power to draw on," I add as a reassurance. They nod, girding themselves before launching into some spellwork of their own.

As they prod it, a few other Murk drift through the throne room entrance. They stop just inside, watching us warily. Hender goes over and starts talking to them in hushed tones. I hope he's talking us up and not inciting a rebellion.

"I don't know," one of my comrades says finally, frowning at the Heart. "It doesn't feel like something that can be *killed*. It doesn't feel alive to begin with." He pauses. "Orion fueled it with the suffering of the fae of the seasons—isn't that right?"

"Yes," I say, watching the summer and winter fae around us carefully, but hearing that stated out loud doesn't appear to provoke any of them. Talia will have reported as much when she returned to the Mists—they probably all already knew.

My mate herself eases past the others to step closer to the Heart. Its orange glow ripples over her body. She looks as if she's restrained a wince. She stares into it for a moment that stretches so long I start to itch to wrench her away from it. Then she glances back at us, a sliver of that glow dancing off her eyes.

"Can you move it?" she asks. "Is it attached to this spot?"

One of the other Murk says a few testing magical words and curls her fingers, and the mass shifts a little toward her like a snowball about to hurtle down a hill. She halts abruptly but shoots a smile at Talia. "I think we can manage that. But moving it won't change the spells it's powering."

Talia worries her lower lip under her teeth, her expression pensive. She ponders for a moment longer before going on. "I wonder… It *is* a Heart, even if it's a false one. What if we brought it all the way to the true Heart and let it decide what to do with this one? All this energy came from it to begin with. It knew how to bring Madoc back to life. It knew how to connect to his soul and some of the other Murk's again. All the magic comes back to it in the end."

Her words hit me with a sense of rightness. We'll let the true Heart find the answer. Maybe that will bring many of the Murk still tied to this malformed thing back to where they belong.

"It could go badly," I have to say. "They could clash, or the energy could start dissipating once we reach the Mists and cause some kind of harm there—we don't really know. Are you sure?"

Talia looks at the Murk Heart again and nods firmly. "Yes. Whatever happens, we can handle it. But even the magic in that thing deserves the chance to get back to the home it deserves."

That's such a Talia sentiment that a lump rises in my throat. As the Murk still connected to the false Heart start to murmur and urge the glowing mass across the throne room, Talia steps out of the way. I move to join her, slipping my hand around hers.

"You know," I say, pitching my voice low, "with every passing day I'm more convinced that the real heart of the Mists is you, bright one."

A blush colors Talia's cheeks. She twines her fingers with mine and squeezes. "And you found your way to that heart too."

Yes, I did. And I know that my people will be okay—the ones of them willing to let themselves be okay, at least—as long as this woman is here to shine on all of us.

Talia

Conveying the Murk Heart back to the Mists and across the fae lands is a slow process. Its energy surges and flares in fits and starts, painting the darkened landscape in fiery shades, and the Murk propelling it along have to pull back and wait until it's settled down again before they can get close enough to maneuver it. We manage to set them up in carriages on either side of it and behind, dragging and pushing at the same time, but we can hardly move the vehicles at full speed.

As the strain of the day's chaotic events creeps up on me, I find I can't keep my eyes open any longer. Sylas shifts into his wolf form and sprawls on the floor of the carriage we're in so I can use his thickly furred side as a pillow. I drift off nestled against him.

My dreams are cast in an eerie orange light,

nightmarish images swimming out of the darkness. When I wake up, still groggy, night is just easing back. A thin dawn light is seeping across the sky. And the rhythmic thrum of the true Heart's energy welcomes us back to the domains on the hill.

We draw to a stop on the field beside the Heart. The Murk pull the false Heart within a few feet of the true one and then scoot backward with wary expressions. Five ravens soar out of the sky and land amongst us in human form: Corwin went to gather his fellow Unseelie arch-lords. Celia and Donovan join us a few minutes later.

"Dust and doom," Celia mutters staring up at the Murk Heart. A shudder runs through her. "It's horrifying."

Maybe what's most horrific of all is seeing it next to the true Heart. Orion managed to grow his self-made energy source to nearly a third of the size of the real one in a matter of decades. And it must have been expanding faster as the curse worsened and caused the fae of the seasons to go through even more distress. How much longer would it have taken before he could have fully rivaled their power?

"What now?" Laoni asks, eyeing the thing with equal revulsion.

"I don't know," I admit. "I just thought… it's stolen energy from these lands, from the real Heart. Maybe the Heart of the Mists can take that back."

The idea seems kind of childish now that we're standing here and nothing's happening. More fae are drifting over from the domains around the Heart. There are a couple of clusters of Murk among them. The woman at the front of that group I can recognize as Delta even though I've never met her in person before.

She gazes at the Heart that Orion created and sucks a sharp breath through her teeth. "Those delusions of grandeur weren't all delusion. Too bad he couldn't have put this power to better use."

The true Heart's energy seems to hum a little more emphatically, but I can't see any change in it or the Murk Heart. Maybe it needs guidance. I test the words out in my mind and find that my throat has constricted too much for me to say anything.

If the Murk Heart is destroyed, however that happens, I still don't know what'll happen to my bond with Corwin.

I glance across the clearing to where he's standing with his colleagues. He catches my eyes, and his mouth twists.

It has to be done, he says. *We can't let the curse keep its hold on so many people just to preserve our bond.*

I know. I just… I'm scared.

It's hard to admit that. I've spent so much time being as strong as I can be, even if only on the inside while I played a victim. But I don't want to pretend I don't care.

I am too, Corwin says, his inner voice going raw. He walks over to me so he can stand next to me and wraps his hand around mine. *But I'm here with you no matter what happens. We'll face it together. And if I don't get another chance to say it to you so intimately, my soul, know how much I love you.*

The connection between us opens completely, and a flood of emotion rushes over me. There's a bittersweet edge of fear and trepidation, but the rest is pure, poignant affection.

I taste how much Corwin cherishes every smile he watches cross my face, even when they're not aimed at him. How proud he is of the way I've stood up for both the fae and humankind while we've fought Orion. How much he longs to pull me into his arms and do nothing but hold me against him, forgetting all these other responsibilities.

I choke up for a totally different reason. *I love you too*, I say. *So much.* I let all the tenderness and devotion I feel for him carry through our bond like liquid sunlight. In that moment, it feels as if we're joined by so much more than our clasped hands and the tenuous magic that first tied us together.

The Hearts still haven't stirred. As I grapple with my thoughts, searching for the right thing to say, another raven swoops through the border and lands by Corwin. It's Verik.

"My lord," he says in a low voice, "your mother—I think she can sense something momentous is happening. She's been battering at her door, crying out that she 'only wants to see it'… None of us have been able to calm her."

Corwin's mouth opens, but at first no sound comes out. He swallows audibly. Then he squares his shoulders. "Let her come. If this works, it'll be the end to the plague that stole my father from her. She deserves to witness that moment if she wants to."

Verik takes off again. I watch his raven fly into the border haze with a prickling sensation winding around my gut.

Corwin's mother was wrecked by her grief when her soul-twined mate died from the curse. She didn't lose just her bond with him but his entire presence in her life. And she's still finding the strength to come and witness the end of that curse despite knowing it won't bring him back.

No matter what happens, Corwin will be here. I can't let any part of me hesitate to believe that destroying the Murk Heart is what must happen.

Gathering my resolve, I wait for the arrival of the former lady of Heart's Cadence. She comes through the border on foot, with Zelpha on one side and Verik on the other holding her steady on her wobbly legs. Her stringy hair is pushed back behind her ears, her face as gaunt as when I first saw her. But when her eyes find Corwin, she shoots him a shaky smile.

Then her gaze veers to the Murk Heart.

As she stares at it, her expression hardens until it contains nothing but pure rage. She remains silent, but her anger practically hums off her, calling for the end to this thing that stole so much of her happiness.

Maybe it'll steal a little of mine too, but that's a small sacrifice to make to see the curse lifted off the entire faerie world.

I let go of Corwin's hand and walk up to the Hearts. August makes a faint noise, but no one moves to stop me. I limp around the Murk Heart to the gap between it and the Heart of the Mists.

Erratic energy hits me from one side, and harmonious power tingles over me from the other. I stare up at the pulsing glow that gave me the magic to win yesterday's war.

"This is all the energy you and your people have lost to Orion," I say. "Take it back. Take it into you and make it something good again. Burn away the curse that's been driving them mad and freezing them to death. Please. It should be yours."

The true Heart's light flares a little brighter, but nothing else changes. Frustration and anxiety tangle together in my chest. What if I was wrong? What if we shouldn't have brought the Murk Heart into the Mists at all?

"There has to be something you can do!" I protest, as if I can argue it into acting. That did sort of work with Madoc. But this doesn't feel like the same situation. There's the faintest hint of confusion in the energy tickling over me.

The Heart of the Mists and the Murk Heart have been totally at odds, opposites to each other, from the beginning. No fae was capable of holding the power from both.

Except for me. In me, they're tied together. In me, both streams of magic meet.

If anyone can bind them back together, it's me.

My mouth goes dry. Without giving myself a chance to chicken out, I thrust one hand into the sun-like glow of the true Heart and the other into the quavering light of the false Heart.

Like the last time I touched the Murk Heart, its energy starts to sear into my skin. I clench my fingers, bracing myself against the pain. Someone lets out a shout from the watching crowd—

And a soothing wave of power gushes into me through my other arm.

The light of the Heart of the Mists surges over me, swallowing me completely in an instant. My vision blazes white; my body seems to crackle with an electric pulse all the way down to my bones. All I'm aware of is that sizzling tsunami and the thudding of my heart, faster with every passing second. The rhythmic thrum roars in my ears. It feels as if the brilliant glow is filling all the tiny vacant spaces inside me, turning me into something more than I was before. It rushes on and on—

And then it pulls back again, like an actual wave drawing back into the sea. I find myself standing there before the Heart gasping as if I've just spent a minute underwater, on the verge of drowning.

Voices are exclaiming all around me. The orange glow has vanished. I'm still gathering my senses when another tendril of light extends from the Heart of the Mists and grazes over my temple, right through my skull and down to my own heart.

As it lets me go, I stumble, but the fae around me are already converging on me. Solid hands catch me by the shoulders. Someone touches my arm, another my cheek. The faces of my mates swim in my vision as I blink to clear the last of the blaze from my eyes.

And a softly eager voice speaks from right inside my

head, cutting through the babble I can't quite focus on yet. *My soul?*

A grin springs across my lips so fast I almost crack my cheeks. I spin around and lock eyes with Corwin, his face alight with hope.

And you're my soul, I answer back, joy filling me to the brim. *Even the Heart of the Mists could see that.*

Sylas glances from me to the Unseelie arch-lord and smiles one of his quiet little smiles. "It seems all's ended as it's meant to be, even if not by our conventional patterns of fate."

I grasp Corwin's arm and pull him into a kiss, then plant one on each of my other mates in turn, not caring what anyone looking on thinks of the display. Even Madoc accepts my embrace without hesitation, his arms closing tight around me for a few seconds after. "Our heart," he murmurs, reminding me of what he said to me in the Refuge.

There's a sharp inhalation behind us. I turn to see Corwin's mother approaching the Heart with shaky steps. Its pulsing glow washes over her. She draws in another breath that's part sob, part awed sigh. Then she looks at her son. Her expression is so full of desperate longing it sends an ache all the way through my bones.

Corwin swallows audibly. I can feel his unsettled emotions: old strands of grief that he could never fully put to rest, a wrenching wish that he could help her. But he inclines his head. "Do what you feel you need to."

His mother gives him one last smile, so full of love it

shines like the Heart itself. She turns back to the Heart and walks straight into it with open arms as if offering it an embrace.

The light swallows her up. This time, there's no re-emerging. The glow pulses on. A faint melody whispers through the air and fades away.

She's rejoined her soul-twined mate the only way she can. The Heart finally granted her that peace. Maybe something in that fathomless glow has shifted its perspective a little too with everything that's happened in the past several months.

Are you all right? I ask Corwin, who's blinking a bit harder than usual.

Yes, he says, in a tone that tells me he means it. *She waited so long. It was her time.*

The rest of the watching fae gradually disperse. Madoc gives me another gentle squeeze. Then he pauses and touches my skin at the neckline of my dress.

I drop my gaze and tug the fabric a little to the side. My breath catches. There's—there's a true-name mark forming just below my collarbone, darkening into the usual black lines before my eyes. It isn't one I remember having identified for me before, but deep inside, I instinctively know it's the mark for light.

I jerk my gaze up to meet each of my mates. "What does that mean?" Was something in me permanently altered by the Heart's touch? A faint tingling races through my veins, and I can't help wondering if it's somehow made me a little more than human.

Sylas's eyes have widened, but his tone stays mild. "I suppose we'll have to wait and find out."

Those words jerk me out of my startled reverie with the thought of the one person who's still waiting for me, the one I haven't properly saved yet. I glance around at the fae milling close to the Heart of the Mists, all of them exclaiming over the spectacle that just appeared, and a sense of urgency grips me.

"Jamie," I say. "We have to get Jamie. He shouldn't have to stay shut away, missing out on his life, for any longer than he already has. And my aunt and uncle must be worried sick."

Madoc nods. "There has to be someone among all the Murk who've joined us since Orion's death who knows what mine he brought your brother to. I'll find out as quickly as I can." He hurries off.

Whitt tucks a few stray strands of my hair behind my ear. "Do you want us to restore your brother to his home as discreetly as possible? He doesn't need to know the incident has anything to do with you."

I pause to consider, but alongside my urgency, an unexpected conviction has gripped me. "No. Finding out about me and the fae shouldn't put him in danger now— no more than it already has. He'll be so confused... He deserves to know. And I want to be able to be part of his life, however he'll have me once he gets used to the idea."

Sylas grips Whitt's arm. "Corwin and I are still needed here to sort out the aftermath of all the fighting we've been through. Madoc should probably stay nearby as more of the Murk cross over to us. Why don't you and August take her as soon as Madoc reports back on the correct location? And I suppose you'll need to pick out a few of our Murk allies not yet reconnected to the Heart to get the boy free of that iron mine."

Whitt smiles back at his brother. "It would be my pleasure."

When we reach the abandoned iron mine one of Orion's former followers pointed us to, Whitt and August need to stay well back from the boundaries. The stretch of ridged earth drops into a vast pit that I have to venture into with the Murk to retrieve my brother. A couple of Orion's guards have lingered there, but at the sight of us, they shift into rat form and flee. They can't work any magic at all right now with the Murk Heart gone.

Neither can the Murk descending into the mine with me. Their fledgling connection to the Heart of the Mists isn't yet in place, so it's a long trudge down on foot.

We duck into a sort of cave carved into one of the ridges near the bottom of the pit. When the iron case comes into view in the dim light, my heart lurches. My brother is sealed away in there as if in a coffin.

But he's not dead. He's alive *because* I helped build this all-encompassing shield.

When the fae conjured the iron case through me, they had the foresight to key it to my essence. I press my hands to the top, and that part springs open like a lid. The Murk lift Jamie's unconscious form out of the box, cringing at the closeness to so much of the toxic metal, and hurry with him back up the slope.

They lay my brother on the grass where we've parked our concealed carriage. I kneel next to him, and Whitt comes to stand over me.

"Are you sure about this?" he asks. "Are you ready?"

"Yes," I say to both questions, bracing myself with the water bottle we brought clutched in my hand.

August murmurs the words to bring my brother out of his physical stasis. Jamie's eyelids flutter and then outright blink. He jerks upright with a start before swaying. Slamming his hand into the ground to catch his balance, he stares at me and then the figures around me. "What— Who—?"

His voice comes out in a rasp. I hold the bottle of water out to him. "You should drink something. You've been knocked out for a long time."

His gaze jerks back to me. He studies me for a long time, confusion and a hint of recognition colliding in his face. "You... Who *are* you?"

There's no time like the present. I offer him the gentlest smile I can summon. "It's me, Jamie. It's Talia. I— I know I've got a whole lot of explaining to do. But I promise you that everything's going to be okay now."

"Talia," he repeats in a disbelieving tone, but I can tell he isn't really all that skeptical. He knows my face and my voice, even if it's been years. "This is... very weird. Maybe

I'm hallucinating?" He presses his hand to the side of his head.

I give his forearm a tentative squeeze of reassurance. "Nope, this is real. But definitely very weird. It's a long story."

He blinks and focuses on me again. A lopsided smile crosses his lips. "I guess you'd better get started then."

Several months later

Talia

There are few spots as peaceful as the stretch of grass right outside the summer side of the border castle. It's become my favorite spot to relax when I don't have any official business as Lady Talia to attend to —or any of my own responsibilities that I've volunteered for—and Sylas has conjured several permanent wooden loungers with woven grass padding for me and whoever decides to join me.

Today, I'm nestled against those thin but cozy cushions, soaking in the mid-afternoon sun. A yawn stretches my jaw. I thought I slept all right last night— with Sylas and Madoc taking a turn sharing my bed with me—but I haven't felt really rested all day. I'm tempted to close my eyes and drift off for a nap.

But this is one of the rare days when none of my mates have any pressing duties either. Four of them are sprawled on their own seats around me, taking just as much enjoyment out of the sun's warmth. Harper has joined me too, although after we chatted for a while, Flynn stopped by from the nearby Murk colony where he's set up his home. I can't help suspecting he picked that one *because* its nearness lets him drop in quite frequently.

Seeing the way my best friend's face lit up at his arrival and the delighted smile curving her lips now as they sit side by side on one of the other loungers, I definitely don't mind. He's even wearing a shirt Harper designed for him, trim and simple but with multiple pockets in easy reach of his hands. Flynn is apparently quite a collector of whatever happens to catch his interest at any given moment.

I suspect that my mating ceremony with Madoc months ago won't be the only one between a woman of Hearth-by-the-Heart and a Murk man this year.

The sunlight gives Corwin's bronze skin a summery glow, but even when he comes over to the Seelie realm, he's still a practical raven underneath. It's hard for him to totally relax and not talk business at all. He glances from his lounger to the one Sylas is stretched out on. "Were you and your colleagues able to quell that little rebellion without too much trouble?"

Sylas chuckles. "So little I'd almost forgotten about it. Honestly, it works out well. Every pack that decides to take aggressive offense to the rat shifters creates an opening for a new colony when we banish them off to the fringes."

"Only when it's deserved," August puts in, flexing his shoulders against his seat. "There *are* Murk who've purposefully provoked their neighbors."

"And you've shut them down too," I say. "But from what I can tell when I talk to them, most of them are glad just to be alive and not sent into battle by a crazed king, no matter who their neighbors are."

Whitt smirks, pushing himself up on one elbow. "True. We couldn't have expected an instantly smooth transition. I'd say our efforts at placing the colonies and supporting their independence have gone better than anyone would have hoped."

August rolls his eyes playfully. "Of course you'd say that, since you're the one who planned a lot of those efforts."

The strategist holds up his hands. "Hey, credit should be given where it's due."

Flynn glances over at us. "I got the impression that Delta is working up to some big ask the last time I happened to cross paths with her."

"Well, she can make all the 'asks' she wants, and we'll decide whether they're reasonable," Sylas says. "I don't think she's pushed for more than is fair so far. And she and her colony have been very helpful in wrangling the late stragglers who've been drifting in."

"Not to mention the few of Orion's supporters who don't seem to have gotten the memo that his time is over," Whitt mutters. His attention shifts to the border, sliding along it toward the Bastion. "When the new castle is finished being built and the Murk decide on their third arch-lord, I'd imagine we'll be hearing even more from her." He tips his head to Corwin. "Speaking of women with strong opinions, that supposed not-quite-mate of yours has still been following the sanctions placed on her, I assume?"

A sadness laced with a prickle of anger slips into me from Corwin. He hasn't forgiven Kara for her part in my kidnapping, but I know he wishes she hadn't been placed in such an awful situation to begin with. He and the other winter arch-lords took her extenuating circumstances into account when deciding on her punishment, recognizing that a fractured soul-twined bond can affect one's emotions and judgment badly.

"Zelpha and Domhnall have been checking on her regularly," he says. "So far she hasn't left the boundaries of her domain, as we decreed. I expect we'll revisit her sentence within a few years and judge whether she continues to pose any threat."

He sends a wordless sense of questioning my way, and I nod. I don't want Kara to be miserable. I just want to be sure she won't try to hurt me—or anyone I care about —again.

"Does she even still feel any kind of bond?" August asks. "I'd have thought the Heart would take that away when it confirmed the bond between you and Talia."

Corwin shakes his head. "We're not sure what she's feeling now. She was vague when asked about her current impressions."

"She has a long life ahead of her to mend that injury," Sylas says. "Not every wound can be healed in an instant."

Whitt hums to himself. "Very true. But for all the wounds still being mended, I have to say I'm liking the relative peace we're enjoying now a great deal more than all the turmoil that led up to it."

"Here, here," I say, raising my hand as if in a toast.

A familiar carriage glides from the trees at the other end of the clearing. I sit up straighter, bracing my hand against the lounger when the blood rushes from my head faster than I expected.

Madoc pulls the vehicle to a stop and hops out, carrying a sack over his shoulder and wearing a self-satisfied grin. "I have a letter for you," he says, coming to me first as he fishes an envelope out of his pocket.

My heart leaps at the sight of Jamie's narrow handwriting. Since I filled him in on where I've been for the past several years, we've been passing each other letters back and forth.

Madoc's conveyed most of them on his regular trips to the human world, where he's watching over the human servants who chose to return to their old home. It's been a difficult transition for some of them, but I know they were relieved to finally *have* the choice. A surprising number opted to stay here and continue working for their masters on a more equitable basis.

I guess once you get a taste of magic, it's difficult to let go of it, no matter how much it's burned you.

I tear open the flap of the envelope with my thumb and pull out the folded papers inside. The actual letter is typed. I can picture Jamie sitting at his desk in his bedroom, tapping away at his computer keyboard.

Hey Sis,

Thanks for the tart you sent in that last package. If that's how the fae can cook, then I definitely need to come over for dinner sometime. Once I'm eighteen, it'll be easier for me to get away with taking off for a weekend to someplace with no phone service. Just mentioning that so you can get your invitation prepared ahead of time.

Just joking. Mostly. Obviously the first step is you meeting the family, if you're sure you're ready, I can definitely set something up. Do you want to come by the house, or would somewhere public be better? Let me know what the plan is, and I'll get Aunt Becca and Uncle Walter on board.

I'd also really like you to meet Amy, my girlfriend. I know, first things first, but I think she might even be able to wrap her head around the whole fae thing, if you ever feel like it's safe for us to talk about that with anyone else. I get that it's very hush hush. Not pushing.

College acceptances are starting to come in, so keep your fingers crossed for me. I got into one of my second-tier choices but haven't heard from my favorites yet. Sometimes there's so much stressing about it that I want to run away with the faeries too, but I know what you'll say. Best to get my education so I have a backup plan. Aunt Becca totally agrees, so obviously you'll get along fine.

I'm actually pretty excited about the idea of getting to study something I'm really interested in. And obviously crashing a college party or two could be fun. We'll see.

Since you liked my sketches so much, I'm sending

another one. It's hard drawing from memory, but it felt better doing that than using a photograph. Let me know what you think.

Talk again soon!

Jamie

The other folded page shows a family standing together, the father's hands on the daughter's shoulders and the mother ruffling the son's hair. It's *our* family—I can recognize us instantly even with the roughness to the lines. Our family before Aerik tore it apart.

I guess in a way that family still lives on in Jamie and me, no matter what.

A twinge of anxiety ripples through me at the thought of making final arrangements to reveal myself to the rest of our surviving family. I've put it off for long enough, and it isn't really fair to Jamie to make him keep so much of a secret for so long. I've just got to perfect my story of where I've been and why it took me so long to reconnect with them, one that won't sound at all insane, but maybe in a week or two…

I'll think on it for a few days and then write him back with a definite plan.

Madoc is handing out the other items he picked up on today's trip. He hands a DVD to Sylas. "A new release. Very good reviews, if you like that sort of thing, which I know you do. Those discs are getting scarce, though. Everyone's switching to streaming now. You're going to need to find a way to get internet access all the way out here."

Sylas guffaws, but he looks pleased as he checks out

the latest comedy flick he'll add to his collection before tucking it aside.

Madoc pulls the opening of the sack wide and sets it down in the midst of the loungers with its remaining contents poking out. "I also went looking to restock my snack collection. You all get first dibs on *one* thing. The rest is mine." He gives us a slyly territorial glower.

August leaps up and bounds over with typical eagerness. He counts on Madoc's love of snacks to expand his culinary horizons with human-world flavors. I push myself to my feet, thinking a little treat might be nice, but as I straighten up, my stomach flips. A sudden wave of dizziness washes over me.

My legs stiffen to help me keep my balance. At my abrupt halt, Corwin glances over with a waft of concern through our bond. "Are you all right, Talia?"

"Yeah. I think so. I just—"

My heart skips a beat as the sensations collide in my mind into a pattern I've experienced only once before. I pause, thinking back. It's been two weeks since the last time they said— That's just about the right timing, from what I know about these things… Could it really be—?

I look around at my mates, who are all watching me now. My voice comes out quiet. "I'm just feeling a little off. But it's exactly like—like before when I—" I can't quite get the words out, so I rest my hand on my belly instead.

Understanding flares in all five of the men's eyes. Snacks forgotten, they converge on me like one being, surrounding me and dipping their heads close. As they each breathe in my scent deeply, the heat of their bodies washes over my skin. My pulse keeps skittering giddily on.

Sylas's hand comes to rest on my belly where I touched it a moment ago. August's follows, and then Corwin's, and then Whitt's and Madoc's, until they're overlapping with each other like an echo of our joint relationship.

The Seelie arch-lord speaks first, his voice rough with emotion. "Our family is going to grow again, in a very different way."

A grin stretches across my face. I beam at all of them, lost in the exhilaration of the announcement.

There's no curse on me now, no Murk king out to make me and my mates miserable. The Heart has shone on us all. This baby will be born into a world of joy and compassion, one I'll fight to the death all over again to keep that way.

But surrounded by the men I love right now, I know I'm not going to have to. We're in this together, and like that, we can conquer anything. I will never be caged again.

www.ingramcontent.com/pod-product-compliance
Lightning Source LLC
Chambersburg PA
CBHW030759210726
48290CB00002B/338